LAUREN DANE

THRICE UNITED

Witches Knot

ELLORA'S CAVE
ROMANTICA PUBLISHING

What the critics are saying...

❧

4 stars: "Dane doesn't disappoint with book four of the Witches Knot series. It's an entertaining tale of magic, treachery and love." ~ *Romanrtic Times Magazine*

Recommended Read! "THRICE UNITED has to be one of Lauren Dane's best books ever. I utterly was enthralled from beginning to end reading about this wonderful family of witches and their various mates." ~ *Joyfully Reviewed*

5 Tattoos "THRICE UNITED was one thrilling, sexually charged read that will have you going up in scorching hot, internal flames. What's more, after experiencing Lauren Dane's writing, I can truly say that she has the magic touch when it comes to writing a panty-wetting ménage a trois scene. [...] Readers, you will not be disappointed with this book." ~ *Erotic Escapades*

5 ribbons "Bravo to Ms. Dane for writing this wonderful book! A definite keeper!" ~ *Romance Junkies*

"Once again Lauren Dane has created a compelling and wonderful relationship between three strong and fascinating characters. [...] Revisit the Charvez witches and their extraordinary family as well as meet the other half of Holly's family on her twisting, turning journey to discover her past and her powers and enjoy!" ~ *Road to Romance*

An Ellora's Cave Romantica Publication

www.ellorascave.com

Thrice United

ISBN 9781419956911
ALL RIGHTS RESERVED.
Thrice United Copyright © 2006 Lauren Dane
Edited by Ann Leveille.
Cover art by Syneca.

This book printed in the U.S.A. by Jasmine-Jade Enterprises, LLC.

Electronic book Publication November 2006
Trade paperback Publication September 2007

Also by Lauren Dane

ℰ

About the Author

൧

Lauren Dane been writing stories since she was able to use a pencil, and before that she used to tell them to people. Of course, she still talks nonstop, but now she's decided to try and make a go of being a writer. And so here she is. She still loves to write, and through wonderful fate and good fortune, she's able to share what she writes with others now. It's a wonderful life!

The basics: Lauren is a mom, a partner, a best friend and a daughter. Living in the rainy but beautiful Pacific Northwest, she spends her late evenings writing like a fiend when she finally wrestles all of her kids to bed.

Lauren welcomes comments from readers. You can find her website and email address on her author bio page at www.elloracave.com.

Tell Us What You Think

We appreciate hearing reader opinions about our books. You can email us at Comments@EllorasCave.com.

THRICE UNITED
Witches Knot

&

Dedication

ℬℭ

For Ray — you're the full moon shining off my Camaro's hood.

Ann — thank you for being such a great editor. I'm so lucky to have you.

This book has seen a few versions. Originally it was called Witches Knot and it had loads more characters and less romance. I want to thank those people who beta read this book and helped it to become what it is now — a better, tighter book that is still the book of my heart.

And on that note, thank you, Tracy. Not only for being such a great beta reader but for coming up with the Witches Knot title to begin with. It's a perfect name for this series and melding of different people and magic. I'm fortunate in my friends and I count you as one.

Trademarks Acknowledgement

ဆ

The author acknowledges the trademarked status and trademark owners of the following wordmarks mentioned in this work of fiction:

GQ: Conde Nast Publications, Inc
Jaguar: Jaguar Cars Limited Corporation
Pearl Jam: Pearl Jam A General Partnership
Perry Ellis: PEI Licensing, Inc
Thermos: Thermos L.L.C.

Chapter One

ഇ

Holly Daniels hurried across the packed Red Square, book bag over her shoulder. Head down against the rain, beads of water glittered against the coppery rope of her waist-length braid. A thousand competing responsibilities and commitments ran through her head, dizzying her. She was so preoccupied that she didn't even notice the man perched on the low brick wall outside of Suzallo Library.

Money and how she'd pay for tuition and books next quarter lay heavy on her mind. The stress of the last months had eroded her grades and for the first time since she started school, she worried about the results of her finals. But worst of all, she missed her mother. Loss and isolation sliced through her when she thought about how alone she was. She and her mother had always had each other—just the two of them against the world but cancer had taken that from her and she was left feeling cast adrift.

And there had been the ever-present feeling that she was being watched. More than that, in danger. She swallowed around the lump in her throat and tried to convince herself—again—that she was just imagining things. After all, she was living alone for the first time in her entire life. But she didn't have much talent at denial and wasn't having much success making herself believe that.

Pushing it all away as best she could, she picked up her pace, rushing to catch her bus to get home.

* * * * *

Rhett watched her avidly. She fascinated him and he was still trying to figure out just what about her captivated him so deeply. Certainly she wasn't his usual type. He liked his women tall and blonde, thin with long legs and big breasts. This woman was of middle height with her hair perpetually tied back in a long braid. She wore those funky glasses that reminded him of a woman he dated once in Greenwich Village. *Art school girl glasses,* he thought with a smile. She was definitely not the supermodel-thin, lithe women he usually found himself in bed with.

A month ago he'd walked into Elliot Bay Books to hear a reading by a favorite author. The basement area had been packed to standing room only in the café. All of those humans — all of that blood — had heightened his awareness and so at first he hadn't thought much about it when his skin had seemed so alive.

He'd found a place near one of the doorways and leaned there. It was her hair that first drew his gaze. Like a river of brilliant copper, it twisted in a braided rope on her shoulders and back. Sitting there against her sweater, it had almost seemed alive.

It slid down as she'd turned and their gazes locked. Everything in him had frozen when the shock of recognition — of connection — rode him. The electric sensation shot straight to his cock, hardening it to the point of pain. Her big brown eyes widened behind her glasses and her lips had made a little "O" of surprise.

Suddenly, his brain had been assaulted with visions of that mouth wrapped around his cock, her hair freed and cascading over his hands and arms like liquid fire as he guided her over his flesh. The sense memory of it was so vivid and strong that he'd nearly come right then. As it was, he'd stood there, breathing hard, unable to tear his gaze from her. He'd felt so connected to her that it was as if he could hear her heart pounding from two rows away.

As if she'd known what he was thinking, a flush had stolen over her face and she'd turned away quickly. She'd faced forward for the rest of the reading but he'd been unable to stop staring at her.

After the reading he'd wanted to approach her – to get close enough to scent her better – but the author who'd been speaking was a huge draw and the crowd had been too thick to do it without using his powers to get to her. That had been too big a risk to take when he and Nate had just gotten to Seattle a few months before and were keeping a low profile.

He did follow her home at a discreet distance – after all she was a woman alone and he was a stranger. He'd been watching her – watching *over* her – every evening since then. He watched her as she worked as a waitress at a local bar. Watched her study late nights in the library. Watched her read on the bus. She'd become a part of his life and he wanted more than the sad routine of watching her from a distance. He wanted to *know* her.

While she appeared quite shy and introverted, there was something else there, just beneath the surface. When she smiled, her entire face transformed from serious to sexy. At times she seemed innocent and sweet and admittedly, that called out to him. Made him want to crack open that shy shell and free the siren inside. He wanted to corrupt her inch by delicious inch.

His cell phone shifted in his pocket and Rhett came back to himself. His roommate and best friend Nate had gone back to Atlanta for a while, needing to seek out his Sire for advice, but his plane should have arrived back in Seattle by then.

Still keeping his eye on her, Rhett pulled out the phone and punched in the number.

"Yeah." Nate's rich voice filled Rhett's ear.

"Where are you?" He spoke as he trailed behind Holly at a safe distance. In the last two weeks he'd picked up her fear and felt a driving need to protect her. He wasn't sure why. Well, he had an inkling but he wasn't ready to admit anything to himself or anyone else just yet. So after sunset, he kept an eye on her the best he could and tried not to feel like a stalker.

"Hey, Rhett. I'm walking up the sidewalk to the front door right now. I take it you aren't here?"

"Nah, I'm at the UW."

"Watching her again? Man, get hold of yourself and introduce yourself to her already." Nate laughed as he said it and Rhett could hear him going into the house and dropping his bag. "You know, Rhett, I'm going to have to see this woman for myself. I feel like I know her as much as you yammer on about her all the time."

"She works at The Roanoke Tavern. I'm going in tomorrow night, you can see her then. I'm just going to make sure she gets home safely and then I'll see you at our place. Have you fed yet tonight?"

"My donor is back in town, I just spoke to her a few minutes ago. She's got a friend who would love to help you out."

Just about the only thing that tore him away from watching over his mystery redhead was hunger. "All right. Sounds good." Hanging up, Rhett waited until she'd gotten on the bus and jumped on behind her and found a seat a few rows away. He took in her profile as she looked out the window blankly.

The bus slowly wound its way through the streets, stopping every few blocks, and Rhett's attention remained on her. He could see her pain in the lines around her eyes. Her tension and the sense of sadness that emanated from her made him want to sit next to her and brush a soothing hand over that magnificent hair while murmuring reassurances to her. Instead he dug his fingers into the seat and forced himself to stay put. Something new for a guy who was more the "love 'em well but get the hell out afterward" type.

The bus route was familiar to him and he knew her stop was approaching so he got up and moved toward the door.

Shadowing her as she walked to her apartment building, he stealthily perched in a tree across the street. Once he saw the light in her apartment window turn on and watched her shadow move into the apartment he allowed himself to relax and quickly hopped down.

Hungry, he silently glided back toward the Capitol Hill house that he and Nate shared, her sad face on his mind.

* * * * *

Holly took a long, hot shower and put on sweats, thick wool socks and a sweatshirt to gird against the cold. Her last exam over and done, she was free for the next month until school began in early January. The luxury of time was something she always took advantage of when it came her way. She planned to do nothing more than pleasure reading and working until January. Well, and maybe a little bit of research.

The thought of her first Christmas without her mother made her heart ache. They'd never had anyone else but each holiday they'd built their own traditions, no matter if they were living in a cheap motel in Phoenix or a small apartment in Detroit. But now she was alone.

She cursed the family that her mother would never go into details over. The people who'd turned a fifteen-year-old pregnant daughter into the streets, alone. Over the years, Holly repeatedly begged her mother to tell her about the people she came from. She'd wanted a connection. Family. More than that, she wanted to know what the hell happened that sent her mother packing to begin with. All her mother would do was shake her head and refuse, her lips in a tight white line.

Heating up a bowl of soup, Holly took it to her small table and ate as she thought. At last she gave in to her curiosity and pulled out the deck of tarot cards that she'd been carrying in the bottom of her bag for the last two weeks. They drew her attention time and again and she drew her fingertip over the deck, tracing the deeply colored figure on the top card.

She could no longer ignore that voice, that bright ember inside of her. It was time she dealt with the whole issue of magic. Now that she had a break from school, it was something she needed to confront and explore. After a lifetime of being forced to pretend it didn't exist, Holly barely knew where to start. But everything in her life had been pointing at the burning need to know what lay inside her and why.

Two weeks before, she'd been walking past a shop in Wallingford when an elderly woman walked out and handed the colorful deck of cards to her.

"You should use these. They'll help you free the magic. You don't need them to see. Your gift is there," she tapped Holly's forehead. "You have the sight. But she was afraid to lose you so she made you bury it."

Holly had blinked in shock and surprise as tears stung her eyes. "What are you talking about?"

Despite Holly's demand for answers, the woman had just pressed the deck into her hands and walked back into the shop. Holly had thought to follow but the accuracy of the woman's comments had spooked her and she'd hurried past instead. The deck had been in her book bag ever since. She'd pulled them out several times but had hastily packed them away again, telling herself to wait until after finals.

From a very early age, Holly had known things before they happened. Simple things like when the phone was going to ring or who would be at the door and later, more complex things. She'd had visions, dreams of her mother's cancer for over a year. Holly had urged her to go to the doctor but Elena had been so frightened she refused and told Holly to stop speaking of it.

The worst thing was that as her mother lay dying they both knew it wasn't necessary. Holly knew her mother had a gift for healing. Her mother had taken away hurts and health problems many times over Holly's life, but she wouldn't do it to save herself. She always refused to use the gift on herself. She chose that stubbornness over living and Holly hated her for it as much as she loved her and missed her.

And here she was, not knowing who she was or what the heck this prescience she had meant or how to use it. Elena had forbidden Holly to even speak of her own unique gifts. And so, over time, Holly had just walled as much of it out as she could and pretended not to deal with what did leak through.

Now her mother was gone and she ached to understand herself and her gift. She needed to know where she came from and if anyone else in her family was like her. So many questions plagued her.

Making up her mind, she pulled the cards out of the deck, taking their weight into her hands. She slowly shuffled through them. She'd never seen tarot cards up close before she'd received the deck. They were beautiful—colorful and vivid. She'd looked through a book she found at the library and had learned a lot of interesting things.

Shuffling one last time, she cut the deck. The Empress was at the top. Taking a deep breath to center herself, she thought of her path and a pattern just came to her as she laid five cards on the table before her.

Four of Wands. Unity and family? Five of Cups. Loss and mourning but also seeking to heal. That one made sense. Justice. Questioning why something happened, seeking answers. Okay, that one made sense too. The Hierophant. Seeking knowledge but questioning it too. The last card, The Moon. Hmm, facing fears, personal journey, questions. More questions.

She closed her eyes as a vision hit her, knocking her off balance mentally. And found herself facing a small woman with hair like hers, although auburn more than coppery red. Holly looked into a face that held a chin very much like her own and—her heartbeat stuttered a moment—her mother's lips, complete with the little cupid's bow. Smiling, the woman

19

held her hand out to Holly and she noticed the two men standing at the redhead's side. More than a physical look at the men, Holly got an impression of them. But what was worrisome and sent a frisson of fear down her spine were the dark shadows around the edges of the vision and the same feeling of danger in the air she'd experienced over the last weeks.

* * * * *

In a very large bed a few thousand miles east, Lee Charvez sat up abruptly. Alex, the dark-haired man who'd been kneeling between her thighs, made a surprised sound. "Baby? What is it?" He reached out to touch her, concerned and wanting reassurance.

The other man, Aidan, slid his hand up Alex's body and he disentangled himself and knelt next to her on the other side, exchanging a worried glance with Alex.

"Oh my god," Lee said quietly. "I've got to call *Grand-mére*." Scrambling over the men, she grabbed the phone with trembling hands.

Alex turned and pressed a kiss into Aidan's shoulder and they both watched Lee, anxious to hear what she'd seen.

A voice sounded on the other side of the connection and Lee took a deep breath. "*Grand-mére?*"

"Yes, *chere*? You've dreamed, haven't you?"

"How is it that you always know?" But there was comfort in that, comfort in being known that well by the people in her life and the understanding that she could seek solace and advice freely.

Her grandmother chuckled. "Oh it's not that hard. I can hear it in your voice. I've been feeling out of sorts lately too. Something is wrong with one of our own. Tell me what you saw."

"*Grand-mére*, I can see her face. She has my hair and *Tante* Elise's chin and mouth. She's in trouble. Alone and in trouble.

She feels abandoned. She doesn't know we exist. She needs us. Who could it be?"

Her *grand-mére* gave a long sigh filled with sadness. "*Chere*, before you were born we lost one of our own. There are things—painful, stupid things—it's time we all talked about them. Let's have a family meeting at your *maman's* house, eh? I'll call and arrange it. Tomorrow night. We need to bring this girl back home."

"What are you talking about, *Grand-mére*? Who is she?"

"I think she is your cousin. I'll explain it all tomorrow night." *Grand-mére* made a sad sound and hung up after telling Lee she loved her.

* * * * *

Holly rushed in the back door of The Roanoke Tavern. In a practiced and efficient set of movements she tossed her bag into a locker, pulled on her uniform shirt and tied on an apron. She'd been preoccupied all day after a long, rough night in the wake of her vision. Deeply shaken, she'd tossed those cards in a drawer and hadn't taken the risk of even looking at them again.

But the fact was that she didn't have the luxury of wallowing or worrying. She had a job to do and tips to make. As she did every night that she worked, she took a deep breath and sent out a prayer to the universe for patience and for her shyness to abate.

She'd taken the job there on purpose, knowing that it would force her to break out of her shell as well as bring in some much-needed income. She was fortunate that her rent wasn't too expensive and that her mother had put aside tuition money for the rest of the school year but that was it. Everything else was a stretch, from books to food. On a good night she made several hundred dollars in tips and her hours were flexible enough to work around her class schedule.

She pasted on a smile and walked out into the bar area and picked up a tray.

Roy Pointer, her boss and the head bartender, waved at her as she approached, pulling her into a hug once she was close enough. He frowned as he looked at her face. She knew he saw the dark circles underneath her eyes.

"I'm fine. Just a bit tired. Finals are over now so at least I have the next month free. Well, free to work anyway. Thanks for the extra hours."

Holly knew that he understood how much she needed the work. There was a waitlist of staff who wanted extra hours and she really appreciated that he'd helped her out so much. He had three daughters of his own and thought of Holly as part of the family. Even so, Holly always hesitated to bring her troubles his way. She just didn't feel comfortable in burdening anyone else.

"No problem, Holly. You're one of my best waitresses. Speaking of that, it's a big night. Go on now. Shanna is going off shift and you've got her section." He put a pitcher and four frosty pint glasses on her tray. "Table eight needs these."

She expertly wove her way through the crowd and delivered the drinks.

By the time an hour or so had passed, the worst part of her shyness had melted away. It was always that way. Once she warmed up a bit she was able to laugh and joke with the customers.

Dimly, she heard the bell above the door jingle as someone came in. Looking up as she headed back to the bar, she locked eyes with a tall man with skin the color of café au lait. His chest was broad and he had dreadlocks that reached the middle of his back, eyes a light green that were almost translucent, high-defined cheekbones and his lips were full and bore a natural curve, like he'd been born smiling. The goatee he wore was perfectly trimmed and only emphasized those sinful lips. He was the most beautiful man she'd ever seen.

Speaking of smiles, he gave her one then and it shot straight through her and sent liquid heat to her pussy. She felt the flesh bloom and soften as she stood there, honey gathering. "Oh," she said without meaning to, blinking her eyes.

Her heart pounded as he walked toward her. She felt glued to the spot, unable to move as he caught her in his gaze. He looked at her like he was a hungry lion and she was his prey. *Oh lordy*, he moved like sin on legs, all grace and a bit of menace. She was mesmerized and no small amount intrigued by the idea of being eaten by a man like that.

"Hi. I'm looking for my friend. He's a bit shorter than I am. Black hair, brown eyes? Dresses like he's in a *GQ* ad." His voice flowed over her and she felt her clit throb. She squeezed her thighs together against it and had to bite her lip to stop herself from whimpering.

"I haven't seen anyone like that. Is he alone?" Her voice actually squeaked. She blushed furiously and wanted to dig a hole to hide inside of. *Good lord, Holly, hold it together!*

Did his nostrils just flare? She watched, transfixed, as his pupils got wider and that curve of his lips hitched into another grin.

"I'm a bit early, he's probably not here yet. I'll just wait at the bar. If he comes in, can you point him my way?"

She nodded, unable to speak, and a ghost of a smile touched his lips as he moved to go sit at the bar.

* * * * *

Nate watched her, unable not to. Sitting at the bar, catching sight of her as she moved around the room, he realized he was seduced by the way she moved.

He was sure the voluptuous redhead with the shy smile was the woman Rhett had been talking about incessantly. What was it about her that drew him in that way? Like magic, he couldn't take his eyes off her. His fingers itched to touch her, to touch that rope of hair. Partly, he knew it was the shy thing. Like Rhett, Nate loved shy women. Loved getting them to let down their reserve so he could introduce them to the hedonistic pleasures vampires could show them.

And oh her blood called to his hunger. He could almost taste it in the air between them when she'd blushed. His mouth dried up, knowing she'd be rich and spicy. His cock throbbed, he was so hard just thinking about her, especially once he'd scented her honey.

Which of course posed a problem as Rhett seemed obsessed with her. But Nate didn't think this was a mere attraction. Not on his part or on Nate's. In fact, he had the distinct feeling it was deeper than that. Deeper and stronger and something inherent and unchangeable no matter how Rhett felt about her. They'd need to have a long talk about it to figure out just what was going on and how they'd deal with it.

Speaking of Rhett, Nate felt him walk in the doors and turned to see him coming in from the rain. Rhett's eyes immediately sought the woman out and Nate smiled to himself as he saw that he'd been right about the redhead.

Waiting patiently, Nate watched her until she sighted Rhett. It was a quick glance, then she turned back to Nate with a smile and raised her eyebrows in question and he nodded. Giving a little wave, she walked toward Rhett.

* * * * *

Distracted by a bar full of customers, it took some moments before she really saw him. Savage satisfaction coursed through Rhett as he noted that she recognized him. Not just from the author reading but on a deeper level of connection and recognition. She halted for a moment there in the middle of the bar and he watched her struggle to get past that shock.

Her eyes focused on him again and he sent her a slow, sexy smile, pleased that she had to visibly struggle to get hold of herself and calmly continue over to him.

"Your friend is waiting for you over there." She pointed to Nate. "I...I'll be over to check on you in just a minute."

He took her hand—the hand she'd been flapping around in her distress—and kissed the knuckles, inhaling her, and her scent shot through his system like a drug. *Jesus*. He closed his eyes for a moment and let go of her hand.

"Thank you," he murmured. Leaving her stunned, he walked over to the bar where Nate was watching him with one eyebrow raised.

"Hey, how was Atlanta?" Rhett asked without preamble as he hopped up onto the barstool.

"Fuck Atlanta. Who's the redhead?" Nate asked.

"I don't think it's a 'who' question. I think it's a 'what' question. Now that I've been close to her, I can smell her blood. It's got to be what's been drawing me to her."

Nate started to say something but looked up and smiled as she came over to them. "There's a table that just opened up near the window if you two want to grab it," she said with a sweet smile that made him slightly dizzy. Fuck, he felt like a teenager again.

"Will you still be our server?"

She blushed and then looked worried. "Well, yeah. Is that a problem?"

He shook his head. "Not at all. Thank you. I think we'll do just that," Nate said and got up and they walked over to the small table and sat down.

"Okay, what can I get you two?" she asked as they sat.

"A Mac and Jack's and can I get some chili cheese fries too?" Nate was suddenly famished. If he couldn't have her, he'd take some chili fries instead.

The corner of her mouth quirked up. "Sure." She turned and looked at Rhett expectantly.

"Do I know you?" he asked her, using the power of his gift of thrall.

She looked at him and narrowed her eyes, shaking her head a bit. "No, I don't think so."

Nate raised an eyebrow at the way she threw off Rhett's thrall. Rhett was exceptionally gifted with his voice and Nate didn't think he'd ever seen anyone push it off so effortlessly. Most certainly never a human.

He realized then that part of her appeal was that she was clearly more than human. Just exactly what she was remained unclear but he knew that they'd be finding out.

Rhett must have been thinking along those lines because he hid his surprise at the way she was seemingly unaffected by his voice and held out a hand. "I'm Rhett Dubois and this is Nate Hamilton." She looked at him for a moment, unsure, and then took it, shaking it briefly.

They could both hear her heart pounding, the blood flowing through her veins. Rhett wanted to groan when he scented her desire. Close up she was really lovely. Curvy and lush. Her skin was like porcelain. Her features were pretty, rosebud lips, generous breasts, long, graceful fingers. There was something about her, a combination of the total package that created a sort of 1940s film goddess appeal.

"Uh, I'm Holly. Nice to meet you. Can I get you a drink? Something to eat?" She was flustered and Nate thought that just added to her attractiveness. She appeared to be utterly without artifice and he couldn't recall the last woman he'd met who could get anywhere near how genuine this one seemed to be.

"Sure. Can I get a G and T? I'll eat his fries."

"Okay. I'll be back with your drinks in a minute." She smiled and wove her way toward the bar and they both watched her as she gave their drink orders to the man behind it.

"So wow, the way she tossed off your thrall was pretty impressive." Nate was careful to keep his voice casual.

"That's never happened before. I've never seen a human do that, ever. A few master level vampires, a Faerie I knew once. A witch once or twice."

"She's more than human. I can feel that."

Rhett nodded his head. "Yeah, that makes sense. She does have something very otherworldly about her."

"Rhett, clearly whatever this thing is between you and her is more than run-of-the-mill attraction. And I have to tell you, I think it's more than just you."

"What does that mean?" Rhett hissed but before Nate could answer, Holly was on her way back over with their drinks.

* * * * *

Holly brought their drinks by a few minutes later but couldn't stop to chat. Not that she would have known how to talk to two such amazing men anyway. As it was, the bar was packed and she was rushed off her feet. Plus it looked like they were having a rather intense conversation and she didn't want to get in the middle of it.

Her lips curved into a secret smile when she thought of the kiss that the dark-haired man had given her hand. His eyes. She'd realized that she recognized those deep black-brown eyes from the reading at Elliot Bay the month before.

She'd gone to hear Margaret Atwood speak and even though the room had been absolutely packed, she'd felt something—*someone*. She'd turned around and her eyes had been immediately drawn to him. He was there in a button-down shirt, sleeves rolled up a few times, one button at the throat open. His hair was just a bit longer than it should have been but it looked good on him. His pants fit perfectly and he leaned back against one of the posts, feet crossed at the ankles. When her eyes had locked with his, it was as if he'd grabbed her and squeezed her tight. He'd given her a smile so suave and sexy that her heart had jumped into her throat. She'd had to dig her nails into her palms to keep from drooling and staring at him. Truth was, she'd thought of him often since that night.

And his friend, well, he was delicious. She had to shake her head. She didn't understand it. It wasn't like she was prone to obsessing over men. Sure she liked them, but she certainly didn't walk around mooning over them. Grinning, she resolved to give it some thought when she got home after her shift. Some thought with her eyes closed and her favorite vibrator to keep her company.

* * * * *

Both Rhett and Nate watched her as she moved through the bar, working herself nonstop until last call. Each time they'd gotten to the point of the argument they'd been interrupted and it was pretty clear to Nate that Rhett was doing his best to avoid the topic starting up again each time.

"Listen, we need to talk about this, Rhett. We can't just pretend this isn't going to cause problems." Nate pressed the point yet again. Like it or not, it had to be dealt with.

"Talk about what?" Rhett narrowed his eyes at Nate.

"Come on, Rhett. This woman is not just drawing you. She's drawing me too. And not in the way that I'd just step aside because you saw her first. There's something more here and you know it. I think we should stay here and talk to her after she gets off shift."

"You don't need to stay."

"Oh but I do, Rhett. That's the point you keep avoiding."

Before Rhett and Nate could begin to argue in earnest, two women from a nearby table sauntered over and leaned in, giving them both a view to remember. They sat down and flirted.

Flattering as it was, both men nicely began to get rid of the women but not before Holly came out of the back room and saw it, heaving a small sigh of regret.

Her boss saw her and called out for her to go ahead on home and that he'd see her the next day. She nodded, pretty close to dead on her feet. A hot shower, a cup of tea and bed awaited her.

Emerging from the back just a few minutes later in street clothes and with a last look at their table, Holly left the bar to make the short few-block-walk home.

By the time they'd extricated themselves from the women, Rhett realized that she wasn't there anymore.

"Shit, where did she go?" He looked around the bar, which was now empty but for the bartender and a waitress. "Excuse me," he asked Roy, using his voice at full power. "What happened to Holly?"

"She went home about ten minutes ago."

Rhett knew where she lived, he'd watched her coming and going enough times. "Thank you." He grabbed Nate and they headed out.

"She's gone home. She lives just about a mile from here so she's probably there by now."

"Damn!" Nate began to feel a rising tide of worry for her and suddenly understood Rhett's obsession with watching over her the last month. "I get it now. Why you've been so intent on watching her. She's not entirely safe."

Rhett looked at Nate closely. "What's it to you anyway?" he demanded as they walked through the parking lot toward the car.

"I know you've been ignoring everything I've been saying for the last few hours. Let me say it again. She calls out to me the way she calls out to you. I need to taste her blood, Rhett. I need the answers as much as you do." Nate got into the car, refusing to let himself be pushed aside.

Rhett threw himself into the car and started the engine. "What do you mean? She's mine, Nate!"

"No. Well, yes, but not *just* yours. Let's just talk to her first and we'll go from there."

Rhett gave him a dirty look but he pulled away from the lot and drove the short way to her place anyway.

Parking quickly, they got out and walked up the block. He pointed to the apartment on the top corner of the six-plex. "She's up there. And you're fucking insane if you think I'm sharing her."

Nate stopped Rhett with a hand on his shoulder. "You know as well as I do what she is. Rhett, it wouldn't be the first time a woman was made for more than one vampire. You know the history. My Sire was saying something about my life changing. I thought he was just trying to be mysterious and woo woo."

"What? You believe in that one true mate bullshit?"

Nate gave him a dark look. "I didn't believe in vampires until I became one seven years ago. Since then I've come to understand there are a lot of things in the universe that I can't explain but are still real. Ask yourself this, Rhett. Now that you've scented her close up, had your lips on her skin, now that you've smelled how her pussy ripened for me and then you, has any other woman—human or vampire—ever affected you this way?"

Rhett shook his head. Even if he didn't want to deal with it, he couldn't argue. He'd been obsessed with her for the last month and now her scent, the taste of her skin, of her blush was embedded in his brain. *She* was embedded in his brain and he realized he couldn't *not* think of her.

"We don't even know what she'll say. Let's take it one step at a time." Rhett approached the building and Nate followed with a chuckle that women and men alike seemed to love.

* * * * *

As they ascended the stairs to the second floor Rhett's body went on alert as he heard a muffled sound of distress. Nate was already rushing down the hall. As Rhett came to him, Nate reared back and kicked the door in.

Small bits of wood flew everywhere and the door crashed open, slamming inward, the doorknob embedding in the wall behind it.

In a split second, the vampires took the scene in and a killing fury borne of possessiveness over the woman inside obliterated most of the humanity from them.

There were two men in the apartment. Both currently frozen in fear as they watched two enraged vampires coming into the room, incisors out, eyes glittering with bloodlust.

Scanning the room for Holly, Rhett saw her on the floor, nearly unconscious. Her face was swollen and bloody. One of the men had been kicking her bound and supine body. His eyes swept down to the red-stained boots the thug was wearing. Rhett noted with savage satisfaction that she'd fought back in some measure. The man who had been kicking her had deep furrows dug into his cheek from where she'd scratched him. But that satisfaction and pride were washed away by the rage over seeing her so injured.

The other man had turned her bookcases and shelves out. A book fell from his nerveless fingers to the floor, joining the pile. Her meager possessions were scattered all over the place, most of them broken.

Only a very few seconds had passed but it felt like time had stretched and the tension was about to snap. The two intruders stood frozen, terrified as they stared at Rhett and Nate. Time rushed forward again as a savage growl came from deep inside Rhett and he launched himself at the man who'd been attacking Holly while Nate went for the man who'd been ransacking her apartment.

Nate slammed his fist into the face of the human, knocking him back against the bookcase. Muscles trembling with his need for revenge, his gums ached at the pressure of his lengthened incisors and his vision clouded red. It was a close thing but he managed to rein the need to kill any man who would seek to harm his woman. For the moment, the immediate threat needed to be dealt with so he could take care of Holly. That thought alone kept him from ripping the bastard's head from his body and beating him with it.

Nate rushed forward, past the place where Rhett had dumped the human he'd just knocked unconscious. Kneeling on the floor over a very shaken Holly who was fighting to stay conscious, he again had to push back his fury at seeing her in such a state. "Hey there, Holly. We're here, sweet. Nothing is going to happen to you now. You're safe," he murmured, gently running his hands over her ribs, checking for broken bones. Looking up at him with her one good eye, she winced a little as he touched her. She appeared to be bruised up pretty badly but he couldn't find anything broken.

Nate spoke soothing words, using the power of his voice to try to calm her. Seeing her so injured, so fragile, the state of her humanity frightened him to the point that it made him sick to his stomach. They needed to convert her as quickly as possible. He didn't think he could bear to have her going around bearing all the delicate flaws of a human. As a vampire she'd be strong. And safe.

While Nate dealt with Holly, Rhett stood over the human he'd revived, the man who'd been beating her. Lacking time and patience, Rhett unleashed the full extent of his power. "Who are you and why are you here?" he demanded.

The human—obviously a weakling there on orders— didn't stand a chance against Rhett's voice.

"She's a Charvez. Our boss wanted us to kill her and take anything magical that she had," the man wheezed out despite himself.

"Charvez?" Rhett turned to look at Holly who shook her head. "What do you mean? What's a Charvez?"

"Witches. A line of witches. Protectors of New Orleans. Powerful." The man was struggling to breathe.

While Rhett continued to question the human, Nate looked quickly back to Holly at the mention of the name Charvez and noted her surprise. She didn't appear to know any more than he did about these witches. He stroked a hand over her hair, unable to stop himself from touching her, offering her comfort. "Sweetheart, can you stand?" They had to get her out of there and cleaned up. Preferably with a bit of their blood in her system to speed her healing.

Recognition came into her eye and she started. "You? What are you doing here?"

Relief flooded him when her voice was steady and her eyes, or rather her one open eye, gained focus and appeared clear. Helping her up gently, he put her in a chair and reached around to grab a glass of water. He put it in her hands and watched carefully as she drank a sip and then another. Standing over her, he watched Rhett continue to question the men.

"Why does your boss want her dead?" Rhett's demand was so harsh and laced with so much power and threat that the man's nose began to bleed.

"He hates the bitches. One of them nearly destroyed his entire..." The man started to foam at the mouth and was unable to finish his sentence. His eyes bugged out and magic overflowed. So much that it crawled over the skin of everyone in the room. The air became thick and stifling and suddenly the thug's eyes blanked out as his life ebbed from his body. A gurgled shout from the other man caused them to look in his direction just as he breathed his last as well, and suddenly both bodies were gone.

Shocked, Holly blinked her one eye rapidly. "What the hell is going on?" She winced, holding her side. Nate tsked at her as he pressed an ice-filled towel against the side of her face and sat down across from her.

"I was going to ask you the same thing, sweetheart. What's your connection to these Charvezes and why would someone want to kill you because of it?" Rhett made every effort to keep his voice gentle. Adrenaline raced through his system and his bloodlust had been roused to the point of pain. He needed to feed. Needed to take care of her. Needed to fuck her. Needed to claim her.

"I don't know! Why are you two here?" Confusion and anguish laced her voice.

"We're here because of you."

Nate rolled his eyes at Rhett. The man had great fashion sense but no finesse. "We wanted to talk to you but you left work before we got the chance. We were coming to your door when we heard something and came in to see what was happening."

Setting aside how they'd known where she lived for the moment, she was grateful they'd come in when they did. "You saved me. Thank you." Pausing, she looked back to the place on the rug where the man who'd assaulted her had been lying. "What happened to them? Why did he tell you all of that and where did they go?"

"Rhett has a considerable amount of thrall in his voice and I suspect some pretty powerful magic took those bodies. There must have been a kind of trap spell on them. He was going to reveal something and it killed him."

"Magic? Thrall? Trap spell?" Her head hurt, nothing made sense.

Rhett looked at Nate who shrugged. "The magic smelled male—wizard magic, I'd wager. A trap spell is like a booby trap, you say or do something and it triggers a spell. Usually something very unpleasant. Thrall is the power that some vampires have to mesmerize with their voice. I'm not bragging when I tell you that I'm very gifted with the ability to thrall others."

She stood up and limped backward, toward the phone. She was clearly concussed and not in her right mind. The whole evening had gone tragically wrong the moment she'd walked in her front door and it was just getting worse. "Okay. Uh, thanks for saving me and all but I need to call the cops now." She tried not to panic but was quickly losing that battle.

"Sweetheart, what are you going to tell them? Where are your burglars?" Smelling her fear, Rhett spoke gently, desperately wanting to calm her.

"This is too much," she mumbled, feeling herself losing her hold on reality. Vampires, wizards? God, she was in a coma or something. That explained it. "Ooookay. Well thanks. You two can go now. I'm fine."

"You aren't going to comment on us being vampires?" Nate asked, a hint of amusement in his voice.

"No." If she even thought about it she'd burst into tears from the stress. She just wanted them gone. She needed to sleep, to forget it all. She could still taste her fear, the metallic bite of it lodged in the back of her throat.

"You know, if you took a bit of my blood you'd heal up a lot quicker." Rhett kept his voice casual. He could see that she was right on the edge of a full freak-out and he didn't want to frighten her any more than she already was.

Seeing her eyes widen in fear, Rhett reached out to her and she winced, pain whitening her face as she scrambled back. If he could just take a bit of her blood, it would tie her to him and enable her to see that what he was saying was true. She'd be bound to him if she really was his mate.

"And I don't want you staying here. Why don't you come back home with us? Our place is more than big enough for you to move in," Nate added.

Whoops, it was now officially in "can't take another thing" territory. "Stay back!" she said, her voice trembling. "Get out," she said softly. "I mean it. Go." Scanning the room, her eyes lit upon the butcher block and she began to calculate how long it would take her to grab a knife.

Rhett stopped, his hands palm out so she could see he wasn't a threat. "Please, sweetness, come back home with us. We can protect you better there. We've got an excellent security system, modern conveniences." He looked around the tiny apartment, taking in the worn furniture and meager belongings.

She saw the pity in his eyes and suddenly fury replaced fear. "I don't even know you! I'm not going anywhere with you. Not only did you show up here unannounced—and don't think I didn't notice that you knew where I lived without my telling you—but you're both nuts! Get out!"

"They'll come back, Holly. Whoever wants to harm you is powerful and he won't stop until he's accomplished his goal. As for being nuts," Nate opened his mouth and she watched in horrified fascination as his incisors lengthened. "I'm a vampire and I'm going to share a woman with another man. I guess I am nuts."

Holly's face paled and she struggled to keep her hold on herself. "*Vampires?* Share? What? What the hell are you talking about!"

Rhett laughed and the sound of it washed over Holly's flesh like a caress. "Do you deny that two men just disappeared out of your apartment? I know this comes as a shock to you but you're a witch, it shouldn't be too much of a surprise that vampires exist."

"Each time you open your mouth something else totally ridiculous comes out! I am not a witch!"

Nate cocked his head. "Darlin', trust me, you are a witch." He leaned in and breathed her in. She had to close her eyes for a moment when his hair drew across her face. "I can smell it. Inherent. You were born with your gift."

The desire to grab her and fuck her boneless crested inside him. Somewhere in the back of his mind he was surprised because he normally had better control. But where this woman was concerned, the normal rules didn't seem to apply. He wanted Holly more than anything he'd ever wanted. Wanted to tie her up and tease her flesh for hours. Wanted to watch the flush of desire move up her body as he made her come wearing a blindfold. Wanted to tie her up and fuck her from behind. And, he admitted to himself, wanted to watch while Rhett buried his face in her pussy, fucked her, loved her too. The idea of a relationship of three was suddenly so right. He imagined sleeping with her soft body between the two of them, of Holly being the bridge to making the undercurrents of attraction he and Rhett felt toward each other a reality. He looked from her to Rhett.

"Can't you feel it, Holly?" Rhett asked softly.

"Wh...feel what?" She looked deeply into his eyes and relaxed. She also suddenly felt...well, for want of a better word...okay. The aching loneliness of the last six months—for most of her life—was gone. It was as if these two men filled that void. She was whole and it felt really good.

"From the first moment I saw you last month at Elliot Bay I've been obsessed with you. I haven't been able to get you out of my head. I fall asleep with your face in my mind. I wake up with your face in my mind. I dream of you. Don't lie and say you don't feel a connection to me." He looked at Nate and then back to her. "To us."

"I... This is too much too fast. Vampires? Witches? Soul mates?"

Holly's eyes were starting to look panicked again. If she would only allow one of them to take her blood, they could help calm her.

37

"Holly, can I take your blood? Just a small amount? It would allow you to see that what we're saying is true. It won't hurt you, I promise." Rhett used his eyes to mesmerize her a bit, to relax her so that her inhibitions would drop. He felt guilty but he wanted her safe and she was so frightened that if he didn't take the edge off, he'd be unable to help her.

Chapter Two

ഇ

Lee walked into the front room of her parents' house with Aidan and Alex. Leaning in, she kissed her parents and brightened when she saw that her sister Em and brother-in-law Con were in attendance. Grinning, she hugged them both and sat. The room was tense as they all wondered just what bombshell their grandmother was going to drop.

Finally, after the last group of people had filed in and sat down, *Grand-mère* stood up and the room immediately silenced.

"My loves, secrets are ugly things and we've held on to one of them for far too long. I'm going to tell you all something. It will be news to some of you and bring up sad memories for others but it needs to be aired. I ask you to listen and not speak until I am done. And to remember that everyone makes mistakes."

Lee's heart stuttered as she held her sister's hand.

"Nearly twenty-five years ago, your *Tante* Elise had a different husband. His name is unimportant as is wherever he is now. He was not an exceptionally nice man but we all held our tongues to keep Elise in our family, surrounded by people who loved her.

"My sister had a daughter, Elena." *Grand-mère* wore such a look of bleak sadness that Lee and Em squeezed each other tight against it. "Elena was such a vivacious girl. Beautiful, with the same ebony hair as our sweet Em but the blue-violet eyes of our great-grandmother. She was a healer of such amazing talent. Oh she was so lovely." *Grand-mère* stared off into the distance as if she were seeing this mysterious Elena.

"One summer—the summer she turned fifteen—she became secretive. She snuck out at all hours and disobeyed her parents. There was a boy. We don't know the whole story, never found out who it was. Anyway, one thing led to another and she became pregnant. It wasn't the end of the world but she faced some hard choices.

"But her father, he went mad when he found out." *Grand-mére* shuddered. "He kicked Elena out into the street and told her not to come back. Told her she'd shamed herself and the family. He did it when her mother was out and by the time she'd returned Elena was gone.

"We looked for that girl for years. Elise divorced her husband—the pain of losing her child, of that child being alone in the world, was too much for her to bear. Some of us have had mental glimpses of Elena and her daughter over the years but we never found them. Now I believe that our Elena is dead. I can no longer feel her light. But Lee has dreamed of this daughter and I've had visions. She needs us now more than ever. We must find her. Let her know that she has many people who love her. Bring her back to our family."

Lee sat forward. "I wonder if she'll resent us? It won't be easy to get her to accept us if that's the case. What did Elena tell her about us? Don't you think she would have come to us by now if it was positive?"

Em, ever the empath, nodded. "She's alone now. Imagine what she'll feel when she sees all of this," she motioned to the assembled family in the room, "and wonders why we didn't come for her and her mother."

"More than alone, she's in danger. Last night it was a waking dream. I believe she had the same vision. Tonight's dream was a powerful waking dream. I saw her being attacked." Lee's voice was pinched. Aidan stroked a hand up and down her spine.

"Perhaps I can help?" Con said. "If you can get a general lock on her energy—her light—I might be able to find her. I'm an excellent tracker." As a warrior of the Faerie for over ten thousand years, it was no light claim.

Em leaned forward. "Yes, we can shimmer to where she is if we can find her. I won't feel better until we find her and bring her home where she belongs."

"Let's all work together then to see what we can do to figure out where she is and get her back here, shall we?" *Grand-mére* said seriously.

* * * * *

Back in Seattle, Holly noticed that Rhett was holding his side. Despite the utter strangeness of the situation she couldn't just ignore it. "What's wrong?" Leaning in to look, she made a dismayed cry. "You're bleeding." Getting up, she limped over to the counter and opened a drawer. Gingerly, she pulled out a tea towel and ran cold water over it. Going back to his side, she knelt and moved his hand gently. She couldn't help but gasp when she saw the angry red slice in his skin. It worried her that it seemed to seep blood instead of clotting.

"Magical knife. My body is slow to heal a wound made by a weapon that's been bespelled." He explained this in a pinched voice as she pressed the towel to the gash to stanch the flow of blood.

"Jesus. I'm so sorry."

He laughed and tried not to flinch. It just felt so good to have her caring for him. "Sorry for what? You didn't stab me."

"No, but you got stabbed helping me."

"Rhett, do you need to feed?" Nate asked quietly and Rhett nodded as imperceptibly as he could. He'd lost more blood than he'd first thought. The magic on the blade had sapped his strength. He was weak, and with blood loss it would take a deep feed to heal the wound.

She looked between both of them in confusion. "What? What is it?"

"He needs blood. He may be a vampire but with that kind of blood loss, it'll take him longer to heal. I suspect that the magic on the blade has weakened him as well." Nate knew he was manipulating her, using her compassion and guilt, but he couldn't let her go without their protection.

She closed her eyes for a moment. They may have just turned her world upside down by saying they were vampires—okay, *being* vampires— but they'd both saved her life.

"Uh, okay. So if you take my blood will I go all vampire?" Even as the words came out of her mouth she couldn't believe she was saying them.

Rhett looked at her sharply. "No. That takes several exchanges. You'd have to take my blood as well. Are you offering your blood to me? Freely?" The desire rang strong in his voice.

"It's my fault you're wounded. I suppose it's the least I can do."

Nate had put him in the chair and he wasn't sure that he could stand up to go to her. She saw it and he was touched by the concern on her face.

"So how do I do this?" Her voice was no more than a whisper.

"Come here, sweetness." Nate took her hand and guided her to stand between Rhett's thighs.

"Sit on my legs here so that I can get to your neck. That's the quickest place for me to feed." Rhett's incisors were out and his cock was probably at least as hard as they were.

"I'm too heavy," she mumbled, eyes downcast, face on fire with her blush.

Both men made sounds of utter annoyance. "Don't be silly. Sit down and move your shirt collar back," Rhett said silkily and she responded, hesitantly sitting on his lap. He pulled her closer with one arm and Nate pulled the coil of her hair aside and they both inhaled sharply at the sight of the pulse beat against the flesh of her neck.

Nate moved and knelt in front of her. Running a fingertip down her cheek to draw her attention, he looked deep into her eyes and mesmerized her a bit. "It's okay, sweetness. It won't hurt. In fact, it'll feel really good."

He took her hands and she gasped softly in surprise when Rhett dragged his incisors across her skin, opening the vein.

Nate watched as her head fell back and her nipples pressed against the front of her shirt. He could smell her blood and her body's response to Rhett's bite. He barely held back a moan when her nails dug into the flesh of his hands.

"Ohmigod," she murmured in amazement just before her back bowed and orgasm washed through her.

Nate wanted to put her on that table and fuck her. Wanted to yank down her pants and bury his face between her thighs, pulling more pleasure from her. But he knew this whole thing was moving too fast for her as it was. In fact, he was keeping a close eye out for any more signs of shock.

And when he took her the first time, he wanted her to come to him and ask for it. So for that moment he contented himself with watching her give herself to Rhett.

Rhett's entire body tightened when he breathed in her scent at her neck. When her blood rushed over the surface of his tongue the first threads of a bond formed. She was thick and spicy with just an edge of sweetness. The deep richness of her life's essence flowed into him and the power of her magic pushed the negative magic of the blade right out of his system. He felt the wound on his side healing. She was incredibly powerful and clearly had no idea. They'd have to talk about her potential later on but she had more magic than he'd ever felt. It was almost dangerous, all of that power and no real knowledge how to use it.

Pulling away from her neck, he met Nate's hungry eyes down the line of her body. Her head was still back, muscles still twitching from the orgasm that had come from his taking her blood. Her lips were slightly parted and wet from her tongue. There on his lap she was living, breathing sex.

Rhett gently cradled her as she came back to herself. Her eyes fluttered open and she gave a long, contented sigh. He felt the bond then, like a living thing tying them together, felt her sadness, the void inside of her that he now filled, saw that it wasn't all the way filled and knew for certain that Nate was meant to do that. That the three of them were meant to be together. Regret laced through his heart. He didn't want the complication of having to share his woman with anyone. But at the same time, it wasn't something he could change either. They'd have to work around it. She was there, in his arms, and she was his.

* * * * *

The moment that Rhett's teeth had opened her skin, white heat had arced from his lips at her neck straight to her molten pussy. When he milked the blood from her with long erotic pulls of his tongue it felt like that tongue was stroking through the folds of her cunt. She'd never come so hard in her life and he hadn't even touched an erogenous zone.

As she came back to herself from the near catatonic state the orgasm had produced, she realized that she felt him as if he was perched inside of her. She heard the slow, steady beat of his heart. Felt his hesitance and his yearning to pull her close. Felt the way that he took away some of her emptiness.

She saw herself through his eyes. A glimpse. Gone was the pudgy, shy girl with the red hair and the glasses. In her place was a woman of flesh and curves, sensual and beautiful.

Her eyes fluttered open and she sighed, utterly content. When she locked her gaze with Rhett and blushed furiously, he laughed and kissed the cleft in her chin. "I just made you come, you have nothing to be embarrassed about."

She gave a startled laugh and tried to sit up but a wave of dizziness hit her. Gently, Nate took her from Rhett's lap and sat, cradling her against his chest. "Shh, be still, sweetness. You just gave a lot of blood." He looked at Rhett, who had color in his cheeks again. "Look and see if she has some juice or a cookie or something."

"I can't believe this is happening. I'm dreaming, right? If this is a dream I should take advantage before I wake up. Why do you have clothes on? You're really the most beautifully delicious man I've ever seen," she said sleepily, looking up at Nate.

He chuckled. "Why thank you, sweetness. I'd be quite happy to not have clothes on so that I could make love to you until dawn breaks but you're drunk with giving blood and it wouldn't be sporting of me. I want you to be paying attention—begging for it—when you and I are together the first time."

"Mmmm. You do say the loveliest things." She giggled.

Rhett grinned as he handed her a glass of orange juice and a scone. "Here, honey. Take these, it'll help."

"But I *like* feeling this way. So dreamy and silly. I rarely get to be silly you know."

Rhett's heart ached for a moment and he leaned in and kissed her forehead. "We're here now, you can be as silly as you want to be. Why don't I pack you a bag?"

She drank the juice down and sat up a bit more, narrowing her one good eye at him. "Why?"

"Holly, whoever wants you dead is serious. They'll be back and I don't want you here just waiting for them. We can keep you safe with us. Please. We can look into who these Charvezes are. I know some people who are up on this sort of thing. Let us protect you."

"Why? Who are you and why do you care?"

"Oh that's a long story. One best told in Nate's big, king-sized bed, you naked in between us," Rhett said.

"This can't be happening. Are you teasing me?" The utter unreality of the night returned to her with force.

Nate turned her face so that she was looking into those pale green eyes. "We aren't teasing you. I promise. You can feel a connection between you and Rhett now that he's taken your blood, can't you? You can see what he sees? Feel how he feels?"

"Oh please!" She slowly sat up and moved out of Nate's arms, it was distracting. "You two, looking like fucking Greek gods! You want me? Why?"

"I promise to explain it in detail, but please, let's get out of here. I don't want to risk you being here if anyone else comes for you."

She closed her eye and tried to think around the panic and the fear. Her options were limited. "Okay. I'll come, for now. I'm not promising anything and I want that explanation and soon." Truth be told, she was scared that someone would come back too. The terror she'd felt when she walked into her apartment and realized she wasn't alone, and then the men had started to beat her up—it still lurked in her gut. And she had no one else and no money to go to a hotel anyway. She decided to trust her feelings about the two men for the time being.

She turned and tried to pull a gym bag from her closet but the adrenaline drained her system and she began to feel her injuries.

Nate made a sharp sound, grabbing the bag for her. "Stop that. Let me do it. Tell me what you want me to pack."

"And sit down while you do it for goodness' sake!" Rhett added, helping her into a chair. He wanted to get her back home so they could get some of their blood into her. Either that or they needed a doctor.

She instructed Nate and he filled a few bags and they both carried them while Rhett carried her—much to her distress.

46

"Ready?"

Rhett nodded.

"All right. Stay behind me. It feels safe but let's not get stupid." Nate had been in the FBI for twelve years, and although he'd taken leave just a year before, his training was always there and he wore it easily.

Alert and with adrenaline surging through his body, Nate went into the hallway ahead of them to be sure it was safe. Near the stairs, he turned and made a small movement with his head. Rhett set Holly down gently and put her behind him and she followed, her hand tucked in his.

Quick and quiet, they loaded her into the car, a sleek black Jaguar, and Rhett drove. Dazed, she sat cradled against Nate's side in his seat, his arm around her, fingers brushing against the back of her neck.

She honestly didn't know what the heck to think. It was like she'd just turned off her normal decision-making judgment. Who was this woman who'd taken over her body anyway? She sat there, nestled into the side of man she hardly knew. No, not a man, a vampire! She should have called the cops and gone to Roy's. He'd offer her a place to stay, take care of her. But she'd bring danger down on his head and even though a stranger had taken over her body, she knew that these two men were far more capable of dealing with whatever the heck had happened back at her apartment.

She began to tremble as the horror of the beating came back to her. One of her eyes was swollen shut and her body ached from the kicks and punches she'd endured. The residual adrenaline that had helped her survive the initial attack and aftermath ran out of her pores and she was losing her hold. She needed to be alone in a quiet room where she could cry.

Nate felt her trembling and held her tighter. He murmured comforting words into her hair and met Rhett's eyes for a moment of shared concern.

"Just a moment, sweetness, we're almost home," he said softly. "Hold on, Holly. You're okay now."

Despite her approaching breakdown, her eyes widened in appreciation as they pulled into the driveway of a gorgeous house. It was a two-story with a big front porch that had climbing roses up the front. Stained-glass inserts decorated the large front doors. It was a buttery yellow and had pretty white shutters framing the big windows. It was the kind of house that should have a tire swing in the backyard.

"Wow, this place is something else. You live here? Just the two of you?"

"We like it." Nate wanted to add that the three of them were going to live there but he didn't want to spook her right before they had the 'one true mate' talk with her.

They escorted her into the big house and Rhett set the security system. Nate watched her wince as she moved but she'd insisted on walking in on her own power and wouldn't let him carry her.

They guided her into a large living room with two comfortable-looking couches and two club chairs near the fireplace with a low table between them. There was a nice mixture of modern sleek lines and traditional darker colors and fabrics. A bay window overlooked a side garden that was in need of some work but even in its unkempt state was beautiful. The cutout panes on the sides and along the top of the window were done in gorgeous stained-glass designs. Holly wondered what it looked like with the sun streaming through.

Bookshelves laden with books framed the large river stone fireplace and she itched to go and peruse the titles but she hurt and was too tired to do anything more than just stand there and concentrate on standing upright.

"First things first," Nate said as he gently moved her to sit on one of the overstuffed couches. "You fed Rhett, which saved his life. But you were already injured. I've fed fully tonight." He knelt in front of her, his large hands on her knees. "Please, let me help you and give you some of my blood."

Holly's brow rose and she winced in pain. "Drink your blood?" she squealed. "Oh, I think I'm fine with a few bruises, thank you."

"Come on, honey. Don't you think we're past all of this? At this point, do you really think we'd hurt you?" Rhett asked softly.

"Don't you give me those puppy dog eyes, buddy! I've had a supremely bad day. Drinking blood would just be the crap icing on the crap cake." Panic tinged her voice.

Nate laughed but Rhett was offended. "Are you comparing my blood to feces?"

"Oh my god! You're offended because I won't suck Mr. Gorgeous' blood?"

Before Rhett could muck it up any further, Nate put up a hand to silence them both.

"Sweetness, I would never force you to do anything. What I'm offering, I'm offering in good faith. I'm not lying when I tell you that a small bit of my blood—just a swallow or two—would heal your bruises and make you feel better. If you felt better, Rhett and I would feel better."

He gently touched the bruise on her cheek and softened his voice. "But if you don't want to try tonight, then let me get you some ice for your ribs and something for that eye."

She was stiffening already. She'd never be able to go into work the following day in that shape and she had to have the income. Still, drinking blood was so...eww.

"How about this? Let me have some ice, tell me the things you were going to tell me and then I'll decide."

Rhett was up and in the kitchen immediately and brought back ice packs. They moved the couch pillows around to support her better and keep the packs against her body where the injuries were the worst. He also put an ice-filled towel over her injured eye.

Just seeing the vivid bruises on her flesh made Nate grind his teeth with rage. He moved to the bookcases on the far wall, pulled out a large volume and sat on the coffee table across from Holly. Rhett was close to her, a fingertip moving over the very end of her braid.

"This is sort of like Vampire 101," Nate said, opening the book and flipping through the pages until he found what he was looking for. "My Sire is something of a vampire historian."

Oh his Sire was a vampire historian. All righty then! The unreality of the entire night was beating at her. Digging her nails into her palms to keep a grip, she focused on Nate. Let his voice, the way his lips moved as he spoke, the way his skin glowed in the warm light of the room, take her attention away from the rising tide of hysteria.

"We're predators in many ways. But at the same time, the population of vampires who are born that way is very low. In order for the species to continue to exist, over time vampires evolved and became able to change humans and mate with them. However, it's not without risks. A vampire can attempt to change any human but most of the time—something like eighty percent of the time—the transformation will fail and the human won't survive.

"Because of that, we're very picky about who we change. Also, because of that it came about that there were biologically and genetically compatible pairings. The science of it essentially means that the two or more people involved in the relationship are bound to each other at a cellular level through the exchange of blood."

Holly struggled to follow where the heck he was going and he saw her confusion.

"Sweetness, to put it bluntly, you are my other half, my true mate. The woman I'm meant to be with." He sighed tiredly. "But you're also Rhett's mate. Usually it's just one to one, but sometimes, in rare circumstances, it can be that two vampires have one mate who is human. It's complicated, but you asked why we wanted to protect you, wanted to be with you? It's because we are *meant* to be."

"What!" Holly winced as her side jarred. "So I'm not just *your* true whatchamacallit, but Rhett's too? Isn't that convenient?"

"No, as a matter of fact it isn't. You think I want to share this with anyone else?" Rhett said, frustration edging his voice.

"And it's just a coincidence that this super-unique-mate-dealie happened with two men and you're both friends? I mean, the odds on that have to be pretty astronomical."

"I've been thinking about that all night, actually. Since I walked into the bar and saw you and felt so drawn to you. I think that on some level, Rhett and I are meant to be together too."

Rhett looked at Nate and raised his eyebrow.

Holly, despite her incredulity, had to pause for a moment as a particularly detailed image of the three of them burned through her brain. Okay, so it wasn't really scary at that point. Probably because she hadn't had sex in a year.

She was so tired. Tired of only having one choice, tired of scraping by, tired of feeling alone. The idea of belonging to these two men in some kind of familial unit appealed to her at a really deep level. She was attracted to them both in a way she'd never found herself attracted to anyone before and damn it, she could have them both. It seemed too good to be true and her eyelids grew heavy. She'd had enough.

She heard Nate chuckle. "Sweetness, I'm going to carry you up to the guestroom. You can tell me if you want to take a bit of blood from me when we get up there." She felt him lift her into his arms and she made a small sound of pain. "I'm sorry," he murmured and carried her up the stairs and into a bedroom that was warm and cozy.

He laid her on the bed and Rhett pulled off her shoes and sat next to her. Nate looked into her eye but was careful not to use any of his powers. "What do you say?"

"Just a taste will make me better?"

"Mmm hmm."

"And I won't go all vampy?"

He chuckled and shook his head.

She took a deep breath. "All right."

He held his wrist to his mouth, sliced across the vein-rich skin with his incisors and brought it to her lips. She closed her eyes and tentatively lapped at his wrist with her tongue instead of taking a swallow.

Nate and Rhett both groaned at the sight.

His blood was warm and tangy. Not icky at all. She took a small taste and then another and one more. She pulled back, amazed that already her body was less sore. Rhett took Nate's wrist and ran his tongue over the wound and it closed up. Holly's eye was clear enough to see that Rhett seemed quite pleased to be helping with that task.

It was only an hour until dawn and she was exhausted, having been up for long over twenty-four hours. "Thank you. I really do feel better. I'm bloody and my clothes are a mess. I'd like to take a shower and get changed for bed. I have to be back at work at four thirty."

"You can't go to work, it isn't safe. We won't be awake until after that." Rhett shot up off the bed and began to pace.

Her chin lifted with stubborn defiance. "I have to go to work. That isn't negotiable."

Nate shot Rhett a look that told him to shut up and he did.

"All right. Just please take the Jag. Don't risk the bus. We'll be in when we get up and have fed. We can talk more tomorrow about everything."

She nodded and dug some sweats and a long-sleeved T-shirt out of her bag. "I uh, I need to go to the bathroom to clean up and brush my teeth."

"Oh sorry, honey." Rhett pointed to a door. "Right through there."

She hurried off and took a quick shower, standing beneath the hot water and trying not to think. When she came out she was doubly glad her eye had healed to take in the astounding fact that her bed had two very naked men in it and they were both happy to see her.

She choked off a gasp and put her hands up in front of her. "Whoa! Even if I didn't have to think over a whole lot of things—including the fact that you two are vampires—I'm dead on my feet."

"All we want to do is sleep with you," Rhett said. "Hold you."

"For now anyway," Nate added with one of his salacious grins.

"Do you, um, die at dawn?" She didn't think she was up for sharing a bed with two dead naked guys. Then she gave a nearly hysterical giggle at the thought.

"No, we sleep. A deep sleep and we're not dead. Come on, snuggle in." Rhett held out a hand to her.

She was so easy. She took his hand and crawled in between them, screwing her eyes tight lest she go blind looking at the impressive merchandise on display just for her.

"I set the alarm for you for three. Is that all right?" Nate asked as he snuggled into her back, an arm around her waist.

"Yes," she said and sounded more breathy than she wished to. "Thank you."

"There are towels and soaps, shampoo, that sort of thing in the bathroom. I suppose you saw that already. We'll be sleeping so we won't see you until after your shift starts. I've written out the code numbers for the security system and the keys to the house and the Jag are with the note." Rhett's voice was sleepy as he moved back toward her, pushing her back into Nate who was, *whooo!* still happy to see her.

"I really can't take your super expensive sports car." Dear god, that damned car was worth more than she made in three years!

"Do you have a driver's license?"

"Yes."

"Fine. You're taking it and don't argue." Rhett reached back and took her arm, pulling it over his stomach and entwining his fingers with hers.

She was out of her mind to be doing any of this but boy did it feel good. She'd allow her senses to take over when she woke up later.

* * * * *

"Hello."

Holly found herself staring into pretty blue-violet eyes and sat up quickly, looking around. She wasn't in bed with Rhett and Nate anymore.

"Don't panic, you're dreaming. Wow, you look so much like us." The fey-looking redhead walked closer, cocking her head.

"What the hell is going on?"

The redhead laughed. "I see you have our attitude too. I'm Lee Charvez, your cousin."

"Charvez? Two men tried to kill me last night because of you people. Who are you and why are you in my dream?"

"You're well then? What happened?" Lee looked concerned.

"Oh you wouldn't believe me if I told you. I'm fine, staying away from my apartment for the moment. Back to my question. Who are you?"

"The Charvezes? We're your family. Your mother was my mother's cousin, the daughter of my great-aunt, your grandmother, Elise Charvez. I'm in your dreams because it's my gift. I'm this generation's witch dreamer."

Holly's face blanked at that chunk of incomprehensible information. "A what?"

"Do you know nothing of your heritage? Of your gift?"

"Who the hell are you to talk to me that way? Your precious family couldn't be bothered with a pregnant fifteen-year-old! Tossed her out like garbage. How dare you judge me!"

Lee put her hands up in surrender. "I'm so sorry about that. We're all sorry about that. But it's not what you think. *Tante* Elise looked for you and your mother for years. I'm not judging you, honest. We want you to come home to us. We want you to know us, we want to know you. We want to protect you."

"If she was so sorry why let her daughter get kicked out to begin with?" Holly crossed her arms defensively over her chest.

"We want you to know the story from our side. Please, come to us. Tell us where you are and we'll arrange to get you here in New Orleans. What's your name? Where are you? We want to make it up to you. You have a family that loves you. Your mother is gone, isn't she? My *grand-mére*, your great-aunt, she says that she can't feel your mother's light anymore."

Sickness spread through her gut. The last twenty-four hours had been more than a bit too much to deal with. Lee sensed it and touched her cousin's arm. "I'm sorry. I'd be a mess if I lost my mother. Please, tell me who you are, come to us. If you want, we can come to you. My sister Em and her husband Con are Fae, they could come to you in seconds. We just want you to know we're here and that you're wanted. Aren't you curious?"

"I don't know what I am! No, wait! Yes I do! I'm pissed. I'm hurt. Scared as hell. Tonight I was attacked, saved by *vampires*. Yes, I said *vampires*! The guys who tried to kill me disappeared in front of my eyes. I *drank* blood. Oh god, I drank blood! Someone drank *my* blood. I'm in bed between two naked men, vampires—oh god—who say I'm their one true mate or somesuch. And my cousin pops into my dream to say 'hi, come home now'. This has been quite the day. I gotta tell you, Lee, I've had about enough of today." She finished out of breath and no small amount hysterical.

"Vampires? Mate? Wait, *mates*?"

"*Yes!* I know it sounds totally absurd but it's true, I saw their damned teeth, I drank a bit of blood from Nate and it healed me. I can feel them both, right now, as if they are inside of my head."

Lee smiled. "Oh, *chere*, you need to come to New Orleans to see us. Bring your men, I can't believe you've got two." She laughed, delighted.

"What? So you don't think the pudgy cousin can snag two hot men?"

"No. And you're not pudgy, not that it matters because to vampires mates are mates, period. And to you too, especially if there's been blood exchanged. I'm laughing because I have two men. One of them is a vampire. It must run in the family. Aidan would love to meet you—that's my husband the vampire. My other husband, Alex, is a wizard."

Holly's eyes widened and she stepped back.

Lee's sharp eyes noticed. "What? Tell me."

"They said that the magic on the blade smelled male, that it was wizard magic."

Lee's smile faded. "Blade? Who said that? You must come to us. We can protect you. New Orleans isn't an affiliated city, vampires of all castes are allowed here. Please." Lee took her hand. "What is your name?"

"Holly. And what is affiliated?"

"Holly, can I call you in a few hours? After you wake up? We can set up the details for you to come down here. Aidan will arrange for a plane to pick you three up and fly you here. You can stay at our home or with my parents."

"I can't just up and leave. I have a job, bills to pay. I don't have private planes! I have a studio apartment that is now trashed."

"Let us help you! It's what family is for."

Holly let out a disgusted sound at that. She willed herself free of the dream and sat up, awake, heart pounding.

It was nearly noon, she'd had five hours' sleep. She looked down and saw the two naked men and closed her eyes against their appeal. She scrambled up and quickly put on clothes and snatched up her bag.

She had to get away, had to think, and she couldn't deal with vampires and witches and wizards. She grabbed the note with the security codes on it—even though she had to get away from the men, she didn't want to leave them unsafe. On her way out she left a note of her own, thanking them for helping her and telling them she needed some space and time alone to process everything.

Chapter Three

ഇ

Back in New Orleans at her house, Lee came back to herself and sat up with a sigh. She looked at her *grand-mére* and her sister and shook her head.

"Her name is Holly. She thinks we abandoned her and her mother. Someone tried to kill her last night." She looked at Alex. "With wizard magic."

Alex raised his eyebrows. "How did she know? Did they leave any kind of evidence behind so we'd know what family they were from?"

Lee let out a long breath. "Two vampires saved her. There was a blade involved, apparently. I'm guessing it was they who knew it was wizard magic. They also told her that she was their one true mate."

Em let out a startled laugh. "She gets two men too?"

Con tugged on her ear. "Hey! One of me is two of any other man."

She turned and kissed his chin. "You're absolutely right, gorgeous."

"She's a bit overwhelmed. Had a big twenty-four hours. Being attacked, finding out vamps exist, being told they were her mates, exchanging blood, having some total stranger pop into her dreams telling her to come home. I almost had her until I told her that we'd help her because that was what family is for. Boy did I push a big button."

She turned to her *grand-mére*. "Elena is dead. Holly is devastated. She has no idea about her magic, about us."

"We have got to get her here. With this threat from the wizards, she's a target with no one to protect her." *Grand-mére's* voice was filled with emotion.

"I'll try to dream walk again tonight to see if I can connect with her again." Lee sighed. "I just hope I'm not too late."

* * * * *

Rhett came awake first, being the older vampire. He turned and inhaled where Holly had slept. Her scent filtered through his system, calming him, centering him. He looked at Nate's sleeping face and a familiar but suppressed heat bloomed through him. He had never been much for other men but he had to admit that when Nate made the comment that he and Rhett were supposed to be together in some way with Holly as the bridge, it had intrigued him. He'd felt some level of attraction for Nate for several years. Imagining what the three of them would do together made him ache.

Putting it aside for the time being, he sat up and went into the bathroom. A hot shower would warm him up and take his mind off the very erotic scene in his head.

Nate came pounding into the room a few minutes later.

"Hey! Knock!"

"She's gone!" Nate held her note in his hand.

Rhett turned the water off and grabbed the towel Nate tossed him. He took the note, read it quickly and wanted to punch something.

"Visit from her cousin? Time alone? What the hell is going on?"

"I don't know, Rhett, but I hate the thought of her out there alone."

"She has to go to work. You could see how tight her financial situation was just by looking at her place last night."

"Let's go."

* * * * *

Holly felt physically ill. Just being away from them made her feel awful. She'd been aware when Rhett woke up, he'd been so content and happy. She felt his arousal when he'd showered. Nate's hunger for her when he'd awoken was enough to make her weak in the knees. She could also tell when they saw her note because first there was confusion, then anger, hurt and resolve.

They were coming for her and she had to go but she had no idea where. Her apartment was a mess, a new door had been ordered and a temporary one was up to protect her stuff but it wasn't a secure situation. She'd been trying to figure out where to stay since she'd come to work early and a grateful Roy had put her on shift immediately. She couldn't ask to stay with him and his wife, it was simply too dangerous. But Nate and Rhett were getting closer so she made up her mind.

"Roy, I'm not feeling well," she apologized and it wasn't a lie.

He looked at her with concern, reaching out to feel her forehead. "Then go on home. I'll call in someone to pick up the rest of your shift. You do look tired."

"Thank you." Fighting back tears, she quickly gathered up her coat and the bag she'd taken from the house and headed out the back door to jump on a bus headed downtown.

She rode, watching the night deepen as she transferred and headed south, toward the airport and the less expensive hotels there. She would use some of the money she had laid aside for books next quarter. She had no choice and right then, she just needed the time and space to figure out what the hell to do.

Choosing at random, she checked in to a cheap hotel and sat in the dark, staring at the walls as the pain clawed at her insides. She felt their rising panic as the time passed without finding her. She was afraid to sleep and have her cousin back in her mind. She was so weary and lonely. In the back of her mind, she knew she should have been outraged by everything that happened to her in the last weeks — afraid even — but there was nothing but the exhaustion of spirit and emotion.

Wishing for oblivion and reprieve from the pain in her gut, she crawled between the sheets she curled into a ball and let sleep wash over her at last.

* * * * *

Rhett and Nate stalked into The Roanoke and knew immediately that Holly wasn't there. Nate went toward the back and Rhett headed toward Roy. He wasted no time and used his voice.

"Where is Holly?"

"She wasn't looking well. Said she was sick and went home about fifteen minutes ago. Who are you?" Roy's eyes were slightly glazed as Rhett's voice took over but his concern for Holly was strong enough to ask. It impressed Rhett and reassured him that she had a few people in her life who cared about her.

"Will she be in tomorrow?"

"That girl needs every penny she can get. Not much short of having a limb fall off will keep her home two days in a row, I'd wager."

The precarious nature of Holly's life hit Rhett once again and more anxiety ate at him. "She's in danger. If she comes back in, you will call me at this number." Rhett handed him a business card and Roy nodded as he took it, putting it into the register drawer.

Rhett thanked him and motioned toward the door. Nate saw and went outside to meet up with him.

"Well?" Nate paced.

"He says she didn't look well and went home sick about fifteen minutes ago. He was genuinely concerned about her. The bond is partially formed, she'll be in pain without us."

Rhett shoved a hand through his hair. He hated the idea of her hurting, even if he was hurt himself that she'd run off. For a human, a partial bond would cause something akin to withdrawal pain that would worsen as the hours passed. She'd given blood to him and taken from Nate, the circuit between them was half completed and her need for them—and theirs for her—was based on a physical need as well as an emotional one. They had to complete the binding as soon as possible for all their sakes.

"Let's go to her place. I can't believe she'd be so stupid as to go back there." Nate slammed back into the car and Rhett got in on the driver's side.

But she wasn't at her apartment and the state of the place was concerning. The door was flimsy and would be of practically no protection for her. But her scent, while strong enough to let them know she'd been back there that afternoon, was cold.

Rhett called their assistant-bodyguard-man of business, Jax, and arranged for him to get her stuff boxed up and moved and to be sure the manager didn't give her any trouble and they headed back to the car.

"What now? I know from following her the last month that she doesn't have any places she could go other than the boss and she'd never bring any danger down on him or his family."

"And it's clear that she doesn't have a lot of money so if she ran, it couldn't have been very far." Nate was agitated. He hadn't fed and his need for her—to be assured that she was safe—rode him hard.

"Let's get fed and then we'll continue to search for her. If we can't find her tonight, we'll get Jax to assign some of his men to watch for her during daylight. Damn it, I can't believe we hadn't done that already. I just didn't think she'd do this." Rhett reined in his frustration. "Her boss seemed to think she'd be back tomorrow. We'll have some humans assigned to watch the tavern during the day and keep her safe and in place until we can get there to grab her."

"Oh is that woman in for it when I get hold of her," Nate growled as they pulled away from the curb. He was furious at her for running and putting herself in danger. Angry with himself for not thinking to put human bodyguards on her. Hurt by her rejection of them but understanding that she would, knowing how hard it must be for her to face all of the stuff she'd had thrown at her in such a short period of time.

After a quick stop to feed, they drove all over the county looking for any sign of her. Rhett could feel a whisper of her through the link he'd formed by taking her blood. He felt her aching fear. It made him frantic. Nate just sat, quiet and steady, looking out the window, breathing in the night air, hoping for a stray scent of her—anything to aid them in finding her.

Daybreak rode the horizon and they both felt her at rest at last. Hoping for the best and without any more options, they headed back home and arranged for people to watch for Holly at the tavern during the daylight hours when they couldn't be there to protect her.

* * * * *

When Holly awoke she felt like she'd been run over by a truck. Her muscles ached, her skin itched and her eyes hurt. It was like the worst case of the flu she'd ever experienced.

All she could think about was Nate and Rhett and how she'd probably scared them to death. What the heck was she going to do? She couldn't run forever. She couldn't keep spending money she didn't have on this motel and hiding.

And really, she wasn't the type for hand wringing and indecisiveness so she knew she needed to face her situation and at least talk to Nate and Rhett face-to-face and work it out.

So one decision at a time. Needing to get back to work and knowing the bus ride home would be long, she checked out and headed north, back to Seattle and into the heart of the issue.

* * * * *

Once she was at work she was able to lose herself in the busy lunch rush and then the late afternoon happy hour crowd. But at dusk she felt them wake up, felt their resolve to find her. Knew they were on their way.

Holly knew she should go but she couldn't. All day long she'd done her shift as her mind worked through the situation in the background. The inescapable truth was that she wanted them to find her. She wanted to be with them. And somehow she understood that the fire on her skin, her yearning and feeling of nausea wouldn't go away until they got there. For better or worse, she was beginning to believe in the idea that they were meant to be together. In some sense anyway. What that meant beyond those words wasn't quite clear to her yet.

They walked in through the front door half an hour later and she turned as their presence called to her. Alarmed at how good it felt to see them both, her hand went to her throat. Tears sprang to her eyes and the angry look on Rhett's face faded.

The bar was insanely busy. Rhett and Nate made eye contact with her to let her know they were there and had no intention of leaving without her. Once they'd done that, they also felt the edge of her fear and near panic and decided to sit down at the end of the long bar to wait for her.

Long minutes later there was a lull enough that she was able to go over to them. They both watched her approach without speaking but when she reached out to them mentally, she felt no anger. Just relief that she was all right and there.

"I'm sorry. I...I was just overwhelmed and I didn't know what to do. The break-in, you two, this dream I had where my cousin showed up. I just had to get out," she said quietly, fighting tears.

Rhett took her hand and put it over his heart. "It's okay. I can't imagine how hard all of this is for you. Nate and I just want to protect you, keep you safe, make you happy. We worry about you. Last night we were insane with fear that you'd be harmed in some way. I'm so grateful that you're all right."

She looked past Rhett's shoulder at Nate, into those pale green eyes, and saw so much emotion there that it scared her, made her heart race. Nate seemed so tough but beneath the surface she knew lurked someone far more complex.

"Order up!" Roy shouted and she jumped and reluctantly turned and got back to work.

They stayed her whole shift, watching her hungrily. She had to admit to herself that it felt good to have them there. Safe.

After a very long shift that ended at ten she went into the back to get her stuff and walked back out into the bar to find them waiting for her.

"Night, Roy," she called out as they headed for the door.

Roy looked up and narrowed his eyes at the men she was with. Appearing satisfied by her apparent comfort with them, he nodded. "Night, doll."

Once outside, Holly put her collar up against the cool evening air. Rhett took her bags and Nate pulled her to his side as they walked to the Jag.

Wedged between them, she felt content and allowed herself the warmth of it. Nate kept his arm around her shoulders and Rhett's hand was on her thigh as he drove.

"Uh, I don't know anything about vampires, well, not real ones anyway. But do you need to feed or something? You rushed over to the bar right when you woke up."

"You felt that?" Rhett asked.

At first she nodded but realized that Rhett's eyes were on the road. She cleared her throat. "Yes. I felt you come awake. I felt it yesterday too. It was like everything was calm and then you were suddenly there, inside of me. I felt you happy, then very aroused," her voice lowered for a moment, "and then I felt Nate wake up and his arousal too. I knew when he found my note, I felt it."

"It's the bond that began to form when the three of us exchanged blood. I couldn't feel exactly where you were but definitely your basic presence. I felt that you were still alive and unhurt but that's all. We need to change that." The light from the streetlamps lit Rhett's face and Holly could see the emotion there and it cut into her heart.

"I felt you panic and I know you were angry with me." Her voice was quiet. "When you woke up today, you felt less afraid. I thought...I thought that you didn't care until I felt your resolve to get me. I felt you both coming over."

"Holly, we weren't afraid because we had Jax, our man of business, watching the tavern. He reported to us immediately when we woke up that you were safe and at work. Never think we don't care, Holly."

Relief rushed through her even as annoyance rose that they'd had her watched. "Oh. Okay."

Nate gave her a sideways look. "We do need to feed but I want to get you home first. I'll run out and eat and then when I come back Rhett can go out." He made it sound like going out for Chinese.

"Okay," she said hesitantly, inwardly cringing at her inarticulate responses. "So uh, do you just vamp on someone? Toss those gorgeous pale green eyes their way and suck 'em dry in an alley?"

Nate laughed. "No. Nothing so exciting. You've been reading vampire novels, I see. We don't take blood from unwilling humans. We have donors. Humans who freely give their blood to us."

She turned to him. "And what do they get out of it? I mean, sorry to sound so cynical and all, but why would people just offer themselves up to be fed on by vampires? Are they like groupies or something?" As soon as she'd said it she narrowed her eyes at him. She could sense his surprise and then his evasion.

He sighed, knowing he'd have to explain but not knowing how to do it and make it okay. "Well, we pay their living expenses a lot of the time. Provide them with a house or an apartment so they can be available when we need them. And yes, some are what you'd call groupies and they…like to be around vampires."

"Like? As in they *like* it when you make them, uh, feel like Rhett made me feel last night when he took my blood?"

Rhett kept his eyes forward and his mouth shut.

"Yes. Feeding from humans causes climax. It's a symbiotic system, we get sustenance and they get pleasure and a roof over their heads. It doesn't mean anything. Not in comparison to what you mean. What *we* mean. I haven't fed from you yet but I'm guessing that taking blood from your mate is different from taking blood from a donor."

"Why don't you feed from me tonight then?"

He looked at her sharply. "You're offering your blood freely?"

"Yes."

"She can't, Nate. Not a full feeding. She fed me night before last and she's been healing from her injuries. We can't feed from her more than every other day or two. It's too much." Frowning, Rhett pulled into the driveway and turned off the car.

"Not a full feeding but a small one. For the bond," Nate said to Rhett and then looked back to Holly. Seeing her confusion, he touched her chin with the tip of his finger. "When Rhett goes out I'll take your blood. It'll tie you to me and me to you. Completely. We've already got the beginnings of a bond, this will complete it because you took my blood two nights ago. Are you ready for that?"

"Hell if I know," she said, feeling totally off balance. "I don't know anything. That should be my new motto."

"Well, let's talk when we get inside. Okay, sweet?" Nate kissed the tip of her nose.

They all piled out of the car and headed for the house. Once inside they went into the living room and sat together. Rhett pulled her close and she accepted that, leaning her head against his chest as she looked at Nate, waiting for him to speak.

"Let's just be totally clear here, okay?" Nate began.

"Please."

"I want you, Holly. Not just because you're my biological match but because you appeal to me. I like your strength and your courage. I love your eyes and the shyness about you. I want to drink of you and tie you to me. I want the threads of our souls...of our hearts to join together. For us—vampires—a mating like this is permanent until one of the parties dies."

A host of emotions rushed through her as her heart threatened to burst through her chest. "I...I just met you day before yesterday for god's sake!"

"Do you want to be anywhere else right now?"

She thought about it long and hard and shook her head. She didn't. Sure she had her faults like anyone else but being flaky or flighty wasn't one of them. She was careful, rational, measured. She didn't fall for movie stars or the latest fads. That she wanted to enter into a threesome with two vampires—vampires!—was astonishing and overwhelming but it felt right. She knew it came at a time in her life when everything was upside down and she felt off balance from losing her mother. At the same time, she felt deep inside that she was meant to meet these two precisely because it was when she needed them the most.

"You say it's permanent. But you'll never age and I'll get old and die. How will you feel when I'm sixty? Eighty? And you both still look so young?"

"Well," Nate paused, taking one of her hands, "we would hope that you'd want to convert."

"Didn't you tell me last night that a majority of humans *died* from failed conversions?" Her voice rose a bit.

"Yes. But you're a biological match to two vampires, both of whom started life as humans. You'll do just fine or you wouldn't be a match for either one of us." Rhett's voice rumbled in his chest, vibrating against her cheek.

"And it would be just us?"

"What do you mean, sweetness?" Nate asked.

"Just the three of us. No other women." She couldn't bear the thought of being cheated on for eternity.

"No other women except for donors and there will be no sex with them. We promise that. The same goes for you." Nate's face bore dismay and annoyance when he realized she'd be feeding on men, making them come.

"I get donors too?"

"Well, if you convert you'll need at least three."

She rubbed her eyes for a moment. "I need to deal with the situation with my family before I do this."

"So you'll convert then? After the situation with your family is resolved?" Nate asked.

She looked at them both, already loving the different features of their faces—the sexy curve of Nate's lips, the intensity of his eyes, the coal-black silk of Rhett's hair, the aristocratic nose. She took a deep breath and stepped out into the abyss. "Yes."

Nate squeezed her hand and kissed her fingertips and Rhett brushed his lips over her temple. Relief rushed through the room.

"You said something about your cousin in the note, and a dream? I meant to ask you." Relief that she'd agreed to convert was clear in Rhett's voice.

"Look, it's an incredibly long story. Why don't you both feed and we can talk after. I feel bad that you haven't eaten yet."

Nate got up. "I'll be back in half an hour." He bent and kissed her lips quickly and she tried not to think that he was going to do to another woman what Rhett had done to her the night before.

She watched him leave with a curve to her lips, *damn, the man looked as good going as he did coming.* He looked back over his shoulder and gave her an arrogant, self-assured grin and placed two fingers to his lips and left.

"Can I take your hair down?" Holly looked to Rhett, giving him her attention. She nodded slowly.

He slowly pulled the braid free and massaged her scalp. Her hair poured over his arms and through his fingers. It was silky soft and the scent of roses permeated it. "God, it's beautiful. Like liquid fire. Why do you keep it bound back all of the time?"

"It gets in my face and customers tend to get miffed if my hair is in their beer." She nearly purred as his fingertips worked their magic against her scalp. "I should cut it. My mother always said that it was my glory. My one concession to vanity."

"No! Never. Honey, your hair is stunning. This color is so rare—gold and copper and the brilliant orange of sunrise. It's so soft." He ran his fingers through it.

She blushed, wildly flattered. "Tell me about you. How long have you been a vampire?"

"Forty years now. Funny how time feels different when you have so much more of it. It seems like yesterday really. Anyway, my mentor was the head of the history department at Boston University. After two years of knowing him, he told me about this man he'd met. Gaius. Only Gaius was more than a mere man, he was an immortal."

Rhett shrugged. "It was the sixties. There was a sense that there were more questions than answers. I went with him to meet this immortal and that night changed my life. I was mesmerized. Gaius then became my friend—a father figure. I had no family to speak of and he became that to me.

"He changed me that summer. In August. I was in the last stages of lung cancer." He snorted a laugh. "At least I stopped smoking. Anyway, he saved my life and I joined his caste and remained at his right hand for four decades. Until a few months ago."

She turned to look at him, seeing the faraway look in his eyes. His sadness cut through her heart. Reaching out, she ran her fingers through his hair and he leaned into her touch, closing his eyes a moment. "What happened?"

"An uprising of sorts. Vampire society is governed by caste structure in most places, except for unaffiliated cities where all live freely without hierarchy. But my caste, the Nento caste, has faced some major power struggles for the last five years. Three months ago the elder who'd been opposing Gaius won and took over. All of those in Gaius' ruling circle had to scatter or take an oath to serve the new leader of the caste. Most of us scattered. Gaius went back to Germany. He wants to live out the rest of his years quietly amongst the oldest ones."

She took his hand and kissed his knuckles. "I'm so sorry you lost your friend like that. And your whole life, I suppose."

He smiled at her. "Well, it's easier to bear today. Clearly we were meant to be here and find you. And I do tech work, designing websites and Internet storefronts. I can do that anywhere. As long as you're with me, I'm just fine."

"So uh, this is totally rude of me but how old are you?"

He grinned. "I was twenty-six when I was changed. So I'm eighty-six now, in May actually."

"And you have no family?"

"My parents were older when they had me. They passed when I was in college. I have a brother, or had a brother. We weren't close. I have nieces and nephews and I guess grand-nieces and nephews. Nate and Gaius are...were the closest thing I had to family until you."

The way he looked at her warmed her heart. He touched her like she was precious, watched her as if every move she made was important and wonderful. She'd never felt that kind of regard before.

"Uh, my cousin said to tell you that New Orleans isn't affiliated. I guess I know what she means now."

The relaxed and sexy look on Rhett's face sharpened and he sat up, leaning so that he could see her face better. "How did she find you and how did she know about whether or not New Orleans was affiliated?"

She poured out the entire dream to him, including the fact that her cousin was in a threesome with a vampire.

"Hmm. I wonder if we're meant to be together because you have some level of magical ability? You say your other cousin and her husband are Fae? Wow, remarkable. I've only met a Faerie once. She was...interesting."

"Interesting?" Holly rolled her eyes. "Nice euphemism. It's all right, you know, I don't expect you to be a virgin or anything."

He laughed and she shivered. His voice really was a sensual weapon. "Are you?"

"Am I what?"

"A virgin."

"I'm twenty-four years old, Rhett. What do you think?"

His face darkened at her answer. Never in his life had he felt jealousy over a woman's former lovers. This woman...well, he wanted to be her everything. "Well, Nate and I will love you so well you won't remember any of your former lovers. I'll leave when he bonds with you but I'll be back and you and I will finish what we started night before last. I can't be here when you two exchange blood the first time. I'm afraid it would rouse my possessive instincts. Truth be told, this whole thing will be tricky to work around. But this thing between the three of us is meant to be so we'll just have to work it out as we go along."

She laughed and it wove around his heart. "What? You don't have any experience with threesomes?"

"Well," he drew out the word, not wanting to misstep but also wanting to be truthful, "not like what we've got—what we'll have together. Not the metaphysical binding that'll happen between the three of us. Vampires are very sexual beings so yes, I've had threesomes before and I've not had any problem. But this isn't some fun fling. You're my mate. Our mate. And vampires are very territorial and defensive once mated. Our mate is the center of our world. Protection of her is paramount, her happiness is paramount. That instinct will be tested because you will have another mate. You're more than a woman whom a friend and I are sharing for the night or a few weeks. This is something much more important and special. But still complicated."

"Yes. Just seeing her there in your arms, her hair on your flesh, sets me at war with myself. Part of me is turned on by it but another part wants to rip you apart for touching her." Nate came in then and Holly got caught in his gaze as he came toward them. Muscles playing under his skin as he moved, he looked so sexy and yet utterly capable of violence. She felt no fear of him, though she did feel trepidation at what was going to happen between them all.

Nate held his hand out and she took it, allowing him to pull her up from the couch. His eyes held hers and her breathing went shallow. "Are you ready?" he asked softly.

"As I'll ever be," she replied nervously.

Rhett stood up and walked to where they were standing and pressed against her from behind, his cock a brand at the small of her back. "I'm going to feed but I'll be back in a while. Then I'm coming for you."

She turned her head and he took her mouth with his own. Nate was pressed against her front and Rhett against her back. Rhett's tongue flicked out, teasing at her lips until she opened them and he flowed inside. He gripped her hair in his fist and rolled his hips against her ass, which only served to press her pussy against Nate's erection, bringing a growl trickling from his lips.

Nate brought his lips to her neck and his hands moved from her hips around to cup her ass, his hands brushing against Rhett's thighs, and the two of them stiffened for a moment. Holly's mewl of pleasure brought them both back to action.

Rhett broke the kiss, pulling back from her lips slowly, and looked into her eyes so deeply it felt as if he was looking into her soul. "Soon," he said softly and, touching Nate's arm for a moment, left the house.

When the door closed behind Rhett the silence was heavy and thick. Nate stared at her long and hard and she felt a flutter low in her belly. She hadn't felt this ridiculously giddy since the age of seventeen. He made her feel like a girl experiencing her first real crush.

There was something so overpowering about him. Where Rhett was stylish and suave, Nate was dangerous and edgy. Rhett wore Perry Ellis and his hair had one of those cuts that looked effortlessly rakish but cost two hundred bucks at a salon where they got you a glass of wine while you waited. Conversely, Nate's dreadlocks came to mid-back. His pants were leather and laced up the sides. His black motorcycle boots had silver buckles up the side. His T-shirt had the sleeves cut off and he bore tribal circlet tattoos around each of his biceps. Many men paid big bucks to *look* dangerous. Nate *was* dangerous.

"Will you come upstairs with me to my room, sweetness?" His voice was low and silky. But there was something there, energy thrummed along her spine as he spoke. She felt how tightly he reined his actions. There was a precipice there and she stepped out with only Nate to guide her over.

Gulping like a cartoon character, she nodded. The smile he gave her was not reassuring. It did not say, *everything will be all right.* It said, *I'm going to take you places you never dreamed existed.*

Putting a hand at the small of her back, he guided her up the oak staircase leading to the second floor. Pretty colored-glass sconces were set into the walls, casting a warm glow over the stairs and hallway.

Nate opened the door at the very end and stood aside, waiting for her to enter first.

Once inside she was too shocked by the sight that greeted her to even hear him close the door behind them. Astonished and no small amount titillated, Holly gazed around the room openmouthed. An incredibly large four-poster bed dominated one wall. A wall that held rings above the head of the bed with cuffs hanging from them. Opposite where she was standing there were shelves that held things that, while she couldn't tell anyone their specific use, she knew enough to know they were sex toys.

Walking to the large dresser, Nate caught her glance in the mirror hanging there. She watched his reflection as he picked something up just out of her view.

Keeping his back to her, he said in a low, velvet voice, "Holly, sweetness, come here."

She took a faltering step followed by another and another until she reached him.

"Do you understand that I would never harm you?" His face was serious as he asked, looking at her still in the mirror.

She nodded mutely, not having to hesitate for even a moment.

Turning slowly, he touched her cheek with his thumb. So much gentleness there it made her ache. "I'm going to take your blood tonight and in turn, you'll take a bit of mine.

You've already done so two nights ago, but this will be part of the circle. There are some words to say to complete the ritual, and afterward we'll be bound. In vampire culture we'll be seen as married." Her eyes widened and he softened his voice. "Are you afraid?"

She thought about it for a moment and then shook her head. She wasn't. Not of him. She was anxious about the situation. Worried about her future. Wondering about what it would be like when she stood naked before this incredibly gorgeous man, but she had no fear at all *of* him.

The corner of his mouth lifted a bit. "Take my shirt off."

Yippee! She reached out and when her fingers brushed over the taut flesh of his abdomen they both gasped at the contact. She had to tiptoe and he bent down a bit but she managed to pull the shirt off.

It fell through her nerveless fingers when she took him in. Holy cow! Mouth watering, her eyes greedily devoured every bit of him that was uncovered. His abdomen was not just flat, it was hard. His bellybutton was an outie and bands of muscles ridged his lower stomach and disappeared beneath the waistband of his pants. *His very low-slung pants.* So low that his hip bones showed.

Up her eyes dragged, over the broad, muscled chest with the flat nipples, the left one bearing a silver ring. His shoulders were wide and as defined as the rest of him and she wanted to eat him up in three greedy bites.

Finally managing to bring her gaze back up to his face, she was greeted by an arrogant smile and look of total self-assuredness. Despite herself she grinned at him and he threw back his head and laughed.

"Do you like what you see, sweetness?"

"Uh-huh," she replied, feeling incredibly well-spoken.

"Want to see more?"

She couldn't even manage an "uh-huh" this time and so she settled for an enthusiastic nod.

Holding his hands to the side, he tipped his chin at her. "Go on then, sweetness. Take me, I'm all yours."

She felt like it was Christmas morning. Running her palms up the impressive wall of his chest, she gloried at the feel of his muscles jumping beneath her caress. Bolstered that she was having an effect on him, she leaned in and put her cheek against his flesh and breathed him in.

He was warm and hard against her cheek. His heart pounded reassuringly beneath her ear. Something deep inside her roused at his scent. It was comforting and exciting, home and adventure all at once. It was right.

Her hands traced over the muscles of his shoulders and back, down his spine and along the waistband of the pants until they came to the front. Smirking, she went about unlacing them, making a delighted gasp when she saw he wasn't wearing any underwear. *Zippity doo dah!!* Wasting no more time, she pushed the pants down over his thighs. And what thighs they were! Muscular and hard just like the rest of him.

When she bent to pull the snug leather from his body, she ended up kneeling before him. Eye to er, eye with his cock. The lure of the heated skin so close to her face was too much to resist. Leaning in, she brushed her cheek over his cock, breathing him in. The scent of his sex settled into her system, affecting her deeply. She kissed the blunt head and tasted the salt of his semen, the taste bursting through her.

"Wait." Bending down, he gently pulled her upright.

"I thought you said you were all mine?" she said with a slight pout.

"I am, but there are a few things we need to get out of the way first."

"What's more important than what I was doing?"

A smile threatened to come over his face. "You aren't as shy as you seem at first glance."

"Well, duh! I mean, after the supertight leather pants come off what's the point of being shy?"

Nate liked Holly. Aside from the lure of the chemicals that made her his mate, she was interesting. She had this inner core of strength that he admired. And she was funny. His life had been so serious for so long. She brought some much-needed laughter into it.

"Holly, take off your clothes."

"You're awfully bossy." Her voice was quiet as she nervously twisted the hem of her shirt in her hands.

"When it comes to sex I'm very bossy." He tipped her chin up so that he could look into her eyes. "Is that a problem, sweetness?"

"Huh?" she said, mesmerized by the curve of his bottom lip.

Pulling her close, he brought his lips against her own in a crushing kiss. His cock dug into her stomach. His hands held her to him by her upper arms. She was utterly swept away by the act.

After kissing her senseless he pulled back and looked deep into her eyes. "I like to be in charge, Holly. In the bedroom especially. I'm a dominant man."

"No kidding." She grinned at him.

"I'm being serious. I saw you look at the hooks above the bed. Do you know what they're for?"

She turned and looked at them again. "Holding onto for balance? Plants?"

Raising an eyebrow, he continued to bite back a smile. He pulled off her shirt before she could make herself any more nervous about it. Her skin was like milk, so pretty and creamy. The fingertip he ran along the curve of her breasts just above the edge of the lacy bra she was wearing left gooseflesh in its wake.

She blushed at his scrutiny. Undaunted, he reached around and undid the hooks on her bra and slid it forward. Still, she kept her arms crossed so it didn't slide all the way off.

"Holly, don't hide from me." His voice was gentle but steel edged it.

"Easy for you to say," she mumbled, eyes downcast.

"Why is it easy for me to say? Am I not standing here totally naked to your gaze?"

She got pissed then and gestured to him. "Uh yeah! Hello? For god's sake, Nate, have you looked in the mirror lately?"

He looked utterly clueless, which only made her angrier. "In case you haven't noticed, you are fucking delicious, Nate. Gorgeous. Major major hunkalicious. I on the other hand am not."

He narrowed his eyes at her and turned her to face the mirror as he stood behind her. He pulled the bra all the way off and made quick work out of stripping her jeans off. Before stripping her of her panties, he grinned up at her as he caught sight of the front panel bearing the cartoon face of a cat.

"What? Everyone loves a little pussy."

He barked out a laugh. "You're a delight, Holly."

Once she was fully naked, he took her wrists and put leather cuffs on them and laced a sturdy-looking silver chain through them. Wide-eyed, she watched him as he pulled her arms above her head and attached them to a hook suspended from the ceiling, careful to be sure her shoulders weren't overextended.

"Look at yourself, Holly," he said. Ordered.

Her eyes slowly moved from his pale green ones to her own in the mirror. Her hair was like a curtain of flame against her flesh. Her back was arched, arms above her head. Her breasts were heavy and large. The neat triangle of hair at the apex of her thighs framed her sex. She resented the sight of the softness of her stomach and the curve of her thighs that she'd always hated.

He took a breast in each hand and weighed them, thumbs coming up and over the nipples.

She was transfixed by the contrast of those large hands, dark against her own pale flesh, elegant fingers moving around her nipples.

"You're so beautiful, Holly. Inside and out," he whispered into her ear, bringing a shiver as the heat of his breath flowed across the sensitive skin there. He smoothed his hands down and over her stomach and through the curls shielding her pussy.

"I need to taste you. Here," he said, running his tongue over her neck. "And here." He pressed his middle finger through the folds of her pussy.

"Oh my," she whispered and he gave a chuckle so wicked that she grew moist and lethargic just hearing it.

"Are you still all right with offering me your blood, sweetness?"

Somewhere, she found the energy to look up to meet his eyes in the mirror and nod. He whispered in her ear what she needed to say and she licked her lips and very softly said, "You and I, we are one. One heart, one soul. My life force is yours for pleasure and for sustenance."

With hooded eyes he nicked her flesh open and covered it with his mouth while she watched.

Shivers worked through her as she felt her blood leave her own body and enter his mouth. Each pull was like a tug on her clit. When he stopped, moving back to lave his tongue over the wound to close it, her climax bloomed within her and she pulled against her bonds and cried out, back arching, going up on her toes.

He put his lips to her ear and repeated the words back to her and then, keeping his hands at her waist to support her, he walked around to face her and took her lips. The metallic tang of blood coated her tongue and she realized that it wasn't just her blood but that he'd nicked his own lip and she was taking his blood into her body. The thought was scary and yet erotic at the same time.

Total disorientation swam over her and she experienced double vision. She swayed a bit in Nate's embrace and he moved his lips away but kept her within his embrace.

"Shh, it's the bond. Close your eyes a moment and you'll get used to it."

She pressed her face into the warmth of his chest and breathed him in as he held her. The beat of his heart and the rhythmic stroke of his hands up and down her back comforted and gentled her.

Some time later she heard a tap on the door and felt Rhett come into the room.

"Jesus, you've chained her up already?" Rhett murmured as she felt him move toward them.

Nate laughed and it rumbled against her face. "Do you object, Rhett? Doesn't she look exquisite this way?"

"She does," he agreed. "I love the way your hair is like a cloak of fire over your back," Rhett said, pressing a kiss on her shoulder.

The nausea and disequilibrium passed and she carefully opened her eyes and felt the world adjust with relief. "I thought that it was like having both of you inside of my head before but this is way more than that."

"The mate bond is sort of like the integration of our senses together. I can feel your excitement, Holly. The wetness between your thighs. I can feel the way that it turns you on to have Rhett standing behind you, the material of his pants brushing up against your ass. I can feel your fear, your feelings of inadequacy." Stopping, he looked at her closely and the depth of tenderness in his eyes nearly tore her apart. "So alone. Oh, sweetness, you're never alone with me and Rhett in the world."

Tears welled in her eyes and her bottom lip trembled as she fought off her turbulent emotions.

Nate reached up and unhooked her hands but left her wrists bound to each other. He led her to the bed and laid her down on the cool comforter. She looked up at them both and watched as Rhett pulled his sweater off and then shrugged out of his slacks and socks.

The two of them stood side by side, naked. Staring down at her. She flushed scarlet.

"It's our turn to bond, Holly," Rhett said, lying down beside her on the bed. "I took a lot of blood from you night before last so I'm just going to take a taste and you'll do the same."

"O-okay."

He brushed a hand down her body and marveled at her curves. She was so beautiful. He couldn't believe he'd never thought of curvaceous as hot before but she was luscious and delicious. His blood pounded in his ears as he moved down her body.

"I'm going to turn on the shower, she'll be cold when you're through," Nate said quietly to Rhett, who looked up at him and nodded.

Holly had to hold herself with a will of iron to resist writhing under his gaze. When he parted her thighs and nuzzled the sensitive space where her leg met her groin she moaned and spontaneously said the binding words to him.

He nicked her and again the shooting pulses of desire as he drew blood from her pushed her into orgasm. He was suddenly on top of her, weight supported on his upper arms, cock teasing her sopping wet pussy folds. Speaking the words back, he then broke open a wound on his wrist and she licked at it and instead of being creeped out, the flavor, *his* flavor, burst through her system.

Knowing what to expect this time, she kept her eyes closed as the feeling of not double vision but triple vision hit her. She felt Nate in the bathroom, setting out towels and pretty-smelling shampoo and soap, warming the room with the heat lamp. She felt the space where she was lodged within him.

Rhett undid the restraints and kissed each wrist and she felt her place within him as well. His total contentment with the situation puzzled her. She felt him brush up against the walls she had constructed around her heart. His resolve to break through those walls gave her a moment of utter terror. He meant to strip her bare of her defenses and make her see what it was to be his mate.

Saying nothing, he helped her up and into the bathroom where Nate waited in the shower stall.

Although calling it a shower stall was absurd. It was nearly half the size of her apartment and had three showerheads. Built-in benches ringed the walls.

Holly took the hand Nate held out to her, climbing into the enclosure with him. The sharp edge of his hunger for her slammed into her, doubling as Rhett joined them.

Nate gently moved her beneath a showerhead and she groaned as the hot water warmed the gooseflesh that had erupted.

Rhett's hands slicked over her body, soaping her up, and she had a moment of total incredulity as she saw the situation from the outside. Two gorgeous men with her. Naked. In a shower.

Holly Daniels was going to have hot kinky sex with two vampires. "Hee!" she giggled and both men looked at each other and laughed.

She lathered up Nate's chest while Rhett massaged shampoo into her scalp. She moved her soapy hands lower and he thrust his cock between her slippery palms without a bit of hesitation.

She found herself pushed back against the cool tile, Rhett's mouth on hers, his tongue sliding against her own. A whimper escaped as he nipped her bottom lip. A gasp followed when Nate's lips cruised down the column of her neck and found a pouty nipple, sucking it into his mouth, grazing it with his teeth.

Reaching out, she had Rhett's cock in her hand and would have grabbed Nate's but he'd slid down her body and put her thigh up on his shoulder. When he parted her with his thumbs and stared his fill, she made an embarrassed sound. Nate stilled her as she tried to pull away, a big hand at her hip, while Rhett pushed her harder against the tile.

Her mortification at being spread open to his gaze that way was gone the moment that Nate swept the flat of his tongue through the folds of her pussy. Rhett's mouth moved from her lips to her nipples, holding her breasts close together so that he could lap across them both at the same time.

She'd already come twice from being bitten by them and yet this climax—building up slow, with electric ferocity like a storm—was inevitable. Rhett dropped to his knees and his tongue joined Nate's. Looking down her body, she saw them there, heads bent over her pussy, tongues moving over and through her. Ribbons of pleasure shot through her, tied her to them more closely. A scream ripped from her lips as the storm broke. Wave after wave of delicious pleasure swept through her body, singeing her nerve endings, setting her senses aflame.

Her eyes were closed and her muscles still twitching as she was picked up and dried quickly but gently on the way back into the bedroom. Rhett laid her on the bed and she rolled up onto all fours and looked at them. She could feel the sexual tension between the two of them, the curiosity heightened by the dual tonguing they'd delivered.

"Your turn," she said in a near purr. She felt like a goddess at that moment, beautiful and desired. She licked her lips and Nate groaned. The corner of her mouth lifted and she raised a brow. "I'm sure we can find a way for everyone to be happy all at once. I'm game if you two are."

Nate's deep chuckle caressed her and he showed no hesitation when he walked to her.

"I believe I was here earlier, before you waylaid me." She grabbed his cock and licked around the meaty head.

"Don't let me stop you now, sweetness," he growled and watched as her lips wrapped around him. Watched as he disappeared into her mouth.

Rhett, cock in hand, moved behind her on the bed and she arched her back as she felt his crown nudge against her gate. Slowly, he worked his way inside of her, hissing at the feel of her superheated pussy. Despite the fact that she was slick from three orgasms, he had to clench his teeth to keep from coming after he'd seated himself fully. Her pussy hugged him so tight he was just moments from climax it felt so damned good.

Tracing up the line of her jaw with a fingertip, Nate wove his hand through the fragrant, still-damp curls of her hair. Gripping tight, he delighted in her sound of surprise as it quickly turned into a moan of desire. The sound vibrated through his cock.

Throwing open the link, he felt what she felt almost completely. He could sense that part of her that she kept walled off from them. Resolving to deal with that later, he concentrated instead on what he *could* feel from her. Felt his own taste on her tongue, the way the scent of his skin made her wet, the fire on her flesh and the fierce digs of Rhett's cock into her pussy.

Looking up, he locked gazes with Rhett and realized Rhett had also thrown open the link and was feeling Nate's cock slide in and out of Holly's mouth. Knew that Rhett wondered what it would be like if it were his own mouth instead of Holly's. Knew that Nate knew, and that created a feedback loop of pleasure, desire and yearning that neither man could bear and each thrust forward and exploded into Holly's body, one with a hoarse roar, the other with a long moan.

Sandwiched between the two thrusting bodies, Holly was buffeted by the immense wave of pleasure. It broke over her and she saw stars as their unified orgasm flowed through her body.

The three of them collapsed sideways onto the bed and rearranged themselves into a mutual embrace of tangled legs, arms and hair.

"Wow," Holly breathed out some minutes later.

"I always thought the one true mate stuff was total bullshit. Obviously I was wrong," Rhett said, drawing fingertips in a light circle at her hip. "And I'm glad."

Unable to stop himself and wanting to be inside her desperately, Nate quickly pulled her astride him, positioning himself true, pressing the head of his cock just inside her until she gave a surprised gasp.

"Can you take me?"

"Always." Holly was mesmerized by the look of absolute hunger on his face and touched by the way he gentled his need for her. Sliding slowly down the length of his cock, she felt it all the way up her spine. He filled her up, not just physically but emotionally. He left her no room to put a part of herself away. Instead he demanded everything of her. His scrutiny of those protective barriers brought a slither of cold fear down her spine at the thought he and Rhett would find a way past them. Lay her bare in a way she'd never been before.

Nate looked up into her face and watched fear skitter across her features but wouldn't flinch. He wanted her to know he was resolved to making her his completely, no reservations, no holding back. He wanted her to see the love in his face and know that he'd always be there to catch her when she fell.

His world narrowed to that set of moments. Of his mate astride his body, riding him slowly, bottom lip caught in her teeth. Of their bed, the scent of sex rising from the sheets. Her skin so soft against his.

In no hurry to come, he lay back and let her set the pace. Let her ride his cock slow and steady.

For a time, Rhett was content to watch them, a casual hand stroking his cock. But his need for her began to build until he moved to kneel beside her, leaning to kiss her perfect shoulder and over her collarbone. Taking her lips, he sighed into her mouth at the feel of her hand wrapping around his cock. God how he needed her to touch him—felt complete when he was in her attention—when she was giving her love to him.

Nate's fingers intertwined with Holly's around Rhett's cock and they stilled. Drawing a deep breath, Rhett looked at Nate and then at Holly as their pale-as-cream and milky coffee flesh pressed over his olive tones. The strength in Nate's grip added pressure to Holly's silky embrace. And again the three of them made a circuit of pleasure, of giving and receiving, that was electric.

Holly gave out first, throwing her head back as Nate's other hand delved into her pussy and lightly tickled over her clit. The contractions of her inner muscles pulled Nate in and the sound of their pleasure and the new but erotic experience of a man's hand on his cock moved Rhett to join the other two.

He nearly came again when Holly licked his cum from her fingers.

* * * * *

Dawn came quickly and Holly lay between them as they headed into sleep. Something that eluded her as her own racing thoughts kept her awake.

She had never felt more alive—more happy and complete—and more frightened of losing it all in her life. Terror ate at her.

Permanence wasn't something she had a lot of experience with in her life. Growing up, she and her mom had moved around a lot. Her mother paid their bills with a long series of odd jobs. They'd lived in a lot of cheap motels and rooming houses. Because of their impermanence, Holly hadn't had a lot of friends and when she did make them, they had to move and she lost them. So after a while, she stopped letting people get close to her rather than deal with the pain of losing them.

Even as an adult she hadn't let many people in. She didn't date a lot. She hadn't been ashamed of their living conditions precisely but she didn't want pity either. Plus, she wasn't a beauty, she knew that. She didn't go to the prom or other big dances and she'd remained a virgin until her first year of college three years ago.

By that time they'd been in Seattle for a few years. Her mother had been working as an assistant in a nursing home and they'd shared a small apartment. Holly finished high school and got a job as an office assistant. Her mother had insisted that all of the monies from Holly's job went into a savings account for college and after a few years she had a bit of a nest egg. Holly had done well enough in school that despite all of their moving she'd been able to get a scholarship to attend the University of Washington. That money, together with her small savings, had gotten her through the last three years.

Reggie, the guy she'd dated for her first year in college—the one she'd lost her virginity to—was a really nice person and someone she'd counted as a friend but he'd been a senior and had gone away to graduate school at the end of that summer and she hadn't really gone out much since.

But the two men beside her were not content with having all of her minus what was behind the walls. They wanted it all. Panic choked her. She already felt totally exposed through their three-way link. She didn't think that she'd be able to let those walls down without a fight and worse, now that she'd shared such deep intimacy with Nate and Rhett, she cringed to try to imagine life without it.

Chapter Four

℅

In the kitchen, making a meal, Holly smiled at their thoughtfulness. The pantry was fully stocked as was the fridge. She had Pearl Jam playing loudly in the background as she danced around. She had the night off and planned to deal with her living situation. She'd spoken with the police two days before, severely skirting the details, only saying that she'd come home and the place had been tossed. They'd taken a report but didn't seem very hopeful about finding anything. And after she'd watched her burglars dissolve into nothingness, it wasn't like she could disagree. She also spoke to her landlord. He was willing to let her out of her lease because he didn't want to upgrade the security on her apartment or the building.

Despite the fact that she felt at home, the truth was that they hadn't invited her to live there and she didn't want to assume anything. Yes, she knew they wanted her in their bed and that they wanted her in their lives but she didn't know to what extent they wanted her around physically. Things were chaotic enough as it was. She didn't know much of anything and that made her feel totally out of control and that had to end as soon as possible.

When Rhett awoke it was like something inside of her that had been dormant stirred to life. She felt him reach out to her through that link, assure himself that she was nearby. She knew he was satisfied by that, that her presence comforted him. Part of her clicked into place and that felt right. Panic and comfort warred inside her.

Instead of going to join him in the shower like she wanted, she stayed downstairs and continued to make dinner. She'd seen them both eat at the tavern so she supposed that particular popular vampire story was a myth and they did eat regular food. She didn't know what to do, whether or not to ignore these intimate feelings or even whether they were one-sided. So she chopped the ginger and tipped it into the jar with the rest of the marinade for the noodle salad and waited.

* * * * *

Rhett opened his eyes and saw that she wasn't there in bed between him and Nate. Her scent was still strong though and her residual warmth lingered on the sheets and he leaned in and inhaled. Opening the link, he reached for her, understanding she was nearby. He relaxed a bit but was unhappy with the level of uncertainty she was giving off.

Shaking his head, he got up and walked to the bathroom to shower. She didn't believe in herself enough, didn't believe in them enough and that had to end. He just had no idea how yet. It was early days, they had time. Of course, someone was trying to injure her and they needed to deal with her family. God only knew how that would affect her wellbeing.

He dried off and felt Nate wake up and do the same thing he'd done, make sure she was still there and then wonder how they'd break through her defenses.

Rhett nodded to Nate as they passed and he headed downstairs and Nate into the shower. Vampires woke up cold and a hot shower, especially in winter, was the best way outside of a very deep feeding to warm up.

Standing in the doorway to the kitchen, he watched her work. There was an efficiency about her that he admired. She was naturally graceful as she worked, gliding about the big kitchen like she belonged there. She *did* belong there, if only she'd let herself believe it.

She turned — the vehemence of his thoughts alerted her — and gave him a tentative smile. "Hi. Hope you don't mind. I was starving and came down to see what I could scrounge up but you two have a really well-stocked pantry. I'm making enough for three, I know you guys eat and well, you can just...mmpfh!"

He cut off her rambling, nervous, stream-of-consciousness sentence with the pressure of his lips upon hers. Calming, she opened her lips under his with joy and his heart soared to be received in such a way. His hunger for her rose as their bodies pressed against each other. Her curves molded to the harder lines of his body, made for him.

Holly fell under his spell as his hands slid up her sides, over her ribs, came to cup her breasts, testing their weight. A soft sound came from her lips and she arched into him as he kneaded and traced over the nipples through her blouse. Suddenly she realized that she had his shirt gripped in her fists. Concerned that it was some expensive designer job, she let go with an embarrassed cry.

Startled, Rhett looked into her face "What? Did I hurt you?"

"No. I just," she smoothed the shirt where she'd been holding it, "I was ruining your shirt."

Incredulity spread over his face. "The shirt?" Buttons flew as he pulled it open with a yank. Tossing it aside, he looked back in her direction. "You think I care about a shirt when your hands are on me? When your breasts are filling my palms and your taste is on my tongue?"

Picking it up, she saw the designer label and winced. Exasperated, he pulled it out of her hands. "Honey, I don't care about the shirt. It was just some wrinkles."

"And now you've ruined it by opening it that way!" She was appalled.

"It's just a shirt! Why are you so upset? I've got twenty more in my closet upstairs. There's only one of you, one moment like that in time. In the balance, you win out every time."

"Twenty more? My god, Rhett, that shirt must have cost you at least a hundred dollars."

"Three hundred and fifty. But so what? It's only money, it's just a thing."

Her back went up at that. "I find that it's only people who *have* money that like to say that."

Rhett groaned aloud.

"What are you groaning at?"

"You. You're going to find a way to hold yourself back over this, I can feel it."

Raising her eyebrows at him, she noticed Nate breeze into the room out of the corner of her eye. He picked her up, placed her on the counter and moved to stand between her thighs. "Mmmm, what smells so good?" He nuzzled her neck. "Other than you, that is?"

Her hands toyed with one of the twisted strands of his hair while she let herself enjoy the feeling of his lips on her throat.

"Soba noodle salad with chicken and don't try to distract me. Rhett and I were having a discussion."

"You and Rhett were having a fight over something stupid. Let's end it now and talk about important things like getting your things moved into the house and when we're going to deal with your family."

"Having a fight because she's holding herself back from us," Rhett said and Nate shot him a disgruntled look.

"I was doing no such thing! Jeez! I just didn't want to wrinkle his shirt and he threw a tantrum and ripped it!"

"I didn't throw a tantrum and you're using whatever you can to keep from fully uniting with us through the bond. You're scared, Holly, and you know it!"

"Scared? Oh I don't have any reason to be scared, do I? Hmm, three nights ago I meet these two men in my bar. I go home and get attacked by thugs or whatever they are who try to *kill* me and then these two guys from the bar burst in and save me. Turns out that these thugs are magical thugs and they disappear before my eyes after telling me some mystical stuff about being a Charvez. Then I find out the two guys from the bar are vampires and I actually feed one and take blood from the other!"

She hauled in a deep breath and tried to hold off hysteria. "And then the vamps tell me that I'm their mate. We do some blood stuff and I'm suddenly wired into your systems and you're in mine and there're hooks in the ceiling and sex with two men who are very nearly strangers who live in a fucking mansion! My supposed cousin barges into my dream, my house isn't safe, I don't know what is going to happen to me. Yeah, nothing to be scared of."

Placing her palm on his chest over his heart, Nate looked at her through solemn pale green eyes. "This beats for you. I don't know how much more simple I can make it for you, sweetness."

Rhett did the same with her other hand and the two of them stood there and opened themselves up to her.

"Everything is about us. About you. All of the other stuff is incidental and we can work past it. But you have to let us in, Holly. You can't hold back."

"I can't just yet," she whispered and winced at Rhett's stricken look. Nate took a deep breath and nodded and leaned in to kiss her softly, gently.

"Soon, Holly. I can't be patient forever."

"Now can we talk about getting you moved in here and the situation with your family?" Rhett asked as he pushed a strand of her hair out of her face.

"Move in?"

"Did you think we'd just fuck you, take your blood and toss you out? After we both told you about being our mate?" Nate raised a brow. He was really good at looking imperious.

"Oh I don't know what to think!" she exclaimed and got off the counter and began to toss the noodles with the chicken and veggies.

Rhett sighed and began to set the table. Nate put out glasses and opened a bottle of wine. The two of them sat and watched her, waiting as she brought the big bowl to the table and sat down with them.

They ate in silence for a while and finally Rhett grabbed her hand and kissed her fingertips. He pulled and she came to him, sitting astride his lap.

"Can we start over? Before the whole shirt thing?"

"I'm sorry," she said quietly.

"Me too. But, honey, nothing is more important to me than you, especially not a shirt."

She ran her fingers through his hair and he closed his eyes and soaked it in. When she brought her lips to his, she felt his entire system fire through the link. His body hardened against hers as she felt the sharp edge of his hunger roar to life. His hands slid up her back and very soon after she found herself lying on the table, looking into Nate's face.

Nate pulled her sweater off and freed her breasts from her bra with a fevered groan. His dreads made a curtain around her face as he leaned in to kiss her lips and then down her neck and to the curve of her breasts.

Rhett pulled her jeans open and off and her panties followed. She heard him move the chair and settle between her thighs as Nate continued to tease and tantalize her breasts with teeth and tongue, big hands stroking over her belly and up her ribs.

Her hands cradled Rhett's skull as he moved in to lap at her pussy. He ate her like she was the best thing he'd ever had, as if the very thought of letting even a drop of her honey go untasted was a terrible crime.

Damn, he was really good at that. Holly groaned low as Rhett fluttered his tongue over her pussy, giving special attention to her clit, his fingers slowly stroking into her body. Without conscious thought, Holly's hips churned. She pressed herself into Rhett's face and he made a pleased hum that vibrated through her.

Heat arced up Holly's spine as she caught the glint of Nate's incisors as he moved his mouth over her nipples. The sight of those sharp predator's teeth turned her on. The juxtaposition of the savage power hinted at in those teeth and in those muscles contrasted with the gentleness with which he treated her amazed and touched her deeply.

"Bite me," she whispered and Rhett and Nate struck simultaneously. Screaming out, climax rode her, holding her in its tight maw. Her pussy clasped at the fingers stroking into her. Her nipples stabbed toward the ceiling and her body flooded with pleasure as she gave her life's most basic essence to these men.

Rhett only took a small amount, he was sure Nate did as well. They'd both need to feed later but for now, she was all he needed. Standing, he nudged the head of his cock against her entrance and slid inside, bit by agonizing bit. Her inner muscles still rippled with the memory of the orgasm she'd just had. Looking up, he watched Holly's eyes slide from him up to Nate's face. Watched a different sort of light come into her when she connected with him. He felt a moment of intense desire to own her, for it to be just the two of them. Frustration and resentment warred with what he knew to be their reality. Sharing was what had to happen, there was no way around it, even if he had to deal with his feelings.

Sensing his tumultuous emotions, Holly broke her gaze with Nate and got up on her elbows to look at Rhett with tenderness and concern.

Seeing this moment, Nate backed off. Quickly pulling on a shirt, he quietly left to go feed, leaving the two of them alone. Rhett felt a bit petty for a moment but then realized that there would be decades for them to work it all out, to share each other. Tonight, right then, she was his.

Leaning forward, he picked her up. Her legs wrapped around his waist and he carried her upstairs and into his bedroom. They'd slept in Nate's the night before, another thing they'd have to work out. Rhett's room was old-world elegance rather than new-world goth. A large cherry sleigh bed with light-colored linens dominated the room. Built-in bookshelves lined the walls and a window seat graced one bay window.

Laying her down gently, he followed, never leaving the haven of her body with his own. He settled within the cradle of her thighs and rocked slowly—not really thrusting—just enjoying the feeling of being enmeshed with the woman who made him complete.

"I love you, Holly." He said it softly and the fear in her eyes eased and she gave him a small smile. He felt the elation move through her but also her fear of losing what they had. Losing them. Fear that it wasn't real or lasting. "It's not going to go away, honey. It's real. Why can't you see it?"

Emotion flooded through her body. Taking a deep breath, she shook her head, unable to speak. She could see it, she just didn't know if she could believe it. Believe in herself. When it came right down to it, she still had no idea why two men who looked like them would be interested in her.

Instead she stretched her neck and kissed him. Grabbing his bottom lip between her teeth, she rolled her hips, taking him deeper, relieved that he let her distract him for the time being.

He rolled over and she was astride him. Her hair tumbled over her shoulders and arms, so long it stroked over his abdomen. Time seemed to stop as their gazes locked and after a few beats, they found a rhythm.

Rhett's hands kneaded her breasts, nipples peeking between his fingers. Each pinch or tug shot straight to her clit. The head of his cock stroked over her sweet spot each time he met her body with his own upward thrust. She leaned forward, her clit brushing with deliberate friction as she ground into his body, teasing them both with a swivel of her hips.

As she looked up at him, his beauty startled her. The depth of what he made her feel yawned beneath her like a big, scary crevasse. But she couldn't deny that it also felt sweet and frankly, it was useless to resist it. If she lost him, she'd lose him. But she couldn't keep from loving him. Not with his inky black hair spread around his head, framing his face. Those gorgeous brown eyes looked right into her soul, her heart. He looked like a thoroughly fallen angel—beautiful beyond description but life etched beside his eyes, in the cant of his smile.

Rhett felt her open the door into herself a bit as she gazed down at him. Above him she rose, the curve of her breasts gently swaying with her movement. Her skin had the loveliest pink flush. So filled with life, her eyes shone with the greedy lust that consumed them both and the glow of the depth of connection they held.

One of his hands trailed down her body, the tips of his fingers finding her clit and circling it slowly, occasionally sliding down to touch the spot where they were joined. The sensation was delicate as he stretched the folds of her sex, bringing her skin to stroke against itself.

He watched her eyes slide half shut and that juicy bottom lip catch between her teeth. "Come for me again, honey. Give me another," he urged her softly.

Her head fell back as a deep moan came from her lips as orgasm washed over her. Clamping down on him, the inner walls of her pussy rippled, pulling at his cock, sucking him back into her body each time she pulled up, retreating.

Arching up, back bowed, he made one last thrust up into her body, holding that position as his body emptied—pouring his pleasure—into hers.

After the world stilled again, he moved, tipping her to the side so that he could wrap his arms around her, pulling her into the shelter of his body.

* * * * *

Nate walked into the house and straight into the bathroom adjoining his room. Rhett had gotten his time with Holly and now it was his turn.

The well of his hunger for her appeared bottomless. He woke up aching for her—aching to be inside of her, to hear her voice, feel her skin under his hands, beneath his lips, responding to him, warming to his presence. He wanted to know her in every situation, to hear her giggle, to watch her come with her arms tied, rope knots up her back, to see her skin pinken after he flogged her.

He knew Holly would be the perfect sub. She was strong—really strong—and knew she was capable of surviving and overcoming. While she clearly had self-esteem issues, he felt like once she understood just what she did to his system, how much he desired her on every level, she would joyfully submit to him.

He knew they'd never have a *stronger* bond but he also knew it would be *different* than the one she had with Rhett. Each one of them would fill a missing, empty spot in the other. In that sense he could share her with Rhett but it was still difficult to know that the woman you loved also loved someone else.

He gave them an hour and was just getting ready to go into Rhett's room and take her out bodily when the door opened and he heard her footsteps coming toward him. In the background he caught Rhett's promise to be back in a while and an imperious reminder that they would flesh out the details of their living situation just before he took the stairs and left the house.

Nate went and stood in the doorway, watching her come to him. One of Rhett's robes was hanging from her body provocatively, the creamy flesh of her shoulder exposed. She was all the more alluring in that she had no idea of her appeal.

"I've got a bath running for us now." Taking her hand, he led her into the bathroom.

Clutching the front of her robe close to her body, she looked up at him shyly. Putting his hands over hers gently, he moved them apart so the robe slipped open and down, hanging from her elbows. Most of the material pooled in a spill of midnight blue silk at her feet, framing her.

Pulling the robe the rest of the way off, he laid it aside and stepped into the large tub. Sitting down, he widened his thighs and waggled a brow in her direction.

Blushing, hands over her body, she stepped into the water and quickly sat down, back against his chest.

Making a tsking sound, he placed her hands on the side of the tub before filling a cup with water to pour over her hair. Gentle hands massaged shampoo into it, massaging her scalp.

"Do you feel all right, sweetness? We didn't take too much blood, did we?"

Dragging her eyes open, she tipped her head back to look into his eyes. "I feel wonderful."

"You *are* wonderful."

He felt something inside of her deny it and he shook his head. "Listen to me, Holly. You can't keep us out. We're all a unit, a group. If you don't open to us fully, it won't work. It's going to be hard enough with two vampire males sharing a mate, let's not make things worse. You have to trust what you know is true."

Sighing, she nodded as she got to her knees. Turning to face him, she soaped a washcloth and began to cleanse him. Loving the feel of her hands on him, he lazily accepted her ministrations, knowing they were each learning the other.

Beads of water glittered like diamonds against the pale peaches and cream of her flesh. Wanting to take care of her, he washed her hair and massaged her dry after they finished. Taking her back into the bedroom, he moved close, breathing her in. She smelled *his* and Nate's system roared with possessiveness.

He loved the way it seemed as if she was unable to stop running her hands over his skin. Her small hands stroked across the muscles of his chest and upper arms, down over the hard, flat surface of his abdomen, just above the flesh of his cock as it jutted up against his body, seeking her attention.

Wanting to give her the freedom to explore him, he stood as still as he could, loving the way her hands felt against his muscles. Although she'd been shy, curiosity and desire emboldened her bit by bit.

Reaching back to the dresser behind him, he pulled out the wrist restraints and held them in front of himself. When she saw them, her breath hitched and her pupils widened. Knowing she liked it, that she responded in such a way, made it hard for him to think a moment. Holly made him complete in a way he understood at that moment he'd been waiting to feel his whole life.

"Hold your hands out," he said softly and she immediately obeyed. Caressing her wrists, he kissed her pulse point, feeling it jump beneath his lips as he did. Smiling wickedly, he put the restraints around each wrist and made sure they were tight but not painful.

"If this ever goes into a place where you're uncomfortable or afraid, or you just want me to stop, I want you to use a safe word. That way you can struggle and cry out but I won't stop unless you say the word. It's more fun that way. You can feel free to say or do whatever you want but you'll always have the safe word and it only means one thing." Wearing a faint smile, he led her back toward the bed. Positioning her just so, he wove a chain between the two wrists and pulled it taut to the hook at the head of the bed, securing it there.

"Our safe word is red." He looked down at her and shook his head. "Never mind. I could easily see calling you red with that hair. How about pasta? Something you wouldn't normally say during sex. Okay?"

She wasn't an expert or anything but she knew enough to know what a safe word was. Clearly he was into BDSM and a part of her deep down thrilled at the anticipation of what he might do.

"Pasta. Got it," she said with a nod, proud that her voice didn't break.

"I'm never going to hurt you, sweetness," he assured her as he got on all fours over her body. "And I'm not interested in humiliating you either. We can work things through as we go. Find things we like, things we don't."

Nodding, she arched, trying to make contact with his body and he laughed. "Eager? Good, let's see what we can do about that."

And he was gone, off the bed. Out of the corner of her eye she saw him pull something out of a drawer. Her eyes widened and something twisted in her stomach when he turned. In his hand he held a small flogger. Twirling it deftly, the wide leather tails made a slithering sound that brought a gush of honey from her pussy. With a flick of his wrist the straps hit his palm and a gasp of delight burst from her. He looked into her eyes, surprised and very pleased if the sight of his ever-hardening cock was any indicator.

"I like the way it sounds too," he said silkily, moving to her. The flogger came down quickly, the tails caressing the flesh of her breasts.

"Oh!" Her voice was breathy as he struck again, the tips of the tails just barely touching her nipples. The sound of contact echoed, a louder crack, but only pleasure radiated from the strike.

What followed was the most intense thing she'd ever experienced. With expert precision, the tails of the flogger caressed, flicked and slapped her flesh from the tops of her thighs to her shoulders. Some of the strikes stung but others, particularly those on her breasts and against her mound, were more like a soft stroke of the leather. A fire built in her flesh, her cunt was swollen and slick, nipples hard. She began to slip under the intoxication of the sensation, to slip away into a place that was soft and warm. She left it to him, gave up her safety and pleasure to Nate's hands.

When her flesh had taken on a rosy hue and her eyes were glassy—fallen under the lethargy of desire—Nate laid the flogger aside. Kneeling over her, he licked from the top of her mound to the hollow of her throat. The blood so close to the surface of her skin from the flogging incited him, called out to his senses.

Taking her lips with his own, he drowned in her taste. She was everything and his body, his heart and mind simply accepted it. She was what he needed, what he craved most, and she was all of that simply by existing.

Her tongue was shy against his for a few moments, but soon her body was arching to touch his. Her teeth nipped at his lip and because her hands were bound, she wrapped one leg around his ass to pull him closer.

Fingertips traced the inside of her upraised arms, over the curves at the sides of her breasts, down each rib and over the swell of her hips and thighs. He rubbed the shaft of his cock against her, the head caressing her clit. She was slippery and the breath hitched in her chest.

Opening the vein-rich skin just above her breast, he sipped her.

A quick intake of breath and a long sigh turned into a keening cry as her orgasm hit. Quickly, he adjusted his hips and his cock slid into her. The muscles of her pussy clutched with pleasure, welcoming him.

"Yessss," he hissed, hilting himself within her.

She moved her legs to hook her ankles just above his ass. Back bowing, her body pulled against the chains but the restraints kept her arms above her head. Kept her body displayed just the way he wanted it.

The sheath of her pussy caressed him, pulled at him, drew him in with a heated embrace. Her lips were parted and glossy and he couldn't help returning over and over to taste her there. Her eyes were glassy and held only him as she gazed up into his face. They fell into each other as he moved over her and into her.

Torturing them both, he delivered sinuous, slow strokes, drawing the lovemaking out for long minutes. But the call of her body was too strong after a while and he poured himself into her, his cock never wanting to leave the silky clasp of her body. She was a miracle, the very thing that made everything right in his world, and that shook him and comforted him at the same time.

He was still wrapped around her body, a fingertip tracing the bones of her cheeks and brows, when he heard Rhett come in downstairs.

"We need to go downstairs and talk about things," he said, reaching up to undo the restraints, gently rubbing her wrists before kissing them softly. He took in the pinkened hue of her flesh from her climax and the kiss of the flogger. Marking her that way turned him on immensely.

"Things?" Her words were slurred a bit. She was still under the influence of his bite and of the flogging.

Chuckling, he kissed her nose before rolling out of bed. He pulled on a pair of drawstring pants but stayed shirtless. The man looked *good*.

Holly hoped her clutching the sheet looked nonchalant instead of desperate to hide her body. Grabbing for the robe, Nate sighed and picked it up, wrapping her in it himself.

"You're beautiful," he murmured, tying it at the side, kissing her forehead. She wished she could believe it.

Taking the hand he held out, she followed him out of the room and downstairs.

* * * * *

Looking up, Rhett's stomach clenched when he saw them walk in together. Holly bore the flushed, extremely satisfied look of a woman who'd been fucked well and truly. He also saw the pink flesh of her chest and realized that Nate had most likely flogged her.

Nate's gaze locked with Rhett's and he sat Holly down, moving to get himself a glass of wine. Rhett knew Nate recognized his feelings and was giving him a bit of distance. They'd all have to work together to get past the anger and the jealousy. When he walked back into the room he deliberately sat on the low table across from where she was on the couch so that Rhett could sit next to her. Meeting his eyes, Rhett nodded at him, thanking him for the gesture.

"We need to get your stuff out of the garage and into the house." Rhett kissed her hand.

She looked confused. "Huh?"

"From your apartment. It all arrived here about three hours ago. I'm surprised you didn't hear it. Then again, the kitchen is on the far side of the house from the garage."

"Come again? You did what?" Incredulous, she sat forward on the couch.

"You said you were going to call the landlord today and our assistant said that the guy was letting you out of your lease. It's all packed safely, don't worry, I'm certain that they did a professional job of it," Nate said matter-of-factly.

"You two arranged to have my apartment moved? Here? Without even bothering to ask me?" Neither man seemed to notice the dangerous tone in her voice.

"You didn't think we'd let you go back to that tiny apartment where you were unsafe? Not when you're meant to be with us and when this place is so safe?" Rhett looked so arrogantly self-assured when he said it that she had to swallow a frustrated scream.

Pushing up off the couch, she began to pace. "I can't believe you just moved my stuff without even discussing it with me. I'm not your child you know! You can't just make decisions without even bothering to talk to me about them."

"Are we wrong in thinking you want to be here with us? I know it's a bit farther from campus than your old apartment was but you can drive. You don't need to take the bus, although you could if you really wanted to."

Coherent thought fled as she saw red. She counted to ten and then thirty-five. "In the first place, I don't have a car. In the second place, I don't recall being asked to move in here at all. In fact, I don't recall you two *asking* me about any of this." Her teeth were clenched to hold in her anger.

"Holly, you're our mate, we're yours. What did we have to ask?" Rhett said, obviously clueless as to why she was so angry. "We love you. Where else would you be?"

"Which leads to the next question. Where are we going to sleep? How do we divide up time?" Nate moved to the couch and put his feet up on the table.

She just looked at the two of them sitting side by side on the couch and snorted in frustration. She wanted to be there and their behavior was well-meant if not totally arrogant and patronizing. Sighing, she looked at Nate's feet on the coffee table and pushed them off with her outstretched foot. "Jeez, feet off the table!"

"Does this mean you'll stop being pissed, forgive us our cavemen attitudes and move in here?" Nate asked with a barely repressed smile.

"Damn it! Can you read my mind?" She stomped a foot in frustration.

"Sort of. Some thoughts and emotions come through loud and clear. You know that. We've had a few moments like this over the last days. We'll try not to if we can help it. We want to respect your privacy," Rhett said calmly.

"If you'd open to us, you'd feel us too," Nate said and Holly felt the annoyance and hurt in his voice.

Giving a long, put-upon sigh, she turned and walked out of the room. They both jumped up to follow her up the stairs.

At the end of the hall she turned back to them. Pointing at Rhett's door she said, "You're here."

He nodded.

Nate tipped his chin to his room when she passed by before walking to the far end of the hallway. "What are these?"

Nate moved toward her to open the two doors at the end of the hall. "Both of these rooms are empty. We can turn one into a study for you, a place to do your homework. The other can be your bedroom."

"Or our bedroom," Rhett said. He looked at both of them earnestly. "I liked the three of us in the same bed. I don't mind having some personal space that's each of ours, but I'd prefer to all sleep together."

Holly thought about it. Truth was, she liked waking up between the two of them and preferred the three of them sleeping together every night.

"Okay, how about we have one room be a study and your personal space and the other one can be our bedroom, a place we all share most nights?" Nate was willing to spend most nights as a threesome but he wanted at least one night a week with her all to himself.

"Most nights?"

"Some nights I want to just have it be me and Holly."

Rhett looked angry for a moment and then nodded. "Okay, but I get one night with her alone too."

"Uh, hello? Do you two plan on including me in this or shall I just wait for you to divvy me up?" She glared at them both.

Rhett laughed. "Sorry, honey. Do you have any ideas of how we should split up time?"

They spoke for a time about how to have couple time as well as time as a threesome and much-needed solitary time too.

"Why don't you tell us about the situation with your family and what you want to do while we move your stuff into your room. Which one do you want for your room, sweetness?" Nate kissed her temple.

She pointed to the one that would get the best daylight, they sure didn't need it.

It only took them an hour to get her room together. When all was said and done, she didn't really have much. Some of her kitchen stuff would stay in the garage. The important things, the scrapbooks and albums of photographs her mother had made over the years, sat on the large bookshelves.

As she finished hanging up her clothing, Nate sat on the bed and Rhett in the window seat and she told them all she knew of her family. She'd only briefly told Rhett about the dream the night before.

Nate nodded decisively. "Sweetness, we need to contact them and visit New Orleans. It's safe for us because it's non-affiliated and you need to find this piece of yourself as well as figure out who is trying to hurt you and why."

"James, our assistant who took care of the boxing and moving of your belongings, told me that your neighbors said that someone was there during the early morning hours looking for you. They aren't going to give up and we can't stop them until we figure out who it is."

"What if I don't want them?" She knew she sounded petulant but she couldn't help it.

"You don't have to have them, then. But we need to figure this out and they're necessary to that. We can stay in a hotel. Rhett and I will always be with you. James and Jax, our daytime help, are going to move in for the time being, until we can be sure you're safe. Jax is a former Navy SEAL and he's served vampires for the last fifteen years. He came with us when we left Boston. He used to be Gaius' personal bodyguard so he's more than capable of helping you when we're sleeping."

"A bodyguard?"

"Yes, Holly. Don't pretend you don't need one. He'll drive you to and from work and hang around while you're there, until one or both of us can be around. This isn't a joke. Someone wants to kill you and that can't happen." Rhett's face was set, his arms crossed over his chest.

She sighed. She was not going to be one of those romance novel heroines who argued over every last point just for the sake of arguing. The fact that someone wanted to kill her totally freaked her out and she understood that the two men in the room were a part of her life and could protect her. Were her best chance at having a good life, a safe life.

"I suppose I can just call directory assistance for New Orleans. Lee Charvez. You think she'd be listed?"

Nate picked up the phone and handed it to her. "One way to find out, sweetness."

Sighing, she picked up a pen and a pad of paper from her book bag and got on the bed. Nate rearranged himself so that she was leaning against him while Rhett moved so that he was lying next to her.

She wasn't overly surprised when Lee's number was listed. For good measure she got the number for the sister Lee mentioned, Em, as well.

"I'll call tomorrow. It's two there." She reached to put the phone back in the cradle.

Laughing, Nate pushed the phone back at her. "She's mated to a vampire, someone will be up. Call."

"Oh yeah." Grinning sheepishly, she took the phone and dialed the number quickly before she chickened out.

"Hello?" a male voice answered and sex spun through the phone lines. Both men narrowed their eyes at her, feeling her response, and she shrugged.

"Hi, is Lee there?"

"Can I tell her who's calling?" The voice had an Irish lilt to it. Really sexy.

She had to clear her throat and jumped when Nate pinched her nipple and mouthed, "You're mine."

"I'm her, uh, cousin, I guess. Holly."

"Oh," his voice warmed up considerably, "we've all been waiting to hear from you. Hang on a mo."

She heard him lay the phone down and call out for Lee.

"Holly, you don't know what it does to me to see your body react to another vampire like this. It makes me crazy," Rhett murmured as he slid a hand up her calf.

"Stop that!" she hissed and moved his hand. "I can't very well talk to my cousin with you trying to cop a feel."

She heard laughing on the other side of the connection and realized that her cousin had picked up the phone. "Oh god, sorry," Holly mumbled, embarrassed.

"Don't be embarrassed, Holly. I've got a vampire mate myself, I know how it works. Man, you're going to need an industrial-sized load of patience to deal with two of them."

Against her better judgment, Holly warmed when she heard Lee's voice.

"I'm so glad you called. Can you come down here and stay a while? Or we can come to you. Whatever is easiest."

"I need to know who's trying to kill me and why." Holly just didn't know if she could trust the people who'd spurned her mother.

"I know you have very little reason to trust us and a whole lot of them not to, but we really want to know you, Holly. We want to help you. Show you that you have a place in our family. All three of you do."

"Before I say yes or no, I want to hear straight from my mother's mother why she let a fifteen-year-old girl be shoved out into the world alone."

Rhett gripped one of her hands tightly and Nate ran his fingers through her hair, over her scalp, to soothe her.

A soft cry of grief came from Lee and at that moment Holly knew. Tears stung her eyes.

"She's dead. She was murdered three years ago. She and I were very close, she would have so loved to meet you, to hold you in her arms. She was a beautiful woman. I'm sorry." Lee's voice was choked with emotion and the envy hit Holly, sliced through her heart. Her cousin had had the life *she* should have had. But Holly had lived in run-down tenements and cheap hotels with a mother who hid the truth from her. The loving grandmother was in someone else's reality.

The walls slamming shut around Holly were so tangible that Nate winced. He could hear the conversation and felt Holly's pain, her envy and fury.

"She didn't know, Holly. Her husband, your grandfather, kicked your mother out while your *grand-mére* was out for the day. By the time she'd gotten back your mother was gone and she couldn't find her. She looked. All of them looked for you. She divorced your grandfather in her grief. According to my grandmother, she never forgave herself."

"Look, just tell me who is trying to kill me and why. And how did they know about me if I didn't even know until two days ago?" Holly wanted to curl up and cry.

Lee took a long pause. "You have to come here. Just come here and we'll tell you everything we know. Give us a chance to explain things—show you how much we want to know you—and we'll tell you what we can."

"That's blackmail!" Holly sat up, furious. As if these people hadn't caused enough pain in her life they had the nerve to pull this crap?

"It is and I'm sorry but I can't think of any other way to get you here and we really deserve a chance. You're one of us, Holly. Don't you want to know about your power?"

"Damn it!" All of a sudden her major life decisions were being made by other people and that made her feel helpless and pissed off. "How dare you people do this!" Tears crept into her voice.

Unable to take another moment of her pain, Rhett sat up and took the phone from her. "This ends now. We will bring her but we will not give in to this blackmail in any other way. We'll stay in a hotel and you can meet us there. You will not upset Holly any more, do you understand?"

"I'm sorry. I don't want to hurt her but I can't think of another way. We want to know her. Is that so wrong?" Lee desperately wanted them to understand why she was being so manipulative.

Aidan was trying to take the phone but she knew that that path was a dead end. If vampire guy stuff got tangled up in between her and Holly, they'd never meet. She slapped at his hand and narrowed her eyes at him and he snorted, looming over her.

"You've upset my mate. I know your mate must be there, ready to knock you down for the phone, so let's make this simple, shall we? Avoid the vampire stuff that's bound to muck this all up," Rhett said smoothly but firmly. "We will fly to New Orleans on Wednesday and check into The Château. Holly will call you when we arrive and she's ready to meet you."

"All right. Please know that should you change your mind, I live in a really large house. A really safe house that's warded tight enough to hold out a demon. You'll not be that safe at The Château, even it if is a vampire hotel. We want Holly with us and because you're her mate, we want you and her other mate as well. We do have a story to tell. She has a big family, we're very close. It's difficult for us to know that one of our own is out there, alone and in need."

"She's not alone and she wouldn't be in need if she hadn't been kept in the dark about her identity," Rhett said and Holly sighed and snatched the phone back.

"Now that *she* is on the phone, *she* is perfectly capable of making her own life plans, thank you very much." She touched Rhett's lips gently, she appreciated his protectiveness but she had to do this herself.

"He's just protecting you, they do that. I understand, I really do. Will you come on Wednesday? Aidan has a jet, he can send it for you, it's got a special passenger area that's tight against light but you can fly at night, the time difference isn't bad. We can pick you up at the airport here, take you to my house or to the hotel, whichever you prefer. I would like you to let me ward your room if you stay at The Château, though."

Holly let out her breath. "Okay. We'll fly in Wednesday night. Since we'll be traveling with vampires and I have no idea what they need to be safe, I'll take you up on the offer of the special plane but we can arrange our own ride." She bit back a thank you. Why should she thank the other woman for blackmailing her?

"Great. Oh you won't be sorry, Holly. We really can't wait to meet you. There are so many of us who are just really excited to welcome you back home."

* * * * *

Holly hung up and leaned into both Rhett and Nate, allowing herself a bit of comfort. She eased the door back open a bit and everyone relaxed. She'd been so freaked out but the two of them had fought for her, helped her, comforted and defended her. At that point it was difficult to remember why it was so important to keep them out of her heart.

"Thank you for that." She smiled at Rhett and he leaned in, brushing a kiss over her lips.

"I'm sorry I was pushy. I just couldn't stand to see you that upset."

She nodded. "I got it. I'm trying to get used to it."

Nate threaded his fingers through her hair and she felt like purring. The normalcy of the moment shook her for a moment.

"Debauching you is going to be so much fun." Nate chuckled. "I can't wait to show you off at The Bite."

She tipped her head back to look at him. "The Bite?"

"It's a vampire sex club in town." Leaning down, he flicked his tongue over her fluttering pulse.

"Oh. My. I've been sheltered and I didn't even know it. I uh, well, I've never been to a sex club but I trust you. I work four nights a week though, Friday nights until two, Sunday, Monday and Wednesday 'til midnight. So I won't always be able to work out stuff like that."

Rhett took a deep breath—the subject couldn't be hedged around any longer. "Holly, love, when do you plan to take classes? You're going to have to give up your job to take classes at night, or work shorter shifts."

"My classes are all early in the day except for Thursdays when my last class is at four. I don't need to work shorter shifts. I do my classwork for the week—the major stuff—on Saturday and Sunday afternoon and catch up on Tuesday and Thursday."

"Honey, when you convert you can't be out during daylight. You'll have to take night classes to finish your degree," Nate said softly. The moment had arrived, they needed to confront the issue of her converting. He'd wanted it to go another few days but there wasn't much time before they went to New Orleans and he didn't want to leave it in the air for another week until they got back.

She got quiet for a few minutes. "I guess I hadn't really thought of it. I mean, I hadn't really even thought of conversion even though we talked about it before. I need some time. My entire life has changed and it seems to be continuing on that course. I'm a bit overwhelmed right now. I'm pretty sure you aren't supposed to make any big life changes while you're freaked out and overwhelmed. Turning into a vampire is a pretty big life change."

"How much time?" Rhett asked. "The conversion would make you a hell of a lot stronger. I'd feel better knowing you were safer when dealing with whoever is trying to kill you."

"By rendering myself helpless and unable to respond for half of the day?"

"Okay, that's a partial point. But you're a witch, Holly. You can protect all three of us once you learn more about your power. As a vampire your abilities as a witch will gain in intensity. And most of all, I don't want to live without you," Nate said, kissing her fingertips. "I want to have centuries with you. I found you relatively young. I have lifetimes to be with you and I want that. Some vampires never find a mate or find one when they're already hundreds of years made or born. I'm thirty-nine in human terms—seven years a vampire."

"We don't get sick, Holly. Any aches that you might have now will be gone. You will be stronger, faster, safer. Please don't take too long to make your choice," Rhett whispered as he kissed her knee.

* * * * *

The next evening she sat with Nate, snuggled into his side as they watched a movie on DVD.

"Tell me about how you became a vampire."

He threaded his fingers through hers. "I was an FBI agent in Atlanta. Born and raised there. Anyway, I was on this case. A serial killer who'd been working his way across several southern states. I interviewed a witness, Eric VonDriesen." A smile curved his lips. "Eric was very mysterious. I knew he was hiding something. He had an alibi for several of the killings but I kept watching him.

"We'd cornered the killer, were chasing him through a park just outside the city. He found me first. Cut me and left me to bleed out. Eric came then and saved me. Bit me and changed me.

"I stayed in Atlanta for another year, learning and continuing to work for the FBI. I worked at nights." He shrugged. "Eric is quite influential in the state, he protected me. We had a brief fling. More me being enamored of his power as a vampire than anything else. But then I ended up in Boston and met Gaius and Rhett. Joined Nento. You know how that ended. I took leave from the Bureau six months ago. They'd like me to stay on as a consultant. I'm a damned good profiler."

Her eyes were wide and she threw her arms around him, hugging him tight.

"What is it, sweetness? Eric is my Sire, yes, I love him, but there's nothing between us. Not like you and me. It's been six years since..."

She shook her head and he stopped speaking. "Someone nearly killed you. The idea of you on the ground, dying," she choked back a sob, "I...it just knocked me back a bit."

He kissed the top of her head, ridiculously touched that she was so upset by something he'd pretty much forgotten except for the occasional nightmare. She shed tears for him. Felt terror at danger long past. Being that cared for burrowed deep into his heart.

"I'm here, sweet. I'm not going anywhere."

"What about your family? Do they know?"

"They know something is different. I don't see them very often. I love them and I can still go home from time to time. I won't be able to without telling them in a few years. The aging thing will be too hard to hide."

"Why not tell them?"

"I don't know. They're very old-fashioned. I'm not sure how they'd handle it. They're already convinced that Rhett and I are lovers and are pretty unhappy about that. But I love my parents very much. I won't have them forever and so I try to let them be as comfortable as possible."

"So I guess they'll be relieved about me? Or, well, I'm white so maybe not?"

He laughed then. "My marrying a white girl is pretty small compared to my being a vampire, don't you think? And anyway, my grandmother was white. They might be freaked about me possibly being gay but you being white won't be a problem. We'll have to go down there so you can meet them. They'll love you."

She grinned. "Oh my! I get to meet the parents!"

He chuckled.

* * * * *

True to her word, Holly spent the next few days really thinking over converting. She had come to the inescapable conclusion that she loved them and couldn't bear the thought of leaving them or growing old while they stayed young. She wanted to be with them both for every minute she could.

At the same time, nagging doubts plagued her. It wasn't as if she could let go of a lifetime of self-doubt overnight. Fear ate at her. Fear that she'd never be quite good enough for them and that everyone would know it.

Both men watched and waited, their patience dwindling.

Chapter Five

∞

Holly nervously moved from foot to foot as they waited to deplane. The trip had gone smoothly. The private jet met them at just after dark and they'd flown directly to New Orleans. As promised, the passenger compartment was without windows so there was no chance of light coming in. Even though it was night, Holly felt better knowing that Rhett and Nate had that bit of extra safety around them.

She'd been tied in knots the whole trip. Both men had done everything they could to ease her, to calm her, but she was still a bundle of conflicting emotions. Thank goodness they'd come with her despite her telling them it wasn't a big deal and for them to stay home. They'd just looked at her and kept packing.

Nate walked in front of them, shielding her with his body. She squeezed Rhett's hand as they moved to walk out and down the stairs and onto the tarmac.

"It's going to be all right. No matter what happens with them, you've got us. That won't change," Nate murmured into her ear when they reached the ground. Taking a deep breath, she nodded and hoped he was right.

"I know. It's just…" She trailed off, not knowing how to express what she was feeling, and realized that she didn't have to finish her sentence. Nate knew and relief flooded through her.

"A car should be meeting us," Rhett said, looking around.

Holly felt it when her cousin stepped out of the terminal.

Lee saw Holly and the recognition hit them both with such force that they each gave a sharp intake of breath. Alex looked at her sideways, concern on his face, but she shook her

117

head. The wizard and next in line to lead the Carter family stood, back straight, keeping his eyes moving around the area.

Lee knew he and Aidan had hired extra security for the time being, until they figured out who was behind the attack on Holly.

"She's a Charvez all right. You can taste it from here," Alex said quietly. Holly's magic was strong and he could almost see it shimmering in the air around her. It was Charvez magic, like Lee and her sister had, but also something else he couldn't quite identify but seemed familiar all the same.

He also sensed the slight tension in the air when Aidan saw the other vampires. Aidan's familial caste ran Chicago, where he lived before coming to New Orleans. His grandmother ran the caste now. Alex knew that always when new vampires came into a territory there was a bit of feather ruffling and posturing, especially between males. He hoped it would be better than usual because Aidan knew this was important to Lee and that the two vampires with Holly were family. But as an alpha vampire he couldn't completely override his nature, especially as he was a natural vampire rather than a made one.

Catching Aidan's reaction, Lee shot him a look. He eased back a bit and Alex hid a smile when he saw Holly do the same thing to her vampires.

Alex gave Lee a gentle push forward and they started across the tarmac to where the other three were. Suddenly, his sister-in-law Em and her husband, both Fae, shimmered next to them and more Charvezes came out of the terminal.

"Oh no!" Lee hadn't wanted the entire family to show up. Holly was spooked enough. The last thing Lee wanted was to make her cousin feel more defensive and overwhelmed. But there was no help for it as her mother, grandmother and aunt came out, followed by several cousins.

Holly's face paled and Nate put his arm around her on one side and Rhett did the same on the other, bolstering her as best they could.

"Hold strong, honey," Rhett murmured into Holly's ear and she let herself fall into the link a little bit to feel them both surround her.

They watched as the tiny silver-haired woman who'd come out of the terminal stepped forward and put her hand on the redhead's arm. "Let me go to her, she... Elise would have wanted it this way."

"She's strung tight," Em murmured to her grandmother.

"Of course she is. What she must think of us," *Grand-mére* said and walked to the three near the plane. She stopped just in front of Holly and cocked her head.

"You look a lot like your mother. Not the hair, the hair came from my grandmother. I'm Isolde, your great-aunt. Your *grand-mére* Elise, she was my sister." She moved her hand out and Holly's pulse sped up.

Without permission, Isolde stepped forward and put her arms around Holly. "Welcome home, *chere*. The Charvez women welcome you back to the fold. We've missed you."

Until that contact, Holly'd been holding herself stiff. Now she put her arms around Isolde as the tears flowed silently down her cheeks.

Em watched, nearly doubled over with the pain flowing from her cousin. Sometimes being an empath wasn't the easiest thing in the world. Con pulled her to his side and ran his hand up and down her back. "You okay, *a ghra*?"

She nodded and looked into those eyes she'd dreamed of for so long. Now hers, they held so much love and tenderness that she once again thanked fate for bringing them together. He put his palm over her stomach where their child was growing, a daughter. The first in the next generation of Charvezes would be something altogether new, a Fae witch.

119

"She's hurting so much. They'll help her through," she said, meaning the vampires with her cousin. "We need to be sure to include them in everything, she needs them."

Lee nodded as she looked at her sister and reached out and touched her stomach just under where Con's hand lay. "Can you tell what her gift is?"

Em watched her *grand-mére* and Holly. "They're the same in many ways. Holly's a seer. But there's something else there, I can't quite put my finger on it."

"I see that too. It's familiar but I can't identify it," Alex agreed.

Holly pulled free and wiped her eyes. "This is Nate Hamilton and Rhett Dubois, they're my...mine."

Nate laughed quietly and took the hand Isolde was offering and placed a kiss on her knuckles. "We're hers all right. And she's ours. I'm sure you know what that means."

Isolde looked him up and down, taking his measure, and nodded as if she'd made a decision. "Yes, I do. You're both welcome to the family as well," she said quietly and turned to Rhett, who also bent over her hand with a gentlemanly brush of lips over her knuckles.

"Won't you come to the Charvez home for a while tonight? To have some tea, get to know us? Have you eaten?" She asked Holly but also looked to the vampires.

Lee approached with Em and the vampires all bristled. "Uh, thanks but perhaps tomorrow might be good. While they're all sleeping," Holly said as she took in the scene. The tall blond vampire with her cousin stood very close, definitely inside Holly's personal space. It seemed very aggressive and she felt Nate and Rhett stiffen and move forward.

"I apologize, darlin'," the tall blond vampire said. "I'm Aidan Bell, Lee's husband and your cousin as well. I promise to behave myself even if you do have the most delicious hair I've ever seen. Well, other than my beautiful Lee that is." He touched Holly's fiery tresses and gave a princely bow but kept his eyes up and locked with Rhett's.

Nate growled, surprising Holly.

Lee elbowed Aidan. "Knock this off," she hissed.

"You know, I think we'll go to the hotel. I'll call you tomorrow and you can tell me just what the heck is going on," Holly said coolly, stepping back. The movement separated herself from the Charvezes and pulled her back into her link with Nate and Rhett. It was bad enough that they'd blackmailed her into coming down there—she certainly wasn't going to tolerate any mistreatment of her men.

"Allow us to transport you then, we've got a car waiting. Lee went to the hotel and warded your rooms earlier today." Alex didn't even look in Aidan's direction. He could feel Lee's anger and was glad it wasn't directed at him. His wife might be small physically but she was a force of nature, especially when she was pissed off.

"We have a car," Rhett said flatly. While he was determined to keep a hold on his voice for Holly's sake, the temptation to get into it with Aidan was nearly overwhelming. That the other vampire stood so close to his woman and touched her drove his blood to near-boiling with rage. It was a deliberate baiting behavior and incredibly rude. Worse, he could feel Holly's upset with the whole situation.

"Okay, well…it's really good to have you here, Holly. We've been so excited to meet you—and your mates as well," Lee concluded with a sharp look at Aidan, who actually flared his nostrils at her. "I'm Amelia—Lee. We talked on the phone. I can't believe how much you look like our great-grandmother. You'll see the pictures while you're here. You'll call tomorrow then?" Lee was babbling but she could feel her cousin pulling away from them, offended and hurt by Aidan's behavior and overwhelmed by the show of Charvez force that had come to greet her.

"Yes, I'll call you when I wake up. Jax and I will arrange to meet you."

"Jax?"

"Her bodyguard. With wizards after her, we don't want to take any chances with her safety, especially when we're asleep. In fact, it would be better if you all waited until after dark so that Rhett and I can be there." Nate looked imperious and Lee envied her cousin a moment, the man was truly delicious.

"We can get into that tomorrow as well. Our house is well warded. No one can get in if we don't wish it. And bodyguard or not, if he doesn't have talent, he's useless against a wizard," Alex said, trying not to be defensive.

Finally Holly stepped forward and clapped her hands. "Hello? Can you four just knock it off? I don't know what is going on between you pointy-toothed people but just stop it! I can't deal with it." She looked at Alex. "I know you must feel defensive because this is wizard stuff, but I'm not holding that against you. But I can't have this whole situation devolve into some guy stuff, it's too much and I have enough on my plate as it is."

Before Alex could make a sheepish apology, she stepped to Lee and took the hands Lee was holding out. "I'll call. Thank you for meeting us here." She nodded and turned with Rhett and Nate and they got into a waiting car that their luggage had been loaded into and drove off.

Lee rounded on Aidan and glared at him. "Just what the fuck was that? What's gotten into you? We finally coax her here—under duress and near-blackmail conditions I might add—and you pull that shit? You deliberately made that crack about her hair to yank their chains. If you've pushed her so far away that we can't get her back to us, I'll never forgive you."

Before he could make any answer, she spun and stalked back into the tarmac, chattering with her mother and sister while Alex and Con gave him looks of commiseration.

* * * * *

At the hotel, Holly walked around the suite in a daze. The place was a palace. High ceilings, expensive antiques, helpful staff that were quiet and efficient. She had never been in such luxury before and it was a bit overwhelming. Who'd have ever imagined a vampire hotel? The place had light-tight window coverings and discreetly placed cards offering donors for the special needs of their visiting guests. It was surreal.

Add to that the whole scene with her family at the airport and she was a bit of a mess.

Rhett hugged her tight. "Honey, I hate to do this but I need to feed and I also need to speak to my business manager. I just checked my voicemail and there's something I must deal with tonight. The hotel has teleconference facilities and I'm going to use them when I come back. Nate is here. I'll be back in a few hours."

She took him in for a moment, eyes greedily roving over his features. He was so handsome that it was hard to believe he was hers. "Oh okay. See you then. I'll be all right and I need you to take care of yourself too."

Smiling, he kissed her hard and quick and was gone.

Nate approached her from behind and put his arms around her, pressing a kiss to the top of her head. "I've run you a bath and opened a bottle of wine. Rhett ordered dinner for you and you'll eat every last bit of it."

"Bossy."

He chuckled but she walked into the other room and slid out of her clothes and into the bath without further complaint. He sat on the edge of the tub and handed her the wine. "I think you need this. I'm sorry for how things turned out at the airport. I suppose we should have expected it but when he touched you it pushed my buttons."

"What was all of that about?" she murmured as the warmth of the water and the wine did their work.

"Vampire stuff. Politics. He's a natural vampire, they run most things, think they're better than made vampires. His grandmother runs the city of Chicago, I should have done a bit of homework about this. Plus, male vampires tend to get a bit…twitchy when it comes to their mates and other vampires. He made that comment about your hair to fuck with us. Not that your hair isn't lovely," he added quickly. "He may not have been that aware he was doing it."

"Well, whatever. It's not okay that he's an asshole to you. But you guys have to knock it off. I need to deal with this and I can't if I'm constantly worried that you and he are gonna rumble."

Nate burst into laughter. "That sounds protective. Are you ready to accept all of this at last? Accept that you're ours and we're yours and let go of your worries and let us in? All the way?"

Holly sighed heavily. "I'm trying! I am. It's not easy to give up a lifetime of habits."

"I know. But my patience is thin now. I want you. All of you. I don't want a half mate. I want you totally committed to us and sharing yourself without reservation." He stood. "But I need to feed as well. I'm going into Jax's suite across the hall. I'll be back in a bit, all right?"

Holly nodded, sipping her wine. "I'm working on it. I promise. This lovely red and I have a date. I'll see you when you get back."

He kissed her temple and left her to her thoughts.

She lay there in the bath until the cooling water drove her to get out. She discovered that neither Rhett nor Nate had returned and got dressed and headed across the hall to Jax's suite.

Using the key, she let herself into the room. Smiling at the luxury of the place, she closed the door behind herself and tossed the card on the table in the entry.

Suddenly, a distinctly female sound echoed through the place. Not just any sound but one of *those* sounds. A sound from a very happy woman. Holly's hand went to her throat as she turned the corner and saw straight into the front parlor-type space where a very tall woman in a very short skirt had her arms wrapped around Nate and was grinding herself against his body as he fed. The woman was obviously climaxing and clutching him to her body, begging him to fuck her.

Feeling nauseated, the betrayal of the moment was like a slap to her face. A cry of pain escaped her lips and Nate turned, blood on his bottom lip.

Intellectually she'd accepted the whole feeding thing when they'd told her those days before, but the reality of seeing it was a shock. Worse, the woman he'd been feeding from was supermodel beautiful. Willowy, tall and totally beyond Holly's league.

Nate literally flinched when he felt that small crack in her defenses slam shut to him and their link.

"Who's that, Nate?" the glamazon asked.

"Yes, Nate, why don't you answer that? I'm interested in the answer myself." The cold, flat quality of Holly's voice—a voice so normally rich—sliced through him.

He surreptitiously wiped his mouth and stepped toward Holly, who moved back. He felt her rejection acutely. "This is Holly, my mate—my love. I told you that I'd found her, remember?"

Holly sent him a lethal glare. "Gosh, call me silly but the words you just uttered seem a bit at odds with the fact that I just walked in on you and another woman. A beautiful woman who was wrapped around you with her long, thin, gorgeous limbs." Holly's voice caught in her throat. Her feelings of inadequacy and insecurity shot through Nate and made him slightly sick in a way he hadn't been since he was human.

"Holly," he looked at her and then indicated the ebony-skinned woman who was now sitting on the couch looking every bit like she'd just had a great orgasm, "this is Shelly. She's an old friend. She was one of my donors in Boston but moved down here a few years back." Taking another step toward her, he continued, "Sweetness, you know I have to feed. I never lied about donors. Rhett and I both have them. You knew this. You know you'll need them yourself when you convert. I was just pushing Shelly back and was going to reiterate to her that she wasn't to clutch at me like that when I fed anymore."

Disgust crossed Holly's face then. "Oh well then, it's just fine. I'll just wait in *my* room across the hall, shall I? You can finish with your little friend and give me a ride to my cousin's house. I'm sure I can stay with her. Or not. In fact, don't bother, I'll call a cab."

Nate's face darkened in his anger. This attitude of hers had to stop and it had to stop that very night. He turned to Shelly. "Thank you for your gift. I'm sure you understand why I need to be alone with Holly now."

Shelly cast a curious look back at Holly and then nodded at Nate. "So I'm guessing this means no more sex when you feed?"

Nate wanted to groan when he heard the sharp sound of Holly's exhalation and then the echo of her steps and the slamming of the door. "Yes, that's what it means."

"Too bad. If you change your mind I'd be happy to find myself available."

He smiled at her, knowing it would never happen, and walked her to the door and locked it behind himself. In the hall, he called Rhett and told him to not come back for a while, explaining what had happened and his plans to deal with it.

He stalked into their suite to the room she currently occupied.

"You're not going anywhere, Holly." This was said in his arrogant voice, arms crossed over his chest.

She stopped her furious one-handed packing and dropped the phone from her ear. Mouth open in shock at his audacity, she stared at him, stunned. In that moment of surprise, the shields she'd erected around her feelings failed and her emotions crashed through and over him.

"Holly, how can you carry all of his around?" he said softly, gently, as he walked toward her. He wanted to weep at what she held in her heart.

She moved back with a panicked sound and started to walk around him and he grabbed her in firm but gentle hands. Bringing her body flush with his, he said seriously, "Sweetness, you can't really believe that I'd be unfaithful to you. If I could sustain myself by only feeding from you or not feeding at all, I would. If I could remove the orgasm for my donors I'd do it. But I need blood and an outcome of feeding is climax. If you want to be present every time I feed, fine. If you want me to use male donors, fine. What can I do to show you that I want you to believe, to understand that you come before everything? That all I want to do is make you happy?"

He felt her emotions warring inside her. This insecurity — her worry that she wasn't beautiful or worthy — was eating her alive, closing off her heart to anyone out of fear. He couldn't stand her holding back from them for another day.

Taking a risk, he decided to push those walls down. No, not push. Blow them to little more than dust so that she had nothing left to hold them off anymore. Standing back, he gave her an order. "Come with me, sweetness." He turned and walked toward the room he'd specially arranged for without looking back.

The pull of his dominance rushed over her with dark sweetness. She closed her eyes and tried to resist, but her body called out to him. Her heart. If this was going to be their last night together — and she'd pretty much decided to leave for her cousin's home that next day, alone — then she'd enjoy it.

She walked into the room where he'd gone and saw him like a dream, leaning against the wall at the head of the bed. She also noted the theme of the room, the hooks on the walls and the array of toys on the dresser nearby.

"Get out of those clothes, sweetness."

She reached to dim the lights but he shook his head. "No. I want to see all of you." Her hand faltered near the switch and her heart sped up. It wasn't like he hadn't seen her naked but after that scene across the hall with the gorgeous donor she felt the comparison between herself and other women with a sting.

"I'm waiting."

She narrowed an eye at him but quickly pulled her clothes off and started to go to him. Again he shook his head. She stopped and he pushed away from the wall and moved toward her.

He slowly circled her. He leaned in and ran the tip of his tongue over her shoulders and up her neck, feeling her racing pulse there. "Mmmmm, no one feels like you. Tastes like you," he murmured.

All the while he spoke to her, his hands moved over her body. Fingertips tracing down the line of her back, circling the dimples at the small, skimming the curves of the creamy globes of her ass, over the soft flare of her thighs. He put emotion in every touch, every stroke. He wanted her to see the love in his eyes, feel his adoration.

Her eyes began to slide shut but he leaned into her body and spoke in her ear. "Keep them open. I want you to see what I see."

She blushed then and he hardened his resolve. Reaching back, he pulled something out of his pocket. Gently, he took her wrists and slid the cuff restraints on and she let the shivers of anticipation slide over her body.

Taking her hands, he slowly pulled them above her head and attached them to the chain hanging from the ring in the ceiling. She felt exposed there like that, the lights burning bright, her hands above her head. Naked to his gaze.

He moved away, coming back with a large mirror on a stand, and put it in front of her. Standing behind her, he ran his hands down her arms and ribs. "Look at yourself, Holly." Not a request.

She looked into the mirror and flinched. He sighed and took her breasts in his palms. "Look at these." He thumbed over the nipples and they darkened and hardened. "So beautiful. Big, gorgeous. I love the way they feel in my palms, how responsive your nipples are. Hard and begging for my touch."

He kissed her shoulder and moved her hair aside. "This hair, like a curtain of fire. So silky soft, smells so good. The way you look when you're astride me, the ends of it stroking over my stomach and thighs," he sighed appreciatively, "marvelous."

Hands moved down her ribs and over her stomach. "You're supposed to be soft, Holly. Soft and feminine and curved. So sexy." Fingertips stroked over her thighs. "Here too."

His fingers strummed in the dip of the back of her knees and over the muscles of her calves. Kneeling before her, he looked up into her face for a moment and then kissed her belly and she blushed.

He was so frustrated with her feelings of insecurity about herself. He and Rhett practically worshipped the ground she walked on, showed her nothing but love and respect and she still didn't trust her feelings? He had to strip her bare and then let her re-knit with what the world really was with them in it as a unit, not what her world had been or she feared it might be.

"You still don't see it, do you? I mean to break down those walls tonight, sweetness, be warned."

She shivered at the resolution behind the words and her own response to them. Terror and great hope too. Part of her wanted him to push his way inside of her heart, to free her from her fears, while the other part was utterly alarmed by being that exposed to another person.

"What do you see, Holly, when you look into the mirror?" he asked softly, stroking a paddle down her spine, furry side on her skin.

"What do you mean?" she asked with a slight break in her voice.

"When you look into that mirror do you see the beautiful goddess that you are?" his voice was deceptively soft. She knew all she had to do was open the link wide to know how he saw her but she was so frightened of seeing something there that she couldn't handle, his disgust with her thighs maybe, or perhaps his thought of how pretty she'd be if she lost fifteen pounds.

"I...I like my hair."

He kissed the side of her neck gently. "Good." He sifted the coppery strands through his fingers and then looked back into her eyes "What else, sweetness?" He reached down and held up her breasts. "What about these?"

"They're too big. People always look at them instead of my face."

He was angered for a moment thinking of any other man ogling her breasts but got it under control. She didn't need that. Instead he nodded and gently let go and picked up the paddle and gave her one hard stroke at the bottom of her ass, where cheeks met thigh, where sensation could spread to her clit.

"OW!" she yelped and tried to evade him but he moved quickly and put ankle cuffs on and hooked them into the bolt in the floor, feet slightly apart. She narrowed an eye at him. "What the fuck are you doing?"

"You know the safe word if it's too much," he said without looking into her face. He said it like a challenge. He had to goad her into letting him continue. If he knew her like he thought he did, it would work.

She snorted. "I can't believe you hit me," she muttered.

He stood up before her. "I'd never hit you. Exaggerator. I paddled you and I'll bend you over my knee if you don't stop talking negatively about your body. Your breasts are not too big, they are perfect. I love the way they curve, so beautiful, the cinnamon-pink nipples jutting at the tips."

She gave an impatient sound and he got behind her again and caressed her stomach. He felt her discomfort loud and clear. "What about here?"

"It's...fine. I wish it were smaller, flatter."

Another crack. "Hey! Damn it, knock that off!"

Moving away quickly, he came back with a chair. Reaching up, he unhooked her wrists before sitting down and bending her over his lap, leaving her ankles bound. The bar of the chair at the bottom served as a place to attach the wrist cuffs to.

"Now tell me how beautiful you are. Let me in that fucking fortress, Holly, and see for yourself. See yourself as I see you, as Rhett sees you." His cock jutted into her mound and lower belly.

Refusing, she shook her head, and he brought his palm down on her ass three times quickly, each in slightly different spots.

"Tell me," he said softly.

"Stop this! Who the hell do you think you are to spank me? This is stupid, Nate. Let me up!" She squirmed and he felt her wetness through the denim of his jeans.

He chuckled darkly. "Go on, just say it. Uncle, Holly. Use 'pasta' and this is over. Let me win."

She harrumphed and he grinned at her rigid back. He slid the tips of his fingers down the crease of her bottom. Her skin was so pale, so sensitive, that she bore two perfect handprints on her ass and it was pink from the other strokes.

"Tell me," he urged and she shook her head, her hair covering her face.

He spanked her again in a short burst. Five strokes this time and they began to do their work, radiating sensation up to her clit. Her squirms were more lascivious than panicked. He could smell her desire and they both gasped when he pressed two fingers inside of her and found her slick and hot, the muscles of her pussy pulling at him.

"Hmmm, someone likes being tied up and spanked."

She opened her mouth to deny it but with his fingers stroking into her pussy and the wetness blanketing them both, she had no ground to stand on and instead thrust her ass back, pulling him in deeper. She'd be horrified at how easy she was for him later.

He made a tut-tutting sound and pulled his fingers out of her. "Now, where were we? You were going to tell me how beautiful you are. How strong and smart and self-sufficient. You're going to open those gates and let me in, open the link that you know you should. See yourself through me, Holly. Let go of those views of the fat and shy Holly who can't keep anyone in her life. See the Holly that *is*. The woman who has survived and continues to do so. On her terms but now paired with two men who adore her and want to fully share in their bond with her."

He brought the paddle down on her this time, over and over, in different spots. Each stroke he delivered another compliment, another order for her to give up and trust them, open the link. Over and over, paddling and then fingers inside of her pussy until she'd nearly come and a withdrawal and more spanking or paddling and his infernal pushing to open the link.

Nate looked down at the pinkened skin of her ass and thighs. So delicate and delightful, heated and desire-slicked. The little zone at the apex of ass and pussy and thighs was glistening. He could feel her fighting her emotions and he knew that her control was only paper-thin at that point. He had to end it.

He pulled her head up, her hair wrapped around his fist, forcing her to look in the mirror. "Look at yourself, Holly. Look at the woman bent over my lap, her ass pink from my strokes, hair in disarray, chained. Look at her and tell me she's a fat, ugly, stupid girl that no one wants!" he hissed. "Is that who you're going to hide in your whole life? Are you going to limit your future by hating yourself so much that you won't open up to people who love you?" He had to steel himself, he wanted to comfort her and pull her to him, kissing away her hurts, but he had to push her hard and then he could comfort her.

She burst into tears as he rained three more strokes with his palm. He felt it all rush free and it took all of his control not to dash in and take up the opened link. He waited and this time when he pushed fingers into her, his middle finger slid up and over her clit, flicking over it from side to side.

"I love you, Holly. You're beautiful and stubborn and intelligent and damn it, you have so much love to give and to receive. Just fucking let it go!"

She met his eyes in the mirror and he saw the tears tracking down her face, felt her resistance fall away and her yearning for connection with him. He took her invitation as he brought her off and she arched back as he filled her with his soul, his love, and felt hers in return like a shy gift that he cherished even more for it coming to him in such a tortured way. She was still afraid but her defenses were gone, she was too tired to hold him back and when she opened her eyes she saw herself through his eyes in that mirror and gasped in surprise.

Gone was the pudgy shy girl with awkward looks and in her place truly was a goddess. A woman who was alive with curves and femininity, with a crown of hair that inflamed the senses of the man holding her.

"I'm beautiful," she said with awe. "Because you love me."

He gave her a smile and shook his head. "No, *because* you're beautiful, I love you. Your inner beauty shines through as well as the way you look on the outside. I can't get enough of you."

He reached down and unhooked her ankles and wrists and reached back and pulled out a tube of something that he poured over her skin, cooling it and soothing the sting. "This will make you feel better. I'll let you be on top so you don't have to lie on your back."

She let him help her up and she stood on shaky legs and watched him as he pulled his jeans off before sitting back down. She moved to sit astride him and guide him into her body. He gave a long groan at the exquisite pleasure of it, of being with her in such a physical way, but the strengthened link also fed the emotional sensation. Before it was like a whisper of sensation between them but now it was the roar of the ocean. Her hunger, the sensations of their mating sliding through her, tied them together in ways he'd only heard tales of before. He felt himself in her heart, felt her in his.

A sheen of sweat on their bodies caused them to slide over each other, to cool hot flesh. Grabbing her hair in his fist, he brought her mouth to his and devoured her. Slaked his thirst for her with the sweetness of her lips, the carnal flesh of her tongue, her taste. He took in all of her soft noises of pleasure, all the while just meeting her body when she slid down him with a thrust of his hips.

As he got closer to climax he moved his lips from hers and they slid down her jaw to the spot where neck met shoulder. He nicked her and felt her blood rush into his mouth, into his body.

She arched her back with a cry as she began to come, the tips of her neat, squarely trimmed nails pressed into the flesh of his shoulders as she spasmed around his cock. With each swallow of her blood the pleasure of her climax rushed into his body.

He held her down on him with his hands at her hips as he came with a roar, body thrust up tight into hers, filling her.

Her head fell forward after he'd closed the place he'd fed. "I love you, Nate," she whispered into his ear.

Something deep was pulled free from him at that moment. It was disorienting for a small span of time—the enormity of her love for him, of those words spoken by his mate. After they'd just had an intensely emotional scene, hearing such a declaration pushed him so deeply in love with Holly Daniels that he'd have walked into the sunlight if she asked him to.

The door opened and Rhett was standing there, chest heaving, watching them both, incisors glinting in the light.

* * * * *

Without a word, Rhett pulled Holly up and into his arms, making a frustrated sound because she tasted of Nate. He clawed at his clothes and tore them off as she kept her lips to his as much as she could.

He'd felt the moment that her emotions had burst forth. All of it rushed through the link between the three of them and he'd nearly come sitting in the room downstairs, on the phone with his business manager. He needed her with such intensity that he shook with it.

Naked, he picked her up and stalked into her bathroom at the end of the hallway and turned on the taps as Nate watched from the doorway, amused and also sympathetic.

When Rhett saw how pink her back and ass were, he made the water cooler and had her stand facing the spray to ease any sting. His eyes moved to Nate's and an understanding passed between them. Rhett appreciated what Nate had done to break down Holly's defenses, understood that while they all needed time alone, they also needed to be together as a unit, to strengthen their bond.

"Shhh, let me help you," he murmured as he gently washed her body and hair and helped her out, even let Nate envelop her in a towel.

"Can I stay?" Nate asked and Rhett knew how much it cost him to make the request. He could feel Nate's need for connection. To both of them.

In that moment, Rhett realized that Holly wasn't the only one who had problems letting herself be loved. Nate, for all his arrogance and good looks, needed reassurance too. Needed to know that Holly *and* Rhett loved him. Sharing Holly became easier to bear suddenly because Rhett felt an equality to Nate that he hadn't before.

Rhett nodded and they walked into the master bedroom that they had yet to christen. The bed was large—vampires did love their comfort—and dominated the center of the room.

"Honey, are you all right? Would you rather just rest?" Rhett wanted her more than his next breath but he knew that she'd taken a huge emotional beating that evening and that she'd already had sex with Nate. He didn't want her to suffer in any way.

Her eyes softened and she pushed him back onto the large bed. "I think I can manage," she said with a smirk and Nate chuckled.

"Turn around and sit astride Nate, facing me," Rhett said quietly. "No cocks inside you just yet." He looked at Nate. "Her pussy is mine, Nate, you've had your time. Just slide it against her."

They were both very dominant. Nate had never really realized that. Rhett was so laid-back but the way he was handling the situation showed that he was a top too. They'd have to work out the very complicated situation that caused.

Nate took in the glory of his handiwork on her back and ass and rubbed his cock through her slippery folds. She hitched a breath and he took her hips under his palms and pushed her to him tighter.

Rhett leaned down and with the help of a few pillows ran his tongue through her pussy and over Nate's cock, bringing a surprised gasp from both of them. Rhett chuckled for a moment.

He wasn't opposed to having sex with a man, it just wasn't something he'd felt an urge to do before more than once or twice. He and Nate had had a few moments over the years they'd known each other. Sexually charged moments when their cocks brushed against each other when they'd had threesomes. But Rhett could feel Nate through their link and he wanted to connect with him in that way as well as Holly.

Holly leaned forward to watch Rhett's tongue slide over her and Nate, watch the edge of his teeth lightly graze her clit. One of Nate's hands sifted through Rhett's hair and she felt such tenderness for them both at that moment that it felt like her heart was squeezed. Aside from that, it was really hot to have Rhett's tongue in her pussy at the same time that Nate caressed her clit with the blunt head of his cock. Even better, watching Rhett's tongue move over Nate's cock, and feeling that slight jerk of sensation from Nate through their link.

Rhett tickled the underside of her clit with the tip of his tongue. Over and over, he stroked it, drawing pleasure from her with each quick, wet pass. She could feel that her climax was coming but she wanted him inside of her when it happened.

"Rhett, fuck me, please. I don't want to wait," she begged softly and Rhett circled her clit one last time and moved up onto the bed.

He knelt beside her and pulled her into a kiss. She tasted herself on his lips. Nate's hands were on her hips as he ground his cock against her over and over.

Rhett broke the kiss and moved to sit back against the headboard, legs spread out. She took the hand he held out, coming to sit astride.

"Take me inside then, honey. Let me in," he said softly and she slowly slid down onto his cock as she also threw herself open to him mentally and emotionally.

Suddenly he was in the link fully with both Holly and Nate and it was amazing. He felt his cock slice through her body, felt the heat of her back, the contrast of his cool skin beneath her thighs. He pinched a nipple and he felt it echo to her clit. Nate watched them, his hunger rising, but he stayed back, letting Rhett have this moment, content with just being there.

Rhett leaned in and kissed the fluttering pulse at her throat. The heat from her back, the blood so close to the surface, was driving him hard. He worried that Nate had taken more than he should have and that he'd be injuring her if he took from her.

"Do it," Holly whispered as she arched, taking him deeper. "Please."

"Nate…"

She put her finger over his lips to silence him. "He didn't take too much. Feed from me. I want it, I need it." She leaned in and spoke with her lips against his temple.

Rhett looked over her shoulder at Nate, who licked his lips. He felt Nate's hunger—his bloodlust and his desire for them both. He nodded at Rhett and Rhett kept his eyes locked with him when he dragged his incisors over Holly's jugular and the first jolt of her blood hit his system.

Suddenly she was writhing in his arms, squirming against him as she came. Her pussy was a silken vise around him as he laved over the wound, closing it.

"I love you, Rhett. God help me, I love you both so much I'd die without you," she said in a whisper and it was too much to bear, the weight of worry lifted from him, the words settled inside of him with certainty and he arched up as she moved down, getting into her as deeply as he could, pouring into her.

When he laid her down Nate came to lie next to them, on the other side of Holly.

Rhett rolled to his side and held his head up on his hand. "I love you, Holly. More than I can put into words. But you know that, you can feel it here," he took her hand and put it on his heart.

"And here," Nate said and put her other hand over his heart and she looked between them, eyes filled with unshed tears.

"Yes," she said in a quiet voice. "I can feel it. It's so miraculous. I...I'm sorry that I held back." She looked from one man to the other, needing desperately for them to understand.

Nate traced over a nipple with a fingertip. "I know why you did. It's in the past now. From now on we're three. Right?"

She looked from him to Rhett and nodded. "Right."

Chapter Six

ℬ

"She's here in New Orleans, sir," the man said nervously as he watched his boss's reaction to the news.

"She's what? Has she made contact with the witches?"

Piven wasn't fooled by the calm demeanor of the white-haired man behind the large desk. He gulped. "Yes. They met her at the airport. But she's not with them. They're at The Château."

"They? She's got those damned bloodsuckers with her?"

"Y-yes, sir."

"Have they bonded?"

"It appears so." Piven surreptitiously rubbed his sweaty palms on the thighs of his pants. "We sent some men into the hotel, it's been warded so tight none of them were even able to get on the elevator."

A meaty fist pounded on the desktop and Piven jumped. "Incompetents! I thought you were a high talent wizard, Piven. Why such bumbling? You allow her to escape the first attempt, even having her find out about our anger toward the witches, and now this?"

"I'm sorry, sir. She's protected by the vampires and a bodyguard at all times. She has some kind of protection around her. It's difficult to even see where she is, impossible to scry. I've never seen anything like it. We've got men on the hotel right now and men on the witches too. We'll try once she leaves."

"I don't want you to try, Piven. I want you to succeed. Now get out before I cast you into hell itself for failing me yet again."

* * * * *

Holly woke slowly and stretched. It took her a moment but she remembered that they were in New Orleans and that she had to set up a time to meet with the Charvezes—she still didn't think of them as her family although she had to admit that she felt some kind of connection to them, especially when Isolde Charvez hugged her.

More than that, the memory of the night before, of the way she'd come to totally accept Rhett and Nate, flooded through her, leaving her smiling. It gave her strength to face the rest of the stuff in her life she needed to fix.

Gently, she moved the arms banded across her body and slid from the bed. She stood watching them both for a moment. They did not stir, nor did they look dead. Rhett's rakish ebony hair was tousled about his face, long lashes lying against his cheeks. One of his hands was open, fingers just touching one of Nate's dreads.

He was so good to her. Patient and loving as well as suave and handsome. He took his time with her even when it was clear how much he'd wanted her to just accept their connection. He accepted her fears and did everything he could to help her past them. Often just before dawn, he'd brush her hair until it gleamed. The way he touched her made her feel cherished and loved. But when they were naked together, touching and loving, he was creative and tireless and it seemed as if he couldn't get enough of her. She smiled and touched the spot where he'd fed some hours before.

Her gaze shifted to take Nate in. The sheet was low on his abdomen and it showed the hard muscle of his body. The ropes of his dreadlocks were spread about the pillows and mattress, his lips still in their natural smile.

He was so much more complicated than he wanted to show. Underneath all that leather, past the floggers and the paddle, there was a deeply sensitive man. She'd felt his yearning the night before when she and Rhett had gotten out of the shower. Felt how much he needed to be assured that both of them loved him and wanted him. That, and the way he'd so skillfully destroyed her defenses against them both, made her adore him.

So very different, her men. But each filled a space within her that she'd never had the courage to even look at before. Both had been family to each other and now she was theirs too. In so many ways the three of them needed each other so much. Needed that connection and that belonging.

Reaching out, she pushed a lock of hair from Rhett's face and kissed his lips gently. Her fingertips trailed down the muscle of his arm and she squeezed his hand and pulled the blanket up. She knew he'd wake up cold, they both would.

Walking around to Nate's side of the bed, she pulled the blanket up over him as well but didn't resist the urge to slide her palm up his stomach and into the perfectly manicured beard and mustache. She pressed a kiss to his forehead and tried not to think about the fact that they'd still need donors. She knew they'd most likely be gorgeous women and sighed as the familiar specter of her self-doubt raised its head.

She felt Rhett stir along the link and pushed it away quickly, relieved when she felt him return to rest.

After showering, she called for lunch. She still felt uncomfortable taking their money but for now she had no other choice and she'd have to find a way to deal with it when they converted her and she couldn't work and go to school at the same time. They'd both assured her that it wasn't a big deal.

Nate came from money and consulted with the FBI. Rhett had built up a nice portfolio and ran a lucrative business designing websites. Both men were very, very well off. Still, it was difficult to allow herself to depend on anyone.

Jax brought the food in and ate with her. Holly liked the former Navy SEAL. He was mellow and had a very dry sense of humor but she didn't doubt for a second that he could snap someone's neck in moments and without a qualm.

"How are you feeling today? You looked wiped last night. Some big family you got here," he said as he poured them both a cup of steaming coffee with chicory.

"I didn't expect it. It was...overwhelming."

He looked up and nodded, waiting for her to elaborate if she wanted.

"I don't know what to think. What to feel. They seemed genuinely happy to meet me, which is at odds with people who'd just cast a fifteen-year-old girl out into the street. I don't understand it. And it doesn't erase the fact that we struggled my whole life. Alone." Her voice trembled a bit at the end and she saw the compassion in his eyes but he respected her space and merely nodded again.

"It's gotta be pretty hard to take. But you're going to let them explain?"

"Yes. I have to figure out what is going on at the very least. Someone is trying to kill me and that's connected with them. They strong-armed me to get me down here, they've got a lot of explaining to do."

They finished their meal in relative quiet. That was another thing she liked about him—he respected that she liked silence. He didn't have to fill up every moment with something to say.

"It's nearly four. I'm thinking that we should just wait until Nate and Rhett wake up and then go meet with them. They'll be awake in about forty-five minutes anyway. This way they won't feel so out of control." Jax watched her casually as he said it. He phrased it in a way that made her feel that she was making the decision rather than someone else doing it. She knew it and appreciated it.

"They need to eat first." Her voice had a slight edge to it.

"You know it's nothing to them."

She held up a hand to cut him off. "I don't want to talk about it. It is what it is. Doesn't mean I have to like it."

He shrugged. "That mean you want to go now?"

She gave him a shrug in return. "Let me call them and see what we need to do. I take it you've seen to the arrangements for their donors?"

"Yes, with some help from Bell's people. Someone will be coming here every night. And before you ask, yes, I checked them all out myself. They're all male by the way. Nate specifically asked for that this morning before he went to sleep."

Holly hid her smile. "Of course you did. I wouldn't insult you by assuming that you'd done anything less than your normal fabulous job with security." Inside she leapt with joy that Nate took care to make sure she wouldn't be hurt by the issue of donors.

She went to the phone and dialed Lee's number.

"Hello?"

It was Alex.

"Hi, it's Holly. Uh, is Lee around?"

"Holly! How did you sleep? Is the hotel all right?" Alex was warm and his questions sounded genuine.

"Oh fine I guess. The hotel is beautiful. Thank you for asking."

"Good. Let me get Lee for you," he said and Holly heard him call to her cousin softly.

"Holly, it's lovely to hear your voice. Can we have you and the guys over for dinner here? Of course you know that being with vampires, dinner means around nine. We'd like to see you before that. Have some tea maybe? We can meet here or at The Grove. That's the family's magic and herb shop in the French Quarter. It's up to you. We all want to make this as easy as possible. We could come there for a while, talk. Then decide." Lee desperately wanted Holly to give them a chance. Especially after the problems of the night before.

"I think it's best that I not leave the hotel without Nate and Rhett. I don't want them to be worried."

"Okay, that sounds reasonable. So, why don't a few of us come to the hotel for some tea? They do a lovely tea there. I know, funny considering it's a vampire hotel and all. Then we can decide what the next step should be."

"Few of you?"

"Well, me and my *grand-mère* and my sister Em. Of course Alex and Aidan and Con too. And I swear to you on my life, well, on Aidan's life, that there will be no repeat of last night and I'm so very sorry about…"

Holly interrupted, "That's fine. Can you give me about an hour? They'll be waking up soon but will need to feed." Holly was still working through just how angry she was over the way her men had been treated. She wanted to address it but on her terms, her timeline, her turf.

Lee bit her tongue. She could hear the icy tone in Holly's voice when she brought up the whole scene from the night before. "We'll see you in an hour then."

She hung up and turned to Alex, who raised his brows and gave a sigh. "She's pissed?"

"Yes and hurt. And she should be. We brought her here and then we treated her like crap by treating her mates so poorly. Can you imagine Aidan's family treating me that way? She may be shy, but I get the feeling she's one of those people who takes a lot to get angry but once there, watch out."

Alex quirked up a corner of his mouth and moved toward her. "Hmmm, seems that we'll have to think up some ways for Aidan to make amends."

Lee laughed as he pulled her into his arms.

* * * * *

Rhett sat up, felt Holly nearby and relaxed. She walked into the room and smiled at him.

"Hey, babe. The bathroom is heated up and your donors are here. Go on and shower and feed."

He kissed her quickly and jogged into the huge bathroom, pleased that she'd followed him. He'd been waiting for her to accept them this way. It felt really damned good.

"I'm glad to see you waited for us to wake up." He groaned long and hard when he stepped into the hot spray. "You should come in here," he invited.

She laughed. "I'd love to but your donor is waiting and after that the Charvezes are coming over. I'll take a rain check though. I do love washing your back."

Rhett let her dry his hair, reveling in the tender ministrations of her hands, and he left the bathroom as Nate strolled in.

He leaned in and kissed Holly until her knees felt like jelly. "After I feed, I'm bending you over," he whispered and got into the shower.

"No time for that. The Charvezes are coming over. Afterward. I promise. I'll let you have your wicked way with me."

"You bet you will," he promised and she laughed.

They fed and were dressed and drinking coffee when Jax led the Charvezes in. Isolde pulled Holly into a hug and kissed both cheeks and sat down after extracting kisses from Nate and Rhett. She didn't give anyone the chance not to receive her hugs and kisses, she simply gave her affection without hesitation.

Lee introduced Em and they also gave their cousin kisses on the cheek. Aidan stood back, a bit sheepish, and Alex gave a small wave.

Con snorted and pushed them aside and pulled Holly into a hug. "We didn't get a chance to meet last night. I'm Con MacNessa, Em's husband. I'm pleased to meet you."

His smile was infectious and flirtatious and Em just rolled her eyes at Holly, who couldn't help but smile back.

As they all sat down and Holly started to pour out, Lee cleared her throat.

"First thing, I'd like to apologize for Aidan. He's normally not like that. I guess it was some vampire bullshit, which is no excuse at all of course. Anyway, he'll be on his best behavior from now on and I want Rhett and Nate to feel welcome at any family event. They are as much family as Aidan is. We just want you to know how much we want you in our lives, how much we want to know all of you." Lee looked to Aidan. "He'd like to apologize too..."

Holly held her hand up to silence them all. "Let me be totally clear here. You need to understand that these men mean everything to me. They're part of me. If they are not welcome, I am not welcome. If they are *ever* made to feel the way they were last night again, I will walk out of here without looking back. It was unconscionable to force me down here and then to treat my partners like they were underlings." She leveled her gaze on Aidan. "And to do it for sport, to play with me to amuse yourself at their expense—at *my* expense—it was petty and certainly not something I'd consider courteous. If that's your idea of family, I don't want any part of it."

The room got silent for a moment. Holly felt Rhett and Nate's surprise along the link and then each put a hand on hers.

Aidan stood forward. "You are absolutely correct. It was petty of me and I apologize most sincerely. I am old enough to show better manners and I didn't. I made you all feel unwelcome and that was unfair. I would hate for us to continue on the wrong foot. Would you please, all of you, give me another chance?"

Lee knew what it cost him to make the apology but also heard the steel of Holly's voice. They'd all hurt her.

"My mother always said, 'show me your apology, don't tell me'. If you act like you're family, I'll know you mean it," Holly said, closing the subject.

"Okay, so let's talk about the threat to you, shall we?" Alex smoothly interjected.

"Actually, before we talk about any of that, I want to hear about my mother and how a fifteen-year-old girl with nothing but the clothes on her back was turned onto the street by people who refer to themselves as a close family."

Em looked at her cousin and felt the pain radiating from her. It was different than her anger at Aidan, this was soul deep.

Isolde nodded. "Of course, *chere*. Your *maman* was so young, so vibrant and full of love. She truly was cherished by all who knew her. But her father, he was very strict and so when she got pregnant he wasn't able to accept it.

"Your *grand-mére* was out of the house when it all blew up and when she returned home he'd already kicked your mother out of the house. Elise searched for hours, we all did. We searched the bus stations and the airport. Everywhere we could think of. We kept it up nonstop for weeks until Elise pretty much collapsed with exhaustion. Even then, she hired private investigators and they scoured the country.

"Your mother was just a girl, a penniless girl at that. We didn't understand how she was able to just drop off the face of the earth the way she did. I still don't understand it. We're a family of witches and we couldn't find one girl!" Isolde broke off, emotion in her voice, and Holly held back a sob but only barely. Rhett squeezed her hand and she leaned into him, taking comfort.

"Your *grand-mére*...it broke a part of her that never truly got fixed. She left your *grand-père* and we haven't heard from him since. We've missed your mother so much. Missed *you* so much."

Fat tears began to run down Holly's face and Rhett pulled her to him and spoke quietly in her ear. "It's okay, honey. We're here. Always."

"But she isn't. My mother could have healed herself but she didn't. When she was diagnosed with the cancer it was too far gone. They couldn't do anything for her. But she could have stopped it, she could have saved her own life but she chose to die and leave me instead of using her magic. Magic she hated so much. What did you all do to her that she hated herself that way?" Anguish laced Holly's voice as the thought that her mother hated her magic more than she loved her daughter surfaced yet again.

"I don't know!" Isolde wrung her hands together. "Honestly, *chere*. We loved her. We still love her. We always held hope that she'd come back or at least get into some kind of contact, let us know she was all right. Let us know what happened to her child. But nothing."

"Who is my father? Why didn't he help her?"

"We never found out. Whoever he was, she kept him secret. She wouldn't tell us and he never came for her after she ran away." Isolde was crying now and moved to the couch where Holly was, pushing Nate over so that she could sit next to her.

"Holly, you're one of us. We've loved you for twenty-four years without ever having seen your face. We loved your mother. We so very much want you to be part of us, to get to know you. Don't you want to know us?"

Holly looked into those eyes, shiny with tears, and sighed. "I do, but I don't know if I can trust you. You don't know what it was like for us. For most of my life we had next to nothing. We moved around a lot. She never dated, never wore pretty dresses or makeup. She just worked and made me go to school, pushed me to learn."

"Did she help you with your gift?" Lee asked.

"No! She hated it and I was forbidden to speak of it. She wanted me to pretend it didn't exist. The only time she ever used hers was when I was extremely sick or injured. Never, ever for herself. She worked as a nurse's aide from time to time but she was always careful not to use it."

Em knelt before her cousin and took her hands in her own. "I can feel your pain, Holly. The loneliness and fear, the ache of not belonging, of not having connections with anyone but your mother. You fear that we'll betray you like you wonder if we did her. A few years ago I had so many doubts about myself too. But you're strong. A survivor. I can feel that. You're a Charvez, Holly. And you have a gift for seeing like my *grand-mére*. Let her teach you how to use your talent, your gift. Let us know you, be your family." Em looked up at Rhett and Nate. "They love you, they want what's best for you. We love you and want that too. Won't you give us a chance?"

"Let us tell you about yourself. About the family you come from," Isolde added.

Holly took a deep breath and looked into Em's pretty green eyes and nodded. "Okay. Let's take it slow, but okay. I can only take so much time from work and I'm going to convert, which sounds like vampirism is a religion or something." She laughed nervously. "I have a lot to figure out, including who wants to kill me and why."

"Believe me, we want to know that too. Not just because you're one of our own, not just because all Charvez women could be in danger. But because if they're wizards, we need to stop them and as the next in line to run my family, I'm partly responsible for that," Alex said vehemently.

Over tea Holly told them everything she remembered about the break-in and Rhett and Nate added their impressions as well.

"The comment about a Charvez nearly destroying his 'entire'. His entire what?" Aidan asked as he paced.

"Clearly this wizard has some sort of enmity toward the Charvez witches. And we know of one family who has reason to hold a grudge." Lee looked at Alex and then back to Holly. "Three and a half years ago the dark wizards in Alex's familial clan were destroyed by us—the Charvez witches."

"My grandfather was executed. Most of them were either killed in the battle that day or were executed later. Of those who still live, I can't think of anyone powerful enough to set a trap spell so complex that it would have transported two bodies. That's a very high level spell."

Holly picked up a piece of paper and a pen and traced a series of symbols and words and Alex took it from her when she'd finished.

"Where did you get this?" he exclaimed.

"I dreamed them."

"You dreamed them?" Lee and Isolde burst out, leaning forward.

Holly nodded. "Is that wrong?"

Isolde shook her head and patted Holly's hands. "No, *chere*, there's nothing wrong with you. It's just that dreaming of this type is usually only something the witch dreamer of the line does. But Em, she dreamed of her Con for years." She looked at Alex. "What are they? What do they mean?"

"They're wizard spells. High level wizard spells. A few of the symbols are above my skill level, probably even above my father's skill level."

"How would Holly have seen them then?" Nate asked, drawing lazy circles on Holly's shoulder with a fingertip.

Alex sighed. "Well, the way such a spell works is that it would be said over something owned by the men, probably something the wizard gave to them before they went out to Seattle. A pen, a business card in a wallet, sometimes on the skin if the men trusted the wizard that much. It would have been written in the air around them, like a cloak. But humans wouldn't see it, hell, witches, even seers, shouldn't be able to see it. I'm not even sure most but the highest level wizards could see it."

"So how did I?"

"That's the big question, now isn't it?" Alex mused. "I don't know. It's a question of whether you saw it somehow and it niggled at your subconscious and came out as a dream or whether you dreamed it from whole cloth. You didn't grow up being schooled in magic and we don't know the full extent of your gift. Perhaps you saw something or heard something when they were tossing your apartment."

"Well, if only a few wizards are capable of such magic, can't you narrow it down?" Holly asked.

"I'll work on it. Em is actually the one who would be best at this." Alex looked at his sister-in-law affectionately.

"Well, I don't want to tax her," Holly said, worry in her voice, and Em laughed.

"Oh you're so sweet! Don't worry, it's more a matter of hitting some books than anything else. Con watches me like a hawk, he'd never let me endanger our daughter, even if I were silly enough to do such a thing. Which I'm not. I am, however, really pretty good at research."

"Really pretty good," Lee snorted. "Holly, my sister is pretty much *the* magical historian and research guru. If there's an answer to be found, she'll find it."

An ache sliced through Holly's heart when she watched the interplay between the sisters. It was truly wonderful to see but again, the feeling of loss, of envy, hit her hard.

Em looked at her closely. "We may not have been able to be part of your life when you were growing up, but you're here now. We're here now," she said quietly. "There are more of us. Your other cousin, Simone, is off with her husband right now but she'll return soon enough. You'll love her and goodness knows she'll love you right back. We do have a history together, but there's a Holly-sized spot right here if you'll just give us a chance."

Rhett tightened his arm around Holly. "Honey, why don't you rest for a while?" he murmured in her ear.

"No. I'm fine. Really. I want to hear about my mother. I want to find out who my father was. I want to know about the Charvez witches and I want to learn about my magic."

Isolde smiled. "You're a seer like I am. Oh your *grand-mère* would have been so proud! I can feel the power around you. I'd love to help you focus and train. It isn't something you can do overnight. But we'll do what we can with the time we have.

"As for the Charvez witches, well, in 1773 your foremother Annalisa saved a goddess from a demon. In gratitude that goddess, Freya, gifted the Charvez women with magical powers and bound us all to protect the innocent in New Orleans by a magical Compact. Each of the girl children is born with a different magical gift. Your cousin Lee is a witch dreamer. I believe you've seen some of what she can do in your own dreams. Em and your other cousin Simone are empaths. Your mother was a healer and you and I are seers. We've lived here and protected the people in the area from dark magical forces ever since."

Holly blinked in amazement at the story. "Wow. That's some family history."

Isolde laughed and nodded. "It is, and we're proud that you're a part of it. As for learning about your *maman*, I'd like to tell you more over your *grand-mère's* photo albums and scrapbooks. I have boxes of things that are yours now — boxes of letters she wrote to you and your mother but never got to mail. She'd want you to have them. Speaking of that, your *grand-mère* had a fairly large estate. It would have gone to your mother but now it's yours. It's waiting in an account. Alex is an excellent money manager, he can talk to you about it all."

Holly's face colored. "I would love to see the pictures and learn more but I can't take something from a woman I never knew. I didn't come here for that."

"Of course you didn't! None of us thinks otherwise. But the fact remains that you're hers. You're ours. And she left you something, left it to your mother and now it's yours. It gives you a few more choices." Isolde looked at Alex, who nodded.

"Shall we go to dinner? *Maman* is making a huge feast at the big house and the rest of the family has gathered," Em said, feeling Holly's discomfort and wanting to give her a break.

Holly looked to Rhett and Nate, who nodded at her.

"Okay then, let's go." Holly stood and felt bolstered by the men at either side of her.

"I trust that you've both fed?" Aidan said and Holly was relieved that his tone was much calmer and more mellow than it had been the previous evening.

"Yes, thank you for sending the donors," Rhett answered.

"It was my pleasure to help. Lee and Alex are donor enough for me so I don't need them anymore but I still have quite a few contacts around town."

* * * * *

The ride over to the Garden District had Holly slightly nauseated from nervousness. "What if they don't like me? What if they're jerks? God what if they think I only showed up for the money?"

Nate pulled her into his body and breathed her in. "One, how could they not like you? You're wonderful and loveable. Two, they *want* to know you and have made that very clear from the beginning. And three, no one thinks you're here for the money. You aren't that way and if you were Em would have known it right away."

"You think?"

"Of course I do. Sweetness, they see you for what you are, a beautiful, wonderful, strong and compassionate woman who is part of them. You're so brave to do this, I'm proud of you."

She squeezed Nate's hand and he kissed her temple. He and Rhett exchanged a look with Jax in the rearview mirror. They all wanted this to work out for her. She deserved to have a family who loved her as much as they all did.

She held Rhett's hand in hers as well and he kissed her knuckles and they both heard her heart beat faster at that touch.

"Careful," he murmured.

"How can you know?" she asked with a bit of annoyance.

Nate leaned in and spoke in her ear. "We can hear your heart pound when his lips touched you. When you blush so prettily the blood comes to the surface of your skin and warms. You smell delicious. Intoxicating."

Rhett's tongue slid between her fingers, bringing a gasp of delight from her lips. Nate watched and got harder. Rhett was just pleased that it was his touch that did it to her.

"Rhett, we're nearly there," Nate warned as he saw the other cars pulling onto a residential street. "Don't start what you can't finish."

Rhett's eyes moved up and caught Nate's. "Oh but I could finish it right now. I could slide my fingers up Holly's thigh and beneath her panties and her wet pussy would be only too happy to have me there."

Both Holly and Nate made a soft sound at the image that brought.

"We're here. Do you want me to drive around the block a few more times?" Jax said quietly and Holly let out a strangled laugh. Sometimes it was easy to forget that Jax was around. She was thankful for the darkness in the car to help cover her blush.

"No. Just park. Thank you, Jax," Holly said and turned her palm so that she was cupping Rhett's jaw. "Behave yourself and you just might get lucky later," she whispered in his ear.

Rhett grinned and turned to kiss her palm and each man had to adjust himself before they got out of the car.

Holly stood and stared at the front of the house. It was something special. The lights on inside shone out through the big windows and it looked welcoming. Greenery hanging heavy with flowers edged the large front porch and trailed up the columns that braced the façade.

The others were waiting for her at the front door and as she walked to catch up with them she saw them all there on the porch. Her family. She stopped dead in her tracks and put her hand to her throat with a gasp.

Nate leaned in and Rhett looked around for threats. "What is it? Sweetness?"

Holly looked at the faces there and saw a bit of her mother in every one. Some had the same ebony hair, another had the big, somber blue eyes. Lee's own smile was a mirror of her mother's. Her history was there, a genetic map of her blood and her family. Something she'd yearned for her entire existence was right in front of her and it felt so wonderful and overwhelming and sad and awful all at once, she didn't quite know what to do with all of it.

"Holly," Isolde saw her distress and went to her, pulling her into a hug. "Welcome home, *chérie*." Emotion hung thick in the air as they wept, holding each other tight.

Nate and Rhett felt the extreme flood of emotion come through the link. The conflicting feelings of fear and safety, of belonging and loneliness, envy and satisfaction. She was awash in the moment.

They all stood around on that big front porch and held hands, touched, as they looked on.

After several long moments Isolde pulled back. "Come on inside and let's get you and these boys introduced to everyone."

As Holly followed her great-aunt, she marveled at the house. More specifically, at how the house felt. It was as if it welcomed her, embraced her.

"Now, introduce the family to these men of yours," Isolde said as she indicated the room, full to bursting with people.

Nate was dressed in a handsome deep blue suit. The white linen shirt was open at the collar. His dreads were caught at the back of his neck, held away from his face. He looked casual and yet elegant but still held that edge of danger.

Rhett was in a charcoal gray pair of pants and a French blue shirt and his tie was gray to match. He looked like he'd just walked out of the pages of *GQ* magazine. He looked classy and so very handsome.

Both her mates were so gorgeous and sexy that she kept sneaking looks at them, amazed as always that they were hers.

She held her hands out and each one came to stand next to her. She made introductions and was relieved when they were greeted warmly and with respect.

She lost count of the names and people she was introduced to. The house was filled to the roof with Charvez women and husbands and brothers and cousins as well. They all seemed so at ease with each other and there never seemed to be a question that she was one of them. They all simply accepted her, welcomed her, treated her like one of the family and by extension, Rhett and Nate.

The dining room was filled to overflowing with people and food and laughter. Holly looked around the room and saw so many faces that looked like her own. Of the women there, only she and Lee had red hair—hers more copper and Lee's more auburn—but another male cousin, Lee's twin, had it as well.

After dinner they all went into the drawing room and sat her down. Isolde pulled out two large boxes and several photo albums and began to paint in the part of her mother's life before she was born.

Page by page, picture by picture, she gave her mother life in a way Holly'd craved for decades. She wondered at them all. Saw herself in the faces of these generations of women.

When she opened the book that started with her mother's birth the room quieted.

Lee's mother Marie laughed at one of the pictures. "Elena and I were less than a year apart in age. We were always so close." She tapped on a picture of a group of them in bathing suits, at a beach somewhere. "This was at the beach for my thirteenth birthday. Our cousin Lou broke her wrist and your mom healed it. Even so young she had such power. And she stayed calm even when everyone else was upset. She had such a gift."

Holly nodded—her mother had been an exceptionally calm person.

"Why didn't she come to us?" Marie asked quietly. "One moment she'd come to me and told me she was pregnant and the next I'd come home from a friend's house and she was gone. I never heard from her again. She was like the other half of my heart and she just disappeared. How could she just walk away from us like that?"

Holly took her hand. "I don't know. But there is something seriously wrong with this story. She lived in fear of being found out. We moved all the time. Whenever I asked about you all she refused to talk about it. I only have a few pictures of her because she would flip out if people took them."

"She was running from something," Nate said and they looked at him. "What? Did Holly not tell you I was an FBI agent? Well, on leave right now but I'll be returning to consulting soon."

"Really?" Alex asked with a grin and a discussion launched about the FBI and the missing persons cases that Nate used to work.

"This all seems so pointless. We'll never know why, and Holly grew up without us and needed us and we weren't there," Lee said as she touched a picture of the Charvez cousins of that generation.

"But she's here now. And she knows we love her and that whatever the reason, it wasn't our choice that she wasn't a part of this family until this moment," Isolde said as she looked into Holly's eyes.

Holly looked around the room at all of them and saw herself reflected there in mannerisms and facial expressions, in the shape of eyes or the slant of a pair of lips. Yes, these people were hers and she was theirs.

"Oh, sug, we've missed you so much," Isolde said as she pulled her into an embrace. "We can't replace your momma but we can be your family if you'll let us. I'd love it if you'd consider moving down here." She looked up at Nate and Rhett and back to Holly.

"I don't know. I have to finish school and Nate and Rhett have a house and I can't ask them to pull up stakes."

"Don't answer yet. I shouldn't have asked like this anyway." Isolde smiled wryly. "Get to know us for a bit and talk it over with your men and we'll revisit it later on in the week."

They read through the letters that her grandmother had written to her mother, all unsent but filled with so much love. With hope and longing so strong and poignant that it made Holly want to cry out at the injustice of all of it.

"Won't you move from the hotel to our house?" Marie asked. "Or Lee's? All are safer than the hotel and you'd have a better chance of getting to know us."

"Our house is equipped to deal with day sleepers," Lee said hopefully. "It's big and warded and nearby. Please. We'd all feel so better about your safety. We don't know what's stalking you."

Nate and Rhett said nothing. This was Holly's choice to make. They'd go wherever she wanted to go. Feeling that, she looked up and smiled as each man put a hand on her shoulder.

"Well, it's awfully late now. We can move to Lee's tomorrow if you're sure it's not a big deal. I'd feel better if the guys had a place that was extra safe for vampires."

Smiling, Isolde squeezed Holly's hands and kissed each cheek. "Sug, I'm thrilled that you're here. That you're letting us be a part of your life. Why don't we meet for a late lunch or whenever you wake up? You can see the shop and then I can show you your momma's things that we've got stored there."

"And move in tonight. Really. We've already had a suite of rooms prepared. We can go back to the hotel to get your things, it shouldn't take too very long," Lee pressed and Em nodded.

"Are you sure?"

"Absolutely!"

"Then why don't you go to the house now, sweetness? Rhett can stay with you and Jax and I will go back to the hotel and get the bags. You'll be safest that way. You'll be in a well-warded house with a master vampire, a wizard and another witch along with Rhett," Nate said as they all began to walk to the front door.

"Good idea," Rhett said and put a finger on Holly's lips as she began to complain. "It's the best way to keep you safe."

Holly sighed and agreed when she saw she was outnumbered.

* * * * *

When they arrived at Lee's, Holly had to admit that the house was as spectacular as she'd heard it was. It was

160

gorgeous but more than the way it looked, the house was special for the way it *felt.*

When they walked through the front door and it closed behind them, it felt utterly safe, almost cocoon-like. There was no noise from the street and the house was comforting around them, like an old, worn sweater.

"Wow, this place is amazing." Holly walked through, following Lee and looking around at the gleaming wood, the jewel-toned rugs and the pretty antiques.

"Thank you. We love it here. I'm so honored to have you with us." Lee opened a set of double doors and motioned them inside. "This is your bedroom. There are specially locked shades on the windows to keep the light out."

The bed was huge and there was a lovely sitting area with a comfortable loveseat and some small bookshelves. Holly dropped her purse on the bed. As she looked around the room, she caught the gleam in Rhett's eye and a shiver worked down her spine.

"The bathroom is here and just outside to the left are the back stairs that lead down to the kitchen. We aren't on Aidan's schedule one hundred percent. Alex has a day job and I work at the shop on most afternoons so someone will be up when you wake in the morning. Just head down and grab a bite if you're hungry. Oh and Jax's room is across the hallway."

Shyly, Holly moved to hug Lee and was pleased when her cousin pulled her into her arms with a tight squeeze. "Thank you for having us. I appreciate it."

"You're family, Holly. A Charvez. You're always welcome. Tomorrow I'll take you to the shop. You'll love it."

"Ah and Rhett, I'll have it arranged for donors to come here at sunset." Holly was relieved to note that the two vampires were much more comfortable around each other.

"Thank you, Aidan." Rhett turned to Lee and gave a bow, careful not to touch her and ignite any trouble between himself and Aidan. "And, Lee, thank you for reaching out to Holly."

Lee blushed and Aidan's nostrils flared. Alex shifted a bit and said with a wave, "Yes, well, I'm going to bed now."

"Yeah," Lee said in a slightly breathy voice and Holly had to stifle a giggle.

When they all walked out Holly found herself flat on the bed with Rhett above her. "I've wanted to touch you all night." Unbuttoning her blouse, he pressed his lips to her fluttering pulse at the hollow of her throat.

A small gasp broke from her throat and she pulled his tie loose, tossing it over his shoulder. In the back of her mind she heard it hit the chair but instead of feeling guilty she just moaned as he popped the catch of her bra and her breasts spilled out into his hands.

She opened his buttons as he kissed down her chest and his lips found their way to her nipples. Pulling his shirt off, she cried in frustration when it got caught at the cuffs. "Damn French cuffs!" she mumbled as she tugged the links loose and reached back to lay them on the table next to the bed.

Rhett took advantage of her stretched body and slid up against her like a cat. Her skirt was up around her waist and his hands made quick work of her panties.

Positioning himself between her thighs, he spread her open to his gaze. She looked down her body at his glossy black hair, watched his eyes as he took her in. When his tongue touched her she moaned and he pressed his palms against her thighs, keeping her positioned just so.

Dimly, she felt it when Nate entered the house. Felt it like a shock of warmth down her spine as he moved toward the room with purpose. He knew what they were up to, could feel their pleasure through the link.

Rhett knew that Nate was out there and he drove Holly higher, relentlessly, toward orgasm. She was writhing beneath him, rolling her hips up to meet his mouth. Breathy sounds of pleasure were coming from her mouth as her hands held his head to her.

The door opened and closed quickly and Holly opened her eyes. Her gaze locked with Nate's as he quickly got rid of his clothes. Stalking naked toward the bed, he stopped directly behind where her head lay.

Before she could say anything to him, Rhett sucked her clit into his mouth, grazing it just slightly with his incisors, and orgasm bloomed through her. Back arched, she felt herself being moved and suddenly Rhett was pushing inside of her and her head was off the bed, upside down, and Nate's cock was tapping her lips.

"Open," they said in unison and she arched up to meet Rhett's thrust and took Nate into her mouth and the three became one.

She was caught in a feedback loop of sensation—the thrust of Rhett's cock deep inside her pussy as Nate pulled back out of her mouth. Nate thrusting into her mouth as Rhett pulled back. Helpless to do anything other than receive, she opened herself to the pleasure of it and let them give and in that, took.

Rhett looked up at Nate, watched him as he stroked into Holly's mouth. His breath came in shallow pants, his dreads loose about his chest and shoulders. The ring in his nipple winked in the low light. He saw Nate through Holly's eyes but he had to admit that he'd found Nate to be beautiful before Holly came along. She was simply the way for him to voice it to himself.

Nate took his eyes from Holly and locked his gaze with Rhett's and the electricity of that zinged through the room. Nate leaned down and touched his lips to Rhett's and straightened so as not to strain Holly's neck.

The hum of satisfaction she made vibrated through his cock. Her tongue, soft and wet, swirled around the ridge of the head and her hands slid up his thighs and came to cup his balls. Pleasure rushed through his body. He gasped her name as he climaxed.

Rhett watched her throat work as Nate came, a sight so erotic that it hit him square in the balls. Her lips were shiny and swollen from sucking Nate's cock as Nate pulled back. He lay on the bed next to them as Rhett continued to fuck into Holly's body.

Unable to resist, Rhett leaned down and kissed Holly's lips, tasting Nate there. He heard Nate's strangled moan and felt the bed dip as he leaned in. Nate's tongue met their joined lips and the kiss caught fire. The inferno of their desire brought Rhett's body to the edge as he began to come.

Wave after wave of pleasure rolled through him as he thrust into Holly over and over again. Nothing had ever made him feel as complete as when he was with Holly, inside of her, her body harboring his. She was perfect. She was his.

Nate broke the kiss and dragged his incisors across the flesh just below Holly's ear and the two vampires leaned in to taste her as orgasm took over her body once again.

"Oh god yes!" she cried out and one hand held Nate's head and the other held Rhett, the three of them joined.

Rhett softened and pulled out and lay to one side, moving Holly's body so that she was able to snuggle between the two of them.

"I love you, Rhett," Holly said softly, leaning over to place a kiss on his chest. He pulled her into an embrace, breathing her in.

"I love you too, honey." There was no other answer. He'd said the words before to other women both as a human man and as a vampire, but he realized that first night with Holly that he hadn't really known what love was until she'd come into his life.

Nate growled and pulled her back and she was in his arms. "Sweetness, I've got to have you. Time is ticking toward the dawn, can you take me?"

Touched that such a dominant man could always put her first, Holly nodded and arched into him. "Oh yes, always. Nate, I love you. I love your cock inside of me."

He got onto his knees and positioned her, head down, ass up. "I love you too, sweetness. You're all I think about, all I want, all I need." His hands stroked over her body, cupping her breasts and rolling and tugging on the sensitive nipples until she gasped.

Both men gave dark chuckles at how she responded and she may have been annoyed by it if it hadn't felt so damned good, so right, to have his hands on her.

She looked up at Rhett as Nate drew a fingertip through her, over her clit with the barest of touches. She was still sensitive from her last orgasm and he was careful not to overstimulate her.

Rhett stroked a languid hand over his cock as he watched the two of them, the people he cherished most in the world.

"Fuck her, Nate," he said, his voice tinged with that northeastern flavor.

"My pleasure, Rhett," Nate replied and Holly moaned softly as he sliced through her in one hard thrust.

"Oh! More. More please, Nate," she whispered, pushing back against him.

Rhett got to his knees beside Holly and this time, he initiated the kiss. Nate's lips were firm and warm and his beard was softer than Rhett had thought it would be.

"Hey! No fair! I want to see," Holly grunted as Nate flexed into her.

In one smooth motion Nate pulled out and flipped her over and plunged back inside and then pulled Rhett to him, back into the kiss.

Holly pushed Rhett's hand away from his own cock. With a raised eyebrow, Nate moved Holly's and replaced it with his own.

"I'll take care of that. I want you to touch yourself. Pinch your nipples. Hard. I know you like it that way."

She nodded and watched as Nate pulled out, moistened his hand with their combined wetness and thrust back inside, his hand grasping Rhett's cock. Both she and Rhett gasped in pleasure.

Rhett looked down at her. "Didn't Nate just tell you to pinch your nipples?"

She licked her lips and continued to watch them as she obeyed, rolling and pinching her nipples.

Nate felt the ripple of her pussy muscles around him and knew that she was just as turned on as the two of them were.

"Touch him, Rhett. He likes it when you play with the nipple ring," Holly said breathily as she drew inexorably closer to coming.

Rhett's hands slid up Nate's stomach and then to his nipples and Nate gave a low groan when Rhett tugged on the ring.

Rhett thrust into Nate's hands and Nate thrust into Holly's pussy and she greedily watched them as she touched her nipples. It was so unbearably erotic that Rhett began to come first, his silky cum sliding through Nate's hands and onto Holly's stomach. Holly cried out as the hot liquid touched her flesh and, back bowed, exploded around Nate's cock. Which pulled him in and he thrust deep and hard and unleashed his pleasure.

The combined thrusts and groans and gasps, sweat and seed and heat filled the air until it nearly throbbed with it. At last the three fell back and bonelessly heaped together.

Unity and love and togetherness. The three of them made a family.

Chapter Seven

ℰ

Holly woke up, as always, snuggled tight between the two men. She leaned out and saw that it was already one in the afternoon. Yawning, she extricated herself from bed and made sure they were covered up well. She saw her suitcase was just inside the door where Nate had dropped it when he'd come in earlier that morning. At least he'd tossed the garment bag over the back of a chair so the clothes inside weren't wrinkled.

She pulled out some underwear and a change of clothes from the bag, hanging it where the other two hung in the closet. The shower was nice and hot and it woke her up nicely. She was ravenous by the time she had finished getting ready and she quickly headed down the back stairs and ended up in the enormous kitchen where Lee was sitting, drinking coffee and reading.

"Good afternoon!" Lee smiled as she stood. She hugged Holly before her cousin could bolt and felt relieved when Holly returned it. "Hungry?"

"Starving!"

"Would you like to grab something quick here, a sweet roll or something, and head into town to the shop? We'll meet everyone for a late lunch in the French Quarter at Deanie's Seafood. I promise you won't be sorry." Lee's grin was infectious and Holly found herself returning it.

"Sure! I'd love to see the shop and I've heard great things about the food in New Orleans. I'm glad that the city seems to be recovering from Katrina."

"Deanie's used to be located in a really hard-hit area but they've moved it to the French Quarter this year. It was just too much to try and salvage it where it was. So many restaurants were destroyed after Katrina. It's going to take years more before it's back to normal. You know, we can protect the city from demons but not a hurricane. The aftermath was horrifying. It still is in many parts of New Orleans. But we'll survive, that's what we do."

Holly was touched by her cousin's obvious love of the Crescent City.

"I'll drive you both wherever you need to be today," Jax said as he entered the room.

"Okay, Jax. Thank you." Holly had promised Nate and Rhett that she wouldn't go anywhere without Jax during the daytime.

"Great, thank you, Jax," Lee agreed.

As it was winter, it wasn't the tourism season and the Quarter wasn't very crowded and so they were able to find a place to park on Iberville and walk the few blocks to Deanie's.

A whole table was filled with Charvez women who jumped up to hug and kiss her cheeks. Holly felt the warmth of their greeting. She felt like she *belonged* to their tribe and that was overwhelming.

Em stood and hugged Holly. "Come on and sit down. Hope you like seafood."

Jax accepted all of the feminine adoration with the ease of a man who was used to it. It made Holly grin. But even with the attention, he never took his focus from the room, from who was there and near Holly.

Lunch was a riot of noise and energy and camaraderie. While Holly envied them their ease of communication and the way they all seemed to know each other so well, she also began to feel a part of that. Clearly she didn't have the decades of togetherness that they did, but at the same time, they treated her like family. Teasing and laughing with her. As she relaxed they did too, Holly began to realize that she really wanted to know these people. She resolved to speak with

Rhett and Nate later that day about their plans for where they'd live after she converted.

However she'd felt at lunch, she was totally unprepared for the shop. She could feel it for blocks as they walked toward it. Could feel the invisible tether pulling her toward the glass doors at the end of the block ahead of her.

Suddenly she turned and it was like time had slowed to a crawl. She saw a flash of light and searing pain in her chest. The stench of burned flesh hit her nose and she crumpled to the ground amid screams.

And then a hand on her forearm and the worried eyes of Isolde. "I saw it. Let's get you inside." Her command was urgent and Jax shielded her with his body and hustled them all into The Grove.

At once, the scent of sage and the polished wood of the giant counter washed away the scent memory of the burning flesh. The sound of the jingling chimes calmed her jangled nerves.

Em pushed her into a chair and Con shimmered into the room, looking worried and ready to fight. Lee handed her a mug of tea. "Drink it, *chere*, it'll calm your nerves."

"I saw...I felt something hit my chest. It hurt, I could smell where whatever it was had burned into me. There were screams and I fell." Holly looked up into Isolde's face and met the same worry there.

"You had a vision. Have you not ever had one before?" Isolde asked as she chafed one of Holly's hands in her own.

Holly's cell phone was ringing and Jax answered it tersely. He came to her moments later. "Holly, it's Rhett."

"Rhett?" Holly looked outside, it couldn't have been later than four, sunset was not for another hour. She took the phone. "Yes? Honey, is everything all right? Why are you awake?"

"Are *you* all right?" he demanded.

169

"I apparently had a vision. I'm all right. I'm at the shop. Jax is here. Rhett, it's an hour from sunset, how can you be awake?"

"What did you see? Holly, to wake me so far ahead of sunset it must have been something bad. I want you to come back here now. I need to touch you, to know with my eyes that you're okay."

"I saw, hell, I don't know really." She looked at everyone else as she explained to Rhett over the phone. "I was walking and then I turned around, but time felt different, odd, slow. I saw a flash of light and then I felt this terrible burning pain in my chest. I smelled burning flesh. I'd been hit with something. Attacked. I fell to the ground, people were screaming." The reality hit her, she began to tremble until her voice was shaking so badly her teeth began to chatter.

"Damn it! Holly, please, it's killing me not to be able to help you. Please, please come back to the house now," Rhett begged.

"H-he w-wants me t-to c-c-come back." She tried to speak and ended up handing the phone to Jax who carried on a tense, whispered conversation with Rhett.

"We should get you back to the house. It's safest and we need to do some thinking," Lee said.

"It was a magical attack that she saw," Isolde said quietly. "I saw it at the same time she did."

"Why haven't I dreamed this?" Lee asked, frustrated.

"Let's talk about this back at the house, shall we?" Jax interjected. "I've got a very agitated vampire waiting back there and soon Nate will be drawn out of sleep too. I've seen a vampire kept from his mate when she was threatened, it wasn't pretty."

"We'll shimmer her back right now with Jax. Lee, I felt Holly's distress very strongly, I'm guessing that Alex and Aidan probably are feeling yours through the link. Call Alex and if Aidan wakes up, we'll tell him we're coming right back to shimmer you home."

Just after Em and Con took Holly and Jax's hand, Alex burst through the door and straight to Lee, pulling her into his arms.

* * * * *

They shimmered straight into the living room of Lee's house and Jax led Holly out of the room, keeping an arm around her to support her as he called out to Rhett.

Rhett rushed out into the hallway and saw her and Holly was taken aback momentarily by the flash of anger in his eyes toward Jax. Jax must have seen it too because he stepped away from Holly slowly.

"He's worried about you. Seeing you in this state, and another man touching you, incites his primal instincts," he whispered to Holly and then looked to Rhett. "Rhett, she's very shaky, why don't you settle her on the couch?" he said in a soft voice and it occurred to Holly that she'd love to know just how he knew so much about vampire behavior.

Shaking his head to clear it, Rhett moved quickly to help her. "Let's get you on the couch," he said softly and they heard a thump and a bellow come from Nate.

"Shit. Stay here, I'll go and let him know you're all right." Jax quickly headed upstairs.

Em tucked a throw around Holly as Lee rushed out to get some tea, Aidan on her heels, not letting her out of his sight.

Nate ran into the room and there was a bit of a tussle between him and Rhett until they both found a way to snuggle in on either side of her.

"Everyone else is driving over," Em said quietly as she sat down and tucked her feet beneath her. Con sat on the floor, his head on her lap.

"What the heck happened?" Alex asked. "Isolde said it was a magical attack in your vision?"

Holly told them what she'd seen and explained the way that time had slowed down. "Funny thing, I wanted to say these words but the pain in my chest cut off my wind, I couldn't speak." She then spoke a fluid series of intonations in a language she didn't know.

Alex paled and stood up. "Where did you hear those words?" he demanded and Nate stood up, getting between Alex and Holly, baring his teeth.

Aidan stood slowly and touched Alex's shoulder. "Rhett and Nate are in a state right now. Their only focus is going to be protecting Holly. I know you don't intend to be threatening but your body language is. Sit down and let's all be calm."

Alex put his hands up slowly and sat back down and Nate followed suit and the glow in his eyes receded.

"Nate, honey, it's all right." Holly touched the side of his face with the backs of her fingers. He turned to her and she watched the panic fade from his eyes.

"I know. I just...waking up after you'd been so upset, I felt helpless. I couldn't have saved you. I hate that."

Sitting up, she moved to her knees and embraced him. "I love you so much. I was surrounded by family. Jax was there. They got me back here right away. It's all right. I'm all right."

Rhett moved behind her and put his arms around both of them. "Jesus, if anything had happened to you..." His voice broke.

"Nothing did. Don't you see? My vision, my gift just saved my life." She pulled back but stayed wedged between them. "How many people get to know of a planned attack with such accuracy? I'll be sure to be extra careful now. Coming here, getting in contact with my family, you both pushed me to do that and it may well save my life."

Lee came in and handed her a steaming mug of tea. "Drink up while you answer Alex's question. It's calming. The Grove's special blend."

"Alex, I don't know where I got the words from, they just came to me." Holding the mug in both hands, she leaned back, letting herself relax against Rhett and Nate.

Within minutes, the room began to fill with people. With family. Holly looked up at them all in amazement. They were her family and they'd come because they were worried about her.

"Do you recognize the words, Alex?" Holly asked as she saw her uncle come in and gave him a smile. He approached her and hugged her tight and then sat across from them, not letting her out of his sight.

"Yes. Holly, that was a wizard spell. Not just any spell but one of a very high power level. Master Class."

"Is a wizard acting through her? Using her to try to get back at someone?" Rhett asked.

"I don't think so. We can't really do that, well, some dark path practitioners could temporarily possess someone but she wouldn't have such a strong memory of the spell. Wizard power is inherited. In other words, because my grandfather was so powerful, my father, being his son, was also powerful. So of course my brothers and I, being his sons, are at that level of power too. That spell she just spoke was a spell that turns magic around, like a rebound of energy. Only the child of a master line would be able to speak it."

"Another Charvez mutation?" Isolde asked. "Em has the power of an empath but also a bit of the power of a seer."

"I don't know," he said doubtfully. "Witch magic and wizard magic are very different. The language we use to manipulate and control our magic comes from our power levels. As you know, our spells are not in a written language but an arcane system of symbols which, used together, create sounds and spell words. Now, we could trade certain elemental spells when I first met Lee because the three of you were at a sufficient power level to handle those. But the spell Holly used is not something you could use. I could spell it out phonetically but you would not be able to say it." Alex pursed his lips as he thought.

"Weird," Holly said.

Nate did a shocked double take and he began to laugh. Others began to join him and a minute or two later the tension was broken and Holly had stopped shaking.

Jax poked his head into the room. "Nate, Rhett? Donors are here."

They wouldn't both leave her at the same time so one went to feed and then the other.

"This is connected to wizards. We know this. We don't know why, but at least we know something," Nate said as he returned.

"True." Alex turned to Isolde. *"Grand-mére,* what was Elena's power level like? Did she have any unusual talents?"

"She was an exceptional healer. From an early age she was so strong. But nothing more than that. She had the Charvez talent for charming people but she didn't have Lee's level of power and I think that even untrained Holly has more all-around power than Elena did."

Holly turned to Rhett and then Nate. "Can I speak with you two alone?" She looked back at everyone. "We need a few minutes." She stood up and held out her hands to the guys. "You ready?"

They nodded, and hand in hand, they went upstairs.

Once in their room Holly went to the loveseat and sat. "I want to stay here to be trained. To learn how to use my powers and to find out what the hell is going on."

Nate sat on one side and Rhett pulled up a chair to sit across from them both. "Okay, that's reasonable."

"Are you sure? You have a house in Seattle, you were starting lives there. I'm sorry to do this to you."

Rhett leaned forward and took her hands. "Honey, we love you. You need to do this and you won't be safe until we figure out who's behind this and stop them. We go where you go."

"But..."

Nate interrupted. "But what? It's not like I can't do consulting work from here. Rhett's web design stuff is portable. We'll get our own house here in the Garden District near your family and after all of this is over we can revisit where we'll live for the long term."

"I agree. I'll call my business manager and get him looking for a house right away. I only have one condition," Rhett said.

"Anything. You two are so good to me. What can I do for you?" She really couldn't believe how fortunate she was. Despite the death threats, she had family. A big family, complete with two husbands, and it was so incredibly wonderful that she could hardly believe it.

"You need to convert."

"I said I would already. Is that what you're worried about?"

"No. I want you to convert tonight or tomorrow night. I want it done and I want it done soon and I won't feel okay until it happens," Rhett said.

"I agree," Nate said.

She sighed and closed her eyes as she thought.

"Do you think we'd do anything that would harm you?" Rhett asked, frustrated.

"No! It isn't something I think I should do right now." Holly stood up and began to pace.

"Are you going to keep trying to put this off?" Rhett continued.

She rounded on him. "Why are you pushing this so hard? Can't you just wait until it's a better time?"

"Is it that you think less of us? That you'll be giving up your humanity to become a monster?" Hurt laced Nate's tone.

"No. How could you think that?" Sighing, she knelt before him and took his hand, placing it against her cheek. "I could never think that. I love you both so much. But I'm afraid. Aside from never seeing the sunrise again I'll be helpless for twelve hours a day. Right now, if I get training to use my power, I can protect you two in the daytime. If I convert now instead of when we fix all of this mess, I'll need protection in daytime too."

"She has a point," Rhett said with a sigh. "The whole issue of her being unable to respond in daylight is a real one. She'll be newly converted, which will mean she'll be useless at the high sun point. Why don't we shelve this for now? It's not like we don't have time to address it later. Let's do some planning. Figure out where we're going to be living and get this asshole who's trying to kill her taken care of and then we can deal with this."

"Okay but this isn't going away, Holly," Nate said.

She looked up into his pale green eyes and put her hands on his lap. "I know. I'm sorry if I hurt your feelings. I love you. I love Rhett. I want to be with you for centuries, I promise."

He touched her cheek gently and tipped her chin up with a fingertip and kissed her nose. "I love you too, sweet."

Going back downstairs, they sat on the couch and she looked at her great-aunt. "Train me. I can't go back to school right now. I need to finish but I have to figure out what is going on and I'll feel better once I start to understand things. Not knowing how to use my power is holding me back."

There was a collective gasp of happy surprise throughout the room and Isolde said with a smile, "Of course. We can begin with the basics tonight."

"Are you up to that?" Nate asked, concerned.

"I have to be. This is part of the puzzle."

"Okay, but why don't you rest for an hour or so? Then you can start refreshed," Rhett said and Nate nodded in agreement.

"Does this mean you're staying here in New Orleans for good?" Lee asked hopefully.

"For the foreseeable future, yes. Rhett is going to have his business manager begin to look at real estate here in the Garden District. That is, if you don't mind my living close by." Suddenly she felt shy. Apprehensive.

Lee pulled her into a hug. "Mind? Sug, we'd love to have you here! We have a huge storage unit filled with your *grandmére's* belongings. Furniture, books, that sort of thing. Please, she left it to your mother and because she's not alive, it's yours. Help yourself to any of it."

"Oh goodness, thank you. I don't know what to say. I won't be converting for a while though, until we figure all of this out."

"Oh I meant to talk with you about that," Aidan said. "Clearly, you don't know about converting a witch. I didn't know either," he said smoothly.

"Know what?" Rhett asked suspiciously.

Lee laughed. "You're gonna love this."

"Well, the conversion has already started if you've taken her blood and she's taken yours. Which she has at least once because you've both bonded with her. Apparently, just the exchange of blood begins the conversion between mate pairs of vampires and witches. Lee has begun to need small amounts of blood. She's also got increased speed and strength and she can see better at night. In about five to ten years she'll start to feel sensitive to light at high day and have to stay out of it in about twenty. Her aging has slowed down immeasurably.

"Each time she takes your blood, it will move her further along. There's no need for full conversion if you don't want to.

It's already happening, it'll just take about twenty years before she needs as much blood as we do and can't be out during the high day. I'm guessing Holly's already got better speed and more strength."

"Ah, and it also means you can get knocked up," Lee added.

"What?" Holly turned to Rhett and Nate. "You said I couldn't get pregnant!"

Rhett quickly put his hands up in defense. "I didn't think you could. I didn't know about this whole witch thing. But you've only taken our blood a few times. We'll be careful now that we know. I'm assuming you want kids at some point?" Rhett asked.

"Okay, this is not a conversation for this moment." Holly turned back to Aidan. "So essentially, I'm already on my way to vamphood and I could be knocked up? Surprise!"

Aidan laughed at her plucky attitude. "You're a Charvez all right. I'll get all of the documentation we've collected over the last three years to you. And please feel free to stay here with us as long as you need to. You're welcome here."

Lee put her hand in his and squeezed in appreciation. Holly smiled shyly in thanks. "Thank you." She turned and took in everyone. "Thank you all for making me...us feel so welcome."

"You can work in the shop and we can start your lessons. We'll make sure you learn about your roots too," Isolde said.

"Really? Great, because I need a job."

Rhett narrowed his eyes at her, annoyed with her money issues. "You don't need a job. You can have a job. It sounds like a great way to be with your family and learn about your roots, but you don't *need* a job. You're our wife, as such, everything we have is yours," he said quietly in her ear.

Alex heard. "And, Holly, I have the portfolio outlining your inheritance. You certainly don't need a job. Even without Rhett and Nate, you wouldn't need a job."

"We can talk about that later." She still felt uneasy taking the money.

Rhett went with Aidan to talk with his business manager about finding a house in the area that would be vampire friendly and Nate stayed in the room as Isolde pulled out a deck of tarot cards.

"Okay, you won't need these once you learn better focus, but while you're learning, they're an excellent way to get your head around the concept of grabbing threads of the future." Isolde tapped the deck but Holly stayed her hand.

"Wait. I'll be right back." She jogged out of the room and returned shortly with her own deck. She told Isolde about the old woman and how she came by the cards and also about the vision she had of Lee when she looked at them before.

"That's wonderful. I think the way the deck came to you was fated. I love how they connected you to us. We'll use your deck." Isolde paused for a moment before leaning and taking Holly's hand. "I'd be honored if you called me either *Grand-mére* or *Tante* Isolde. I'm not your grandmother by blood but Elise was my sister and I'd love to be your grandmother in spirit as well as name. If you're not comfortable, *tante* means aunt."

Holly inclined her head, hiding her eyes. "You wouldn't mind?"

"*Chere*, I mean it when I tell you that I love you like my own granddaughters. That you've come back to us after being gone so long, it's a miracle. Far from minding, I'd love it."

"Okay, *Grand-mére*."

Isolde hugged Holly tight before returning to business. "Now, let's see that deck."

Holly laid out the cards in a way that she felt natural doing and Isolde watched her with a raised brow. The girl was a natural. Not a lick of training and she knew the spread without a prompt.

"Okay, good. Why don't you just tell me what you think the cards are saying to you?"

Holly reached out to touch a card but her eyes slid closed and her head tipped back. Isolde stood up and put out a staying hand to Nate, who'd started to rush over.

Holly watched a tall, dark-haired man in a suit standing near a bank of windows. Another, younger, man stood with him and they both turned to look at her.

The scene shifted and she saw an elderly man with a cane. The head of the cane was a silver wolf with bared fangs. He narrowed his eyes at her and spoke and blood began to run out of her nose and ears.

The scene changed again and it was the old man slumped over in his chair.

The scene flipped and she saw her mother at fifteen, talking with a boy who was just a bit older. They were holding hands. The boy was gone then and the elderly man was there. He was angry. Her mother was crying.

She snapped upright and tears were streaming down her face.

"What is it? What did you see?" Isolde demanded.

Holly told her and they puzzled over it for some time.

"I think it was my father—the boy with my mother. I felt so much love between them. I can't imagine that he just abandoned her." Holly stood up and went to look out the window. "There's just so much I don't know about this whole thing!"

"I know, *chere*. We've gone over and over it for so very long. And with the information you've given us, it's even more strange. She was loved, she knew this. Yes, she was young and pregnant but we loved her and she loved us. That couldn't have changed overnight. I know she wouldn't have just walked away like that without a reason. People just don't make such big changes all of a sudden." Isolde looked sad as she spoke.

"There's someone out there," Em said quietly and Nate grabbed Holly and pulled her away from the window.

"Who?" Nate demanded and Jax went on high alert.

"I don't know. Just someone not usually there. He doesn't belong here." Em closed her eyes and stood nearer to the front door but Con made sure she was away from any windows.

"Wizard," Em said with a nod. "Yes, wizard. I remember the feeling."

Jax started to move toward the door but Alex put out an arm to stay him. "No. You can't fight that kind of magic with physical strength. We don't know what's going on just yet anyway."

Lee sat in the middle of the large area rug and Holly noticed for the first time that there was a magical circle woven into the pattern. Alex came toward Lee to join her but suddenly the glass blew inward, showering into the room. Turning, Holly threw out her hand as strange words came from her mouth—that strange fluid language she'd spoken earlier—and the glass shot back into place.

Magic began to collect thick in the air with static intensity as she continued to speak. Alex held out his hand and joined it with hers, forming a circuit of power as their power flowed outward.

A series of loud pops sounded and suddenly it was silent again. Holly slumped to her knees and Alex held her against his body, pulling her away from the window, handing her to Rhett. While Rhett sat with her on the bench in the hallway, Nate paced. He desperately needed to go outside to hunt down whoever it was that hurt Holly and kill him but Aidan stood near the door with Jax and they spoke in hushed tones with Con and Alex.

"Honey, are you all right? Do we need to get you to a hospital?" Rhett asked, amazed at how calm his voice sounded when he was screaming inside in panicked fear over her wellbeing.

Looking up at him, she nodded. "I'm okay. Let me sit up."

He looked at her dubiously and she sighed. "I promise, I really feel better but I need to sit up."

He helped her sit up but kept her against him. "What was that?"

"That was wizard magic being performed by a witch," Alex said as he approached.

"What? I thought you said that other than simple spells that witches couldn't do wizard spells," Lee said as she handed Holly a glass of water.

"They can't. Or couldn't until today. I don't know how. But not only did Holly perform wizard magic but it was high level wizard magic. As in my level of strength. That popping you heard? It was trap spells being unraveled and dissolved. Nearly impossible for nine out of ten wizards."

"It's all clear out there," Con said as he shimmered back into the room. "Stinks of wizards using blood magic though, according to the missus."

Em smiled at him for a moment and then turned back to Alex and Holly. "Yes. The same way it felt when we went into your grandfather's house."

"It was my grandfather's people?"

"No. Or it could be, but I don't know would be a more accurate answer. I can just feel the stench of the magic—dark magic—and that it was wizard magic. It doesn't give off anything that enables me to say who exactly it was."

"And they broke through these wards," Aidan said, face grim.

"A demon couldn't break through, how come a wizard can?" Lee asked Em.

"I don't know. Unless he knew the spells that created the wards somehow, or had some other back door through them. I'll look into it tonight. The positive is that he couldn't physically enter the yard much less the house. He used his magic to cut through the wards and I think the spell blew out the glass but I don't think any real harmful magic could have breached the house at all," Em said.

"This isn't about anyone else. It's about Holly, I know it," Nate said.

"We don't know that. The guy who broke in said something about hating the Charvezes," Aidan said.

"Yes, but every single attack, every single vision of some injury, has been focused on Holly. He may hate the Charvezes but it's Holly he wants to kill. We've got to figure out why." Nate's mouth was set in a grim line.

"I agree. It just *feels* that way. The more I think about it, the more I keep coming back to Elena. This has to have something to do with her and why she left," Isolde said.

"You three will come to our house tonight. No one knows where it is and it's warded with Faerie magic," Con said and Nate and Rhett nodded.

* * * * *

For the next week they worked on building up Holly's skills as a seer. Isolde was continually amazed that for a woman who hadn't been trained — worse, had actively been taught to avoid her magic — Holly was a natural. More than that, she was powerful. Her unique set of gifts meant that she not only had foresight but that she also had snatches of powerful visions of the past.

No further attacks had been made on her or on Lee's house and they'd found a house in the Garden District, not too very far from Lee. It was a large antebellum Greek revival home on Chestnut Street and Holly loved that she was in a triangle of family, with the Lafayette Cemetery closing the loop. Apparently, the Charvezes had a large family plot there and Holly felt that the Charvezes who'd passed on, including her grandmother, were there keeping an eye on her. Another feature of the home that Holly loved was the sky blue ceiling in the gallery. Like the one at Lee's, it was apparently common in Garden District homes and believed to keep evil spirits away. To Holly, it felt more open and spacious because it looked like the sky.

It had an office for Rhett's business and several extra bedrooms for Nate to convert to an office for himself and his consulting business if he wanted to pursue that as well.

Tulane had a night program that she could attend to finish her degree and she was able to transfer all of her credits from the University of Washington without a problem. Roy was sorry to see her go but was happy that she'd found her family. When escrow closed on the house Con and Em would help move their things from Seattle to New Orleans and the house in Seattle would be put on the market.

Holly was ready to start working at The Grove but Nate and Rhett were concerned about her being out in the daytime without their protection so Con agreed to shimmer her directly into the shop every day and home just before sunset. That way she'd always be in places that were protected.

All of the details were ways of working things out, ways of figuring out who she and the guys were in relation to each other and to the family at large. After that brief period of struggle at the beginning, Rhett and Aidan got on quite well and Nate, Con and Alex all began to create a friendship. Holly *belonged* to something and as she learned more about her family, she learned more about herself.

Despite the stress of feeling under siege, she also began to achieve a level of normalcy with Rhett and Nate. She began to relax once she realized that they were hers forever and once she relaxed they did too.

On the evening after escrow was due to close they all decided to venture out to have dinner to celebrate. They decided on Commander's Palace because it was close to home and the power of Lafayette Cemetery was there to draw on if necessary.

Chapter Eight

ʚ૭

Holly had been rushing all afternoon. They'd moved into the house the evening before and she'd been changing furniture around to make it all just the way she liked it. She'd never had a place anywhere near that large before. The furnishings that Rhett and Nate had, combined with the things inherited from her grandmother, filled the house and made it feel like home.

Her men just patiently smiled at her and moved couches and chairs over and over until she found the way she wanted them. That made her as happy as the house did. Rhett and Nate's never-ending well of patience and love for her, the way they took care of her and went out of their way to be sure she was happy—Holly had never experienced such a thing before. They made her feel special and cherished.

And she wanted that for them too. She tried to do special things for each one of them, to carve out time for them to let them know just how much they meant to her.

She'd never felt totally at home in Em and Con's house, no matter how welcome she knew they were. Same with Lee's house. Even when she'd lived with Nate and Rhett in Seattle, it had always felt a bit like she was a guest.

But this house was different. They were building a home in it. Her books lined the shelves along with Rhett's and Nate's. The painting that Aidan had given her hung over their fireplace—their non-working fireplace. She'd been interested to find out the quirks of New Orleans like how most fireplaces weren't functional in the older houses. Simone, the Charvez cousin she'd become closest to over the month she'd been in New Orleans, had given her a whole series of framed pictures

185

of the family over their history, complete with the one on the mantle that featured their generation—Holly, Lee, Em, Simone, Eric, Niall and Peter.

"Holly, have you seen my shaving kit?" Nate asked as he came into the room wearing only a towel.

As always, his nearness dried her mouth up and turned her knees to jelly. He'd fed and had that glow about him that she'd come to notice vampires get afterward. She'd been so happy to note that all of their donors in New Orleans had been male.

"I told you earlier when you asked me that I put it in your bathroom," she said, trying not to look at him for too long.

"You did?" he asked lazily.

She spun and took him in, noticing too late that he'd baited her.

"You seem awfully stressed out, sweetness," he said in that dangerously velvet voice that slid down her spine and made things tighten low in her belly.

"I have things to do, Nate. Stop it." The words came from her lips but no one, herself included, believed them.

He stalked toward her. "Is that so? Well, you know what always de-stresses you?" He looked at the room and got a slow smile on his face. "Drop your jeans, undo your hair and bend over the arm of the couch."

"Nate…" she started to say but in a flash he was against her.

"Are you going to disobey me?" he said in her ear and she closed her eyes and couldn't stop the smile on her face.

"And if I did?" she said, teasing him.

"Oh, sweetness, it's been too long since you've had a handprint on that sweet little ass of yours, hasn't it?" And as he finished the sentence he ripped the T-shirt she had on down the middle.

"Oh god." She quickly shucked her jeans and reached up to let her hair down, letting it flow over her shoulders and arms the way she knew he liked. Moving to the couch, she bent over it and looked back at him over her shoulder, watching as he let the towel drop. *Oh yeah,* he was interested.

He traced his fingertips over the curve of her ass and then dipped down into the well of her sex and slowly slid into her. She arched back into his hand and let out a cry of dismay when he pulled back. The cry turned into a yelp when he laid an open-handed slap to her ass and then another and yet another.

The flesh began to warm and the vibrations of his perfectly placed strikes began to travel upward to her clit. As always, she was amazed that it could feel so damned good to be spanked.

"Ah, I should have known," Rhett said dryly as he entered the room. "Damn, look at that pretty pink ass." Approaching, he bent over and blew across her heated flesh until she squirmed.

"Oh please, someone needs to fuck me and now!" she pleaded. She'd been on the Pill long enough for it to count and she really, really wanted someone inside of her.

Relief pulled a long groan from deep in her belly as Nate pushed his cock into her. Until he pulled all of the way out.

"No, I think you need to suck my cock for a while and then I'll fuck you." A smile hinted at the corners of Nate's mouth as he waited for her reaction. After a few moments he stood up and tossed a pillow to the floor for her to kneel on.

"Hey, what about me?" Rhett asked.

Holly looked at him and before she could stop herself she replied, "You can help me and then we'll do you."

Both men got very still for a moment. It wasn't like they hadn't had sexual contact with each other over the last two months but it seemed like articulating it was a big deal.

Instead of overthinking it, Rhett dropped to his knees and took Holly's mouth in a devouring kiss. He tasted her tongue and her mouth, her lips, licking and nipping with his teeth. The little sounds and sighs she made into his mouth turned him on beyond bearing. And when Nate pushed his cock against their lips it seemed natural to turn with Holly and lick up one side as she licked up the other.

While Holly sucked Nate's cock into her mouth Rhett kissed down her neck and over her shoulders. When she pulled back, he licked Nate's cock in the wake of her retreat.

Nate could barely stand as he was awash in the sensual onslaught of four hands and two mouths on his cock, on his balls, his ass and thighs. He watched them both, the people he loved and adored, pleasuring him and each other, knowing that this would not have felt so miraculous with any two other people. That it was who they were to each other that made it all so special.

"I'm going to come," Nate croaked out and tried to pull back but both Holly and Rhett had other ideas.

Before he could stop his orgasm, Holly took him as far back as she could and Rhett moved her so that he entered her from behind. His eyes locked with Nate's and he began to slice through Holly's wet pussy over and over as Holly slid her mouth over Nate's cock.

"Holly? When we get home from dinner tonight I'm going to fuck you here," Rhett slid his thumb into her rear passage and she moaned around Nate's cock. "And Nate is going to fuck your pussy. We haven't done that yet and I've been dreaming of it."

"Yesssss," Nate hissed as orgasm clutched him. Over and over, wave after wave of pleasure buffeted him until he was weak with it.

Afterward he held his hands against Holly's shoulders, bracing her against Rhett's thrusts. He leaned forward and watched from above as Rhett disappeared into her body over and over, the shaft of his cock glistening with Holly's honey.

Nate leaned down and whispered into Rhett's ear, "But before that, Holly and I are going to return the favor on you."

Rhett gave out a long groan and unleashed himself deep into Holly who shortly was laid gently down on the floor and flipped over. Rhett lowered his face to her pussy and Nate took her nipples into his mouth, one and then the other, back and forth.

"Oh yes, more!" she urged Rhett, who had begun to flick the tip of his tongue over her clit. "Don't stop!"

One hand burrowed through Rhett's hair, pulling him tight up against her pussy, and the fingers of the other hand dug into Nate's very hard biceps as he feasted on her nipples.

Hips churning, nearly blind with the intensity of the pleasure, her orgasm shot through her. Back bowed, a scream of delight ripped from her lips.

Afterward, Rhett looked up at her with a cocky grin, lips shiny with both of them. The moment that sealed the experience was when both men leaned in and kissed her at the same time.

* * * * *

Simon Decatur walked into Commander's Palace and looked around for his son Josh. His eyes flicked from table to table in the first larger dining room, dismissing each group until he saw her and his heart slammed into his chest.

Her hair was red but her eyes were her mother's, as was the curve of her lips. He could feel the power from across the room. She was at a table filled with other powerful witches and…a wizard too. *Interesting.*

He continued to watch her and he realized with a start that she had his mother's hands. Her mannerisms. This was his daughter. The child that he'd been robbed of by his parents.

Josh walked in and waved but his father never saw him. Seeing his father's distress and feeling his turbulent emotions, Josh reached out and touched his arm. "What is it?" he murmured, following his father's gaze to the crowded table in the far corner.

"Oh my god, it's her."

"Who?"

Simon turned to his son at last. "Your sister," he said, watching the shocked expression of his oldest son, the man being primed to lead the family for the next generation. "You remember when I told you about the girl my father claimed got pregnant by another man and left town with him? That's not some other man's child. That's my daughter."

Josh nodded, stunned, as he remembered the story his father had told him only two years before. He turned and looked at the woman and he could feel her. He could feel that biological spark that tied her to him.

"Dad, what are you going to do?"

"Well I'm not going to let other people push her out of my life again. She's a Decatur and belongs with us." He smoothed down his suit jacket and straightened his tie and noted with pride that Josh did the same.

Holly looked up, feeling the pull of intense scrutiny, and Nate tensed beside her.

He touched her arm and leaned in. "What is it, sweetness?"

She looked into the deep brown-black eyes of the man near the door and felt the shock of recognition. The eyes, the man, it was what she'd seen when she'd used the cards with Isolde that night.

"Sweetness?" Nate said again and Rhett returned to the table, leaning in to hear what was going on.

"I think I know that man," she said, not taking her eyes from him.

"Has he threatened you?" Rhett asked, his voice edged with menace.

"No, nothing like that."

The man leaned in and said something to the younger man with him and they both started over in their direction.

Suddenly Alex looked up and magic crackled in the air.

The two men stopped in front of the table and everyone looked up at them. The older one gave a slight bow. "Pardon me, I'm Simon Decatur and this is my son Joshua."

Alex stood and returned the bow. "Ah, the Scion of the Decatur family. I'm Alex Carter."

"You're welcome in our city. It's a shame we haven't met you yet."

"I haven't wanted to align myself with anyone. I'm still a Carter."

"You need not align yourself with us. While we control the city, we certainly do not do it so exclusively that other wizarding families are not allowed. Please feel welcome to use any of our facilities and services," Simon said graciously.

"Thank you."

Simon looked past Alex straight at Holly. Nate and Rhett felt the power flowing between the two and Aidan's power was stoked simply through Rhett and Nate feeling that their mate was being threatened.

"Have we met before?" Simon asked her softly.

Holly's eyes took on a glazed look and Isolde blinked in surprise and Em gasped.

"Someone had better say something soon because there are three hopped-up vamps here," Josh said quietly.

"You're Elena's," Simon said and Holly nodded.

"Oh my," Holly stood up and at once Simon found himself backed up against a wall, being held up by a very large vampire, incisors gleaming and eyes glowing with bloodlust.

Josh began a spell under his breath and nervous and worried waitstaff began to accumulate. "Stop!" Holly cried out and they all turned to look at her. "Nate, let him down." She turned to Josh. "Please, don't continue that spell."

The manager showed up and quietly spoke with Isolde, who agreed to leave at once.

"Let's take this home, shall we?" Lee suggested.

"I didn't get any Chocolate Sheba," a pregnant Em groused and Con laughed and promised to conjure her some and a slice of the Creole cheesecake too.

"Mr. Decatur, our home is not too very far from here. We have much to discuss, would you please accept our invitation?" Holly asked, voice shaking.

Simon touched her cheek and their connection sparked. "Where is your mother?" He looked sick when he saw the tears well in her eyes and he knew. He sighed sadly and nodded. "I see. I'm sorry. Yes, we do have much to talk about, lead the way."

* * * * *

Once everyone had arrived at Holly's house they went into the large living room and took seats throughout. Simon would have rather had the conversation in private but the way the Charvez witches and the vampires with Holly were looking at him, he knew it was impossible. They were in protection mode.

"First of all, may I ask your name?" Simon asked softly.

"Holly. Holly Daniels, or I suppose Charvez." She answered as if she were in a dream. She knew who this man was but she couldn't wrap her head around it.

"I'm...I have reason to believe that I'm your father," he said quickly.

192

There was a collective intake of air in the room and Nate put his arm around her and felt the shock of it reverberate through her body.

"Oh god, you're so beautiful. A combination of Elena and my grandmother. You have my mother's hands. The way you cock your head, it's hers." He turned and indicated the sandy blond at his side. "This is your brother. You have two more. I can't believe you're here."

"Where the hell have you been?" Holly said, standing up, suddenly enraged. "She was alone! She had me alone in a hospital in New Hampshire. She had no one. For over twenty-four years she had no one! How could you just abandon us?"

Simon took a step toward her and stopped as the suave-looking vampire growled at him. "My father sent me away for two weeks. When I came back Elena had gone. He told me that she'd left, saying she never wanted to see me again, but I knew it was a lie. I loved her. She loved me," he said dreamily as he looked off into the distance as if remembering it like it was yesterday.

"I went to her house but her father said the same thing. Said she'd run off with some itinerant worker. Gave me a letter and it was in her writing! The letter said she didn't love me anymore, that she'd fallen in love with some other guy. I didn't want to believe it but there it was in her own hand and she had gone without even telling me." He sat down and put his head in his hands and pushed them through his hair.

"I didn't know about the pregnancy. I didn't know about *you* until three years ago. We have outside services and investigators who work for the family and one of them deals a lot with the Charvez family and it came up, I don't even remember how now, that one of them had run off pregnant at fifteen and I knew it was Elena. I knew then that she'd left town carrying our child.

"I tried to speak with Elise, Elena's mother, but I found that she'd been murdered and then we tried to get in contact with Isolde but I was told that..."

"We didn't want to dredge up old ghosts," Isolde said, the anguish clear in her voice. "Oh, *chere*, I've done you a great wrong. In my terrible grief over losing Elise I shut down and kept everyone but family out."

"I hired investigators and we found the birth records from New Hampshire but nothing more after about six months later when you pulled up stakes and left. My people tracked you to Minnesota but nothing after that.

"Please believe me, I never, ever would have abandoned you on purpose. I was only seventeen at the time but I would have done right by both of you."

"Wait a minute! Witches and wizards shouldn't be able to reproduce," Alex said.

"See the evidence of that theory right before your eyes, Alex! For god's sake, this answers the question about just exactly why Holly's power is so different but why it seems familiar at the same time," Rhett said, reaching out to touch Holly's hair.

"What happened to Elena? To your mother?" Simon asked, wanting so much to draw Holly into his arms.

"She died of cancer eight months ago."

The shock of it left him pale. "What? Why didn't she heal herself?"

"Good question. I ask myself the same one every day. Why she'd choose death over me. I'll let you know if I ever figure it out." Holly's voice was loaded with bitterness.

"Oh sweet girl. My sweet girl, I've ached to hold you in my arms since the moment I knew you existed. May I?"

A father. The thing she'd wanted so much her whole life. He was standing there, handsome and powerful and yet humble. Asking her, wanting to love her but letting her decide.

Everyone in the room waited for her response, waited to either relax or kick the two wizards out into the street.

She nodded slowly and he moved to her and pulled her into an embrace and the two of them laughed and cried all at once.

* * * * *

After several minutes Simon stepped back and looked into the face of his oldest child, his only daughter. She was so lovely, creamy skin and that pretty red hair. Oh how he wished he could have watched her grow up. But now wasn't the time for regrets, he had a twenty-four-year-old daughter and he had to figure out how to welcome her into his life.

"Are you hungry? We got, uh, kicked out of the restaurant before you two got the chance to eat," Holly asked, looking around Simon — her father — to Josh. "We have some stuff for sandwiches and I baked bread earlier. I'm sure I can toss a salad together too." She needed to do something with her hands, all of the emotions of the evening were too much, she had to focus on some small task or totally fall apart.

"Take her up on it, she's an incredible cook," Rhett said proudly. He and Nate had been trying to convince Holly to pursue cooking professionally.

"Oh my manners!" Holly turned and held out her hands to Nate and Rhett. "Mr. Decatur, this is Rhett Dubois and Nate Hamilton. They're my husbands and my mates."

"Holly, sweetheart, I'd love it if you'd call me Dad. If you're not ready for that yet, at least call me Simon." He looked between the two vampires. Two huh? Well, okay. She was a witch with two husbands. He didn't know a lot about vampire culture but he knew enough to know that they mated for life. And as such, these men were obviously all about her and she about them, and as her father, he would support that.

"Nate, Rhett, it's a pleasure to meet you." He held out his hand and they each shook it.

"I'm sorry about earlier," Nate said.

195

"No, don't be. You didn't know. You thought I was a threat and you protected her. That's what you should do."

"So? Dinner?" Holly said, embarrassed over the fuss being made about her.

Her father grinned at her. "I'm starving. It's been a long day, I haven't eaten since this morning."

In the large kitchen she put together large sandwiches on fresh bread and then tossed a salad of baby greens, crisp green apples, walnuts and gorgonzola cheese. She doubled the ingredients with a smile when she saw the way everyone was watching.

While they ate, Holly told her father about growing up and about losing her mother and how she'd come to meet Nate and Rhett and ended up in New Orleans.

"I think we have some new reasons why a wizard might feel threatened by your existence," Alex said as he drank a cup of coffee.

"A hybrid? But who would know and why wouldn't they just have killed her when she was an infant? When Elena was pregnant? Why wait until Holly was past the age of maturity and had begun to come into her powers as a wizard?"

"Maybe they didn't know until two months ago." Nate combed fingers through his beard as he thought.

"And we need to find out just what the heck the real story is. I need to have a long talk with my father and I think we should do the same with Elena's father."

"We don't know where he is. He left New Orleans after Elise divorced him and no one has seen him since. Not that we really tried that hard to find him until Holly came back to town and this whole thing came about," Isolde said.

"We've got an investigator on it. We'll find him," Nate said. "When we do Rhett and I will have a *talk* with him. Holly is the only human I've ever seen who wasn't susceptible to the thrall in Rhett's voice."

"We can protect you at home," Simon said. "Come live with us for the time being. A house full of wizards, no one can hurt you."

"A wizard is the one trying to kill her in the first place!" Rhett said vehemently. "She's safe here. The place has been warded well and she's learning how to use her powers to defend herself. And Rhett and I are quite capable of protecting her."

Holly felt their need to protect her. She knew they'd both been terribly upset about her having the vision when they were asleep. Reaching out, she touched him softly. "I love you, Nate. I trust that you and Rhett will protect me. Never doubt that," she murmured so that only he could hear.

He looked startled for a moment and then softened and gave her a smile. Rhett heard and brushed his lips over her temple.

Once she was assured Rhett and Nate were all right she turned back to her father. "Thanks for the offer. We'll stay here but I appreciate it. I hope that we can get to know each other. I understand if your wife may not like the idea of an illegitimate daughter. I promise, I don't want anything from you but what you're willing to give."

"We want you in our lives. You're my daughter and I plan to hold you out publicly as such. I'm proud of you. We need to work on your training too. Have you meet your other brothers, Penn and Eli. They're eighteen and twenty. Eli is at Harvard right now and Penn is at Northwestern. I'll call them home tonight. They'll be over the moon."

Simon looked to Alex. "How's her power level?"

"Master status, easily."

Simon grinned with pride. "Chip off the old block I see. Josh is too and Eli is nearly there. Penn is the wild card, he doesn't have the magical focus but he's competitive, if his sister is that powerful, he'll buck up."

"First we need to figure out who's trying to kill her and why," Nate said, bringing the subject back to the topic at hand.

"You're right, Nate. I got a bit distracted there with the proud father thing. Of course Holly's safety is paramount."

They talked for several more hours, Holly learning about the relationship between her mother and father and also about her power as Simon went through some spells with her.

Simon left after two in the morning with a promise to have a late lunch with Holly in two days at the Decatur mansion.

Isolde took her aside before she left. "Are you angry with me?"

She touched the woman she'd come to think of as *Grand-mére*'s face. "No, whyever would I be angry with you?"

"I sent his investigators away. I should have thought about it, but it was just so painful. Elise was my sister and my best friend and it was just the worst time and we could have found you three years ago and it's my fault we didn't!"

"*Grand-mére*, none of that. What's done is done. I'm not angry with you for being inconsolable after my grandmother's death. I know what I felt like when my mother died, I couldn't think straight. I'm here now and that's what counts. It's how it was meant to happen."

Isolde kissed both Holly's cheeks and smiled and walked out to the car, escorted by Alex.

Holly closed the door and leaned against it for a moment, catching her breath and feeling totally drained now that everyone had gone home.

"Come on, sweetness." Nate held out a hand for her to take and she followed him upstairs to the big master suite.

Chapter Nine

ဢ

Arriving at the Decatur mansion that sat on the river, surrounded by tall oaks and weeping willows, they made quite a sight walking through the grand formal entry. The tall, regal father with just a hint of gray at the temples, his cool blue eyes guarded as they always were when dealing with his overbearing, arrogant father. And his two sons—one tall and blond like the father and the other with dark brown hair, stocky and bearing hazel eyes like his mother. The power they spilled in their wake was so impressive that the staff and other members of Simon Decatur Senior's cadre of wizards came out to watch, curious as to what was going on.

The meeting was useless. Power spilled everywhere, threats were issued, but Senior didn't budge from his story about Holly being a gold digger and her mother being a faithless slut.

Simon left the house he grew up in knowing his father was behind the fact that one of his children grew up without both parents.

* * * * *

Daniel Pilotte picked up the ringing phone with foreboding. "Hello?"

"You'd best be keeping your mouth shut. I might be thinking about a trip out of state if I were you," the voice on the other end of the line said.

"It's been twenty-five years, I haven't said a thing. Didn't I tell everyone exactly what you told me to tell them?" Piven made him almost as nervous as Simon Decatur Senior did. The last time he'd talked to either one of them had been three years ago and he wasn't pleased to be hearing the voice once again.

"And anyway, who's to say they'll even find me? They haven't yet."

"The child is in New Orleans. She's quite strong and has vampires, the boy and a few Fae on her side. Not to mention those Charvez bitches."

"Why now though? Why does the girl care? It's not like I was father of the year. She can't possibly think I'd want to have some sort of relationship with her."

"Mr. Decatur Senior has been a bit…zealous in his anger toward the girl. If she tells the boy what happened, he can use that to ruin him."

"And why is this my problem?" Daniel raged. He'd had to stay out of New Orleans for the last twenty-four years because of that arrogant asshole Decatur. Had to leave behind his entire life, not that he wasn't happy to be shot of that bitch of a wife and her precious Charvez family. But he'd grown up there and even with all the money that Decatur had given him, it was a bigger pain each year. And now this demand that he leave the state?

"It's your problem, Daniel, because I say it is. Now keep your mouth shut and your head low." Piven cut the connection.

Daniel Pilotte let out his breath and tried to calm down enough to stop the pounding of his heart.

* * * * *

Holly looked up from the leaves in the bottom of the cup and her heart leapt as she saw Josh come into the shop.

"Hey, Holly!" he called out and another man, a few years younger and darker, more muscled, entered after him and his eyes landed on her and he grinned, a carbon copy of her own right down to the dimple at the left corner of the mouth.

She stood and went to them and laughed as Josh hugged her tight. With an arm around her shoulders he turned to the other man. "This is…"

The other man pulled her out of Josh's arms and into his own. "I'm Penn, your little brother," he said into her hair.

"Is everything all right?" Isolde said as she came into the front of the shop and then she stopped with a smile and took in the boys hugging Holly. She hadn't expected such a warm reception by the Decaturs and it made her glad to be so very wrong.

"Yes, *Grand-mère*, this is Penn, another one of my brothers. Penn, this is Isolde Charvez, my great-aunt."

Penn bowed deeply to Isolde in a sign of respect. "It is an honor to meet you, Ms. Charvez." He and Josh looked around the shop in amazement.

"It's spectacular, isn't it?" Holly asked, pride clear in her voice.

"Indeed. How are you today, darling?" Simon asked as he came into the shop and hugged her, kissing both cheeks. "I hope you don't mind us dropping by. Penn got into town and wanted to meet you. Eli's plane lands in an hour and we're off to the airport to pick him up. I'd invite you along—he's dying to meet you—but I promised Nate and Rhett that we'd help keep you safe."

"Thank you for that," Holly said with a blush. "I know he's just started back to school." She looked at Penn. "That you both did. You didn't have to come back here. It could have waited until the weekend or a break."

Penn snorted. "In the first place, it's not a crime to take a week off. In the second place, you don't get a sister every day and so of course we had to come back here. Right now it's important that we all stand together. Once we find whoever is trying to hurt you and stop him, then we can make long-term plans."

"You're still coming to a late lunch tomorrow?" Simon asked.

"Yes, of course. Con said he'd bring me and Jax at three. Rhett and Nate will be over when they wake up and feed."

"Good! Okay then, we have to be off to the airport. I'll see you tomorrow, darling." Simon kissed her cheeks again as did her brothers. *Her brothers,* who'd have ever thought she'd have brothers?

She waved and watched them go with a smile.

* * * * *

Promptly at five, Con showed up and shimmered her and then Jax back to the house and stayed for a cup of tea as they did a bit of planning for Em's baby shower. Nate came into the kitchen and nodded a hello at Jax and kissed Holly's neck just above where her hammering pulse beat.

"My father came into the shop today. I met Penn. Eli apparently was coming in today too."

"It was all right? They treated you well?" Nate asked.

"Yes," she said with a big smile, the kind of smile that made her glow, and Nate relaxed and smiled back at her, unable not to. He used to be a hard-ass. Now he was a thoroughly satisfied man with a smile on his lips. "They've been so nice to me. Penn told me that he wanted to stop whoever was trying to hurt me. It's odd to go from having no one to having two husbands, a huge family on my mother's side and now a father and three brothers. An embarrassment of riches."

"You deserve it, love." Con dropped a kiss on the top of her head and winked at Nate, who raised an eyebrow at him. "I need to get back home. Lee and Em were talking about the decorations for the nursery. When the babe comes, we'll spend time in Tir na nOg, and it makes the family nervous and their mother gets clingy."

He shimmered and Holly and Nate were alone in the kitchen.

Suddenly she was picked up and put on the butcher block island in the middle of the kitchen and Nate stepped between her thighs. "Hello, sweetness. I missed you," he murmured as he undid her braid, loosing her hair about her shoulders.

"I...I missed you too," she said, a bit shaky as he put his lips to the hollow of her throat.

His hands were at the waistband of her jeans, unbuttoning and unzipping and yanking them down and off, the panties followed. He gently pushed her back so that her legs dangled off the edge.

"Such a pretty pussy," he said softly, the heat of his breath moving over her desire-wet flesh. He took a long lick from her perineum up and around her clit. "Tasty too. God, I love the way you taste. Sweet, salty—like the sea."

She had no words to reply. He always did this to her. His presence, his sexuality and his aura made her speechless with desire. With love and hope and longing and utter joy that he was hers.

"Keep your hands above your head. I'm not going to use the cuffs. My command is your restraint."

She nodded and made an inarticulate moaning, whimpering sound. It was an approximation of assent and the best she could do. Especially once his mouth was back on her cunt, two fingers pressed into her and crooked so that he was stroking over her G-spot while his tongue slid through her folds.

She had to grip the handle of the drawer below her head to keep from grabbing him, touching him. "Please," she managed to whisper as he drove her up and then backed off a few seconds until she lost her climax yet again.

"Oh definitely please, sweetness. So polite when your man's face is buried in your pussy." Leaning in, he flicked the tip of his tongue over her clit with relentless speed as he stroked into her with his fingers.

"Oh yes! Please, Nate, don't stop!" Crying out, she arched her back, her heels hitting the cabinet doors beneath them. He started to pull back but she clamped her thighs tight over his head and held him to her, careful to keep her hands where they were supposed to be. Knowing that if she moved them he might just stop altogether.

He growled against her pussy and sucked her clit into his mouth, stroking the underside of it with the tip of his tongue, and orgasm slammed into her body.

As it always did, the sound of his belt buckle loosening brought shivers of desire through her. Before she could recover she was up and impaled on his cock. He walked her over, pushing her back against the wall of the kitchen as his lips met hers. Their taste mingled as he began to fuck her in great, hard thrusts that had him sinking into her to the root each time.

Each time he struck home, a whimper came from her. Helpless to do more than receive him, she held onto his shoulders tightly. But it was joyous to do it, joyous to have him slide into the haven of her body over and over. He made her feel revered and adored, cherished and desired. Nate aroused things in her, feelings that no one else ever had. Truth be told, she wasn't sure she even imagined she had them before he came along. He was big, bad and dangerous and it gave her a thrill when he was dark and commanding with her. At the same time, she never felt threatened by him, not by his size or his strength. His power was never abused with her. He commanded her, yes, but it was a give and take and he took her gift of submission to him like it was the most precious thing in the world. That such a man could love her never failed to give her an amazed pause.

"I love you," he breathed into her ear as he came. She tightened around his cock and felt each pulse of his semen, each time the muscles tightened and he exploded into her.

She held his face between her hands and kissed him softly. "I love you too, Nate."

* * * * *

Forty-five minutes later she had her hands braced on the counter in the master bathroom, body bent forward as Rhett stroked into her with slow, intense passion. The fingertips of his left hand slid gently down her spine as the fingers of his right hand slowly drew big wet circles around her clit.

She watched his face in the mirror, watched as his eyes took in the line of her back, took in the way the copper fire of her hair slid over her shoulders. Her breasts swayed slowly with each press into her body.

Rhett was no less strong and commanding than Nate but he carried his power differently. Rhett was supple and suave, when he moved it was with grace and intensity. He made love to her like she was the only thing in the universe. Like each stroke into her pussy, each touch of her skin, each kiss and caress, was the most exquisite treasure, as if he simply could not get enough of her. It made her feel like a goddess.

The climax had begun to tingle in her scalp. She could taste it on her tongue. Her muscles began to ready themselves and her pussy fluttered around each invasion of his cock, rippling around him in a heated embrace.

"Holly, you feel so good. How am I ever going to get enough of you?" His voice was soft as he leaned down to kiss between her shoulder blades.

"You can't. You'll just have to keep me around forever." Her eyes met his in the mirror, meaning every word.

She saw the flash of his incisors and her eyes went half-mast. When he struck she felt his tongue pulling her essence into his body as he laved the spot closed. Orgasm flooded her, she felt it around, through her, deep within her.

Suddenly her head was back, her hair wrapped around his fist. "Look at me, honey, know who's giving you this pleasure," he said silkily and pushed deep into her body and met his own pleasure there.

Nate came in afterward and they all showered in the large bathroom and she made dinner and they watched some movies and played cards. The normalcy of it comforted her and excited her all at once. Her life was a thousand years from where it had been three months before and there weren't enough words to say how thankful she was for them.

Sometime after midnight she sat up from where she reclined between the two of them on the couch. "I am so hungry for rocky road ice cream."

"I'll have Jax run out and get some then, sweetness." Nate started to rise.

"Oh please can't we go? Come on, it's late and we know no one is watching, Jax has the whole freaking Garden District under his careful eye. I haven't been outside in a while and I'm going stir-crazy. We can call Lee, she'll be up, and they can all come too. Three big bad vamps, a master level wizard, me and Lee—surely that's enough protection to go to the market. Oh I know!" She bounced up and out of her seat. "Let's get milkshakes at the Clover Grill!"

She was so excited about it that neither could say no. "Call Lee, if they come then we'll go. That big of a magically protected posse and I think we can risk a shake and one of their burgers," Rhett said and Nate laughed.

They both heard Lee's squeal of delight over the phone and within minutes their car pulled up out front and they all loaded into it, Jax riding shotgun to keep a watch for trouble.

"This was a good idea," Nate said to Rhett and Aidan as they watched Lee, Holly and Simone, who joined them shortly after they arrived in the diner. She and her husband lived near the shop, in the French Quarter, so it was mere blocks from their house.

The cousins shared french fries, drank milkshakes and laughed. Holly looked happier and more relaxed than she had in the month and a half they'd been in New Orleans.

They stayed and joked with each other and their servers until nearly three, and then they all trooped tiredly outside.

At the car they were saying good night to Simone and her husband Kael when Simone suddenly grabbed Holly's arm in alarm. Holly stepped back, away from the car, turning as a flash of light hit her square in the chest.

The pain seared her and she realized that her vision had come to pass. She heard the screaming and the panic, and sank to the sidewalk as everything went dark.

* * * * *

"Get her into the fucking car right now!" Jax screamed at them, breaking their stunned reaction.

Sound roared back into their ears. Lee was hurling her own fireball and Alex was speaking under his voice. Aidan had rushed off in the direction of the first fireball.

Nate looked down and saw Holly there and scooped her up, the fear eating him alive. "Holly?" he asked, panic ringing in his voice.

Rhett took in the burn mark on her chest and the bloodless lips and face. He could feel her connection to them weakening. He shoved Nate, pushing them both into the car, and Lee and Alex followed with everyone else. Jax was behind the wheel and they tore down Bourbon to Orleans and skidded to a screeching halt in front of The Grove.

The doors burst open as they rushed her inside, up the back stairs to the large quarters where Isolde and Lou lived.

Nate had to be pried off Holly as they lay her on a bed and Rhett ripped open the sweater to see the horrible burns on her chest.

"We need to get her to a hospital! Call an ambulance!" Nate cried.

"This can't be helped by human medicine," Isolde said. "She's dying. The ball hit her heart, she's badly burned."

"You have to change her, it's the only thing that can save her," Aidan said, holding Lee to him tightly.

Simone lit some healing herbs in a brazier and the sweet clean scent filled the room. Isolde brushed a hand over Holly's forehead.

"He's right. She's not long for this world. If you don't do something she'll die." Isolde looked up at Nate and Rhett, pleading.

"I think you both should do it. You've both got a tie to her, you're both strong in different ways. It'll call her back." Lee's voice was soft but sure.

"I'll do anything I can to save her," Rhett said, his voice breaking. Nate nodded in agreement.

"I'll prepare the room while you start," Aidan said as he pulled his sweater off. "We'll need clean linens. The transformation isn't easy, it won't be pleasant. We'll need washcloths and a few basins of clean water. Some empty buckets too."

Nate looked to Rhett. "You go first, you're older and stronger."

Rhett sank to his knees next to her. "Come back to us, Holly," he murmured just before he struck and began to drink deep.

Everyone sprang into action and soon the room was filled with piles of clean, sweet-smelling linens, fresh warm water and all of the other things Rhett requested. Candles had been lit and the brazier continued to burn the healing herbs.

Rhett stumbled back. "Now, Nate. She's almost gone." His voice was anguished and Nate took his place, feeding at her wrist instead of her neck.

"It'll happen soon." Aidan told Rhett. "Hold on."

Holly had to die first, give up her human body as the virus took over and transformed her system. Nate and then Rhett would begin to feed her just as death approached and then they'd all have to ride out the transformation.

A small sigh escaped Holly's lips and Nate sat back, flushed with the huge amount of very powerful blood he'd taken, and he tore his wrist open and put it over her mouth. At first she did nothing but shortly, she grabbed him and drank. Rhett joined him, opening his own wrist, and took over as Aidan fed Nate. Several minutes later they pulled Rhett back and Lee fed him while they all watched over Holly.

A commotion sounded as Simon, Penn, Eli and Josh arrived and raced into the room.

Alex held them back and explained the situation. Holly shook and sobbed as her body violently fought the change. It felt like a thousand knives were slicing through her veins. Her gut was on fire and she cramped and sweated and heaved. She wanted to die it hurt so badly. Wanted to let go and leave the pain behind and she might have if Rhett and Nate hadn't been there at her side, urging her to live.

Finally, after two hours of the terrible pain and illness, she fell back to the mattress and sighed.

"It's done. Thank god," Rhett said, remembering his own transformation. He'd forgotten about how painful it was and he ached that they'd had to put her through it.

Nate took her pulse. "She'll be okay now. Let's finish cleaning her up. Con, can you shimmer us home? Her first day she should be with us in a vampire-safe space."

"Of course. Is there anything else we can do?" Con asked, his hand on Nate's shoulder.

"No. We just need to find this bastard and remove the threat."

"We're staying at your place. Don't argue, the four of us are very strong and together we're even stronger. We can protect you if he comes for you at your house. We'll drive over now and meet you there. Since it's dawn I'm imagining that you need to rest." Simon's face was set.

Nate waved a hand at him. The adrenaline was going to crash and they'd both need to sleep as Holly already was. Isolde and Simone had cleaned her up and Con and Em took Holly and Nate first, straight to their bedroom, and then came back for Rhett, who had enough state of mind to be sure and arrange with Aidan to get extra donors for Holly.

* * * * *

The three of them lay sleeping deeply while Simon and his sons took up positions in the house and drank coffee and worked out strategy with Alex and a whole host of other Charvezes.

"We have no leads on Daniel Pilotte at all. It's as if he fell off the face of the Earth. I know my father is involved but I don't know how or why and he certainly won't tell me. We need to track him down to get to the bottom of this whole thing," Simon said.

"She needs to scry. It's the only way," Alex said and Josh agreed. "She's got a biological connection with him and since she has wizard magic, she can scry. In fact, I think she'll be very powerful with it because it'll connect with her gift as a seer."

"It's dangerous! I should do it, or one of the boys. She hasn't been trained!"

"Simon, she's incredibly powerful and gifted. Show her how to do it and she will. She has much holding her to this plane, the risks are low. Much lower than her being attacked again, and you know she will."

They slept in shifts and when sunset approached Rhett awoke first and fed, followed by Nate. They took Holly's donor up to the bedroom and had him sit on the bed.

Holly's eyes fluttered and she sat bolt upright on a gasp, clutching at her chest.

Nate knelt in front of her and grabbed her shoulders. "Sweetness? It's okay. You're okay."

"What happened?" She kept feeling the place on her chest where she'd been hit. "I...I was burned, I thought I died! Oh my goodness!"

"You were attacked, honey. And, well, you did die." Rhett added quickly, "But we brought you over. I'm sorry, I know you wanted to wait and do it slowly but it was the only way to save your life."

She looked from one man to the other in confusion. "Are you saying I'm a vampire?"

Nate chuckled despite himself. "Yes, sweetness. The memories of the change will come back slowly. Be glad you can't remember them just yet. But we'll explain it all later, for now you need to feed." He held a hand out to the man at the foot of the bed.

"What? You want me to..." A terrible hunger clutched at her, nearly doubling her over in pain.

"It's the hunger. You need to feed. I'm really sorry we couldn't prepare you for this but it has to be done." Rhett motioned for the man to approach. "This is Alphonse."

She backed up against the headboard, clutching the blankets to her body. She began to tremble and shiver from the cold. "Dude, I am so not sucking his blood! And turn on the heat in here!"

Nate narrowed his eyes at her. "Sweetness, you will take his blood and do it right now! You're cold because you haven't fed. You *need* the blood." He leaned in and whispered in her ear. "Can't you smell it? Dark and rich and delicious? You need it, you want it and he's offering it freely."

She wanted to deny it but she was starving and she could smell him. Her incisors lengthened and Alphonse leaned in and pulled his shirt off.

"Just inhale him and your body will know what to do," Rhett said softly.

Tears of frustration in her eyes, she skeptically leaned in and took a deep breath, pulling his scent into her body. Her eyes went half lidded and instinct took over. Alphonse gave a cry of pleasure when her teeth slid over his flesh and the vein opened.

It was as if every cell in her body had been starved and dry and the blood filled her up, hydrated her. The terrible pain in her muscles began to recede and her cramps subsided.

Nate and Rhett watched to be sure she didn't take too much but each felt guilty that it had to be so shocking the first time she fed. They'd wanted her to change slowly over time instead of having to give up daylight without even getting the chance to enjoy one last sunrise.

She broke off and laved the wound closed, she'd seen them do it enough, and they thanked a shaky-kneed Alphonse and he left the room.

Rhett turned to her and his heart broke to see the tear tracks on her face. "I am so sorry."

"For what?" she asked with a sniffle.

"Last night. Damn it. I knew we shouldn't have left the house and we did anyway and we couldn't protect you and you must hate us for forcing the change on you..."

She put a finger over his lips to quiet him. "What? Are you saying you helped that wizard find me?"

"No! How could you think that?" he asked, shocked.

She rolled her eyes inwardly. "And you?" She turned to Nate. "You really wanted to let me die, didn't you?"

"Of course not! I love you, I want to be with you forever. Seeing you so close to death last night I thought I'd die myself."

"Then shut up, both of you. For heaven's sake! You had nothing to do with my attack and you saved my life because there was no other choice. If I'd had my druthers I would have chosen the long, slow change route, but that's not what the situation was fated to be. All in all, I'm quite happy to be alive. I'd rather be a vampire than dead thank you very much."

"You're crying!" Rhett accused. "How can you say you aren't upset when you're crying?"

"Of course I'm upset! I just had to drink blood! This after having a milkshake and french fries at two in the morning! I'm upset because I had no choice but that's not your fault and it's nothing that can be changed either."

"Women!" Rhett groused.

"I need a shower. I'm freezing and I feel ooky." She got up and walked into the bathroom without looking back and Nate started laughing and followed her, Rhett at his heels.

* * * * *

"You really should have told me we had a house full of people," Holly hissed as they started downstairs an hour later.

"Why? Then you'd have wanted to hurry through the sex or worse, have made us wait," Nate murmured back.

"The whole house probably heard me," Holly said with a blush and both men looked at her, aroused at the scent of her blood rushing to her face.

Nate just gave one of those dark chuckles of his and kissed her hand as he led her down the grand staircase, Rhett at her other side.

"Holly! Darling, how are you?" Simon rushed over and pulled her into a hug and then held her at arms length and looked her over carefully.

"I'm fine. Really. Please tell me you didn't all stay here today? All of you without sleep?"

A husky brunette stepped forward and Holly saw her father stamped on his face. "You're Eli."

He pulled her into a hug and her other brothers followed suit. After they'd calmed down a bit they all let her go but stayed close.

"You think we'd leave you after what happened last night? I know that you grew up without a whole lot of family but we don't walk away!" Lee scolded and pulled Holly into a hug.

"Well, let me at least make everyone a good meal while we talk about what we're going to do to find my grandfather," she said and breezed past everyone into the kitchen.

She began to pull food out of the fridge and the pantry and then she began to assemble pots, skillets and utensils.

"What?" she asked when she looked up to see everyone staring at her.

"You seem really well adjusted for a woman who was murdered and transformed into a vampire," Simone said dryly. "I mean, it's real, I can feel that. I'm just wondering how you can be so calm right now."

Holly pulled out a container of chicken she'd had marinating and put it on the indoor grill and washed her hands. "Well," she began as she tossed the cleaned asparagus into salted water to steam, "what else can I be? I mean now he's in a corner and it's him or me and it's gonna be him because I have everything I've ever dreamed of my whole life—with the exception of my mother—and I'm not giving it up now."

She turned the chicken and put the garlic bread under the broiler and turned to make a quick salad.

"So, tell me what the plan is. I'm assuming you've been strategizing?" she asked her father.

Everyone ate but Holly had no appetite for the food. It smelled pleasant enough and she enjoyed making it but she didn't feel hungry for it. She also noticed that she could hear really well, even Jax talking to his people outside.

"Someone should take some food out to Jax and his men," she murmured to Nate and he nodded and she got up and made a platter of thick sandwiches, cut some cheese and apples and poured coffee into a Thermos.

"I'll take it. Wait 'til I get back before you start talking about the plan." Nate quickly took the food to an appreciative group and came back inside.

"Okay, let's hear it," Holly said as Rhett and Nate each took one of her hands.

"We need to find Daniel Pilotte. He's the key here. I spoke with my father, your grandfather, yesterday and he wasn't giving anything up. I know he's hiding something but I have no way of forcing his hand because he's stronger than I am and I have no way of knowing just what it is he's hiding.

"I am absolutely convinced though that it's him who is behind these attacks. We have to find out what really happened twenty-five years ago when Elena left New Orleans pregnant and alone. That's our leverage because there's something there that kept your mother running scared for twenty-four years and staying out of contact with a family she loved."

"Okay, I'm with you so far. But the investigators haven't found anything." Nate sat nearby and Holly could feel him and Rhett more acutely now, more intensely, as their blood coursed through her veins. It was slightly disorienting.

"True and that's why we think desperate times call for desperate measures. Holly, do you know what scrying is?"

"Um, if I'm remembering right it's when a mirror or a bowl of water is used and spelled so that something can be searched for and seen. But I also remember something about the spell thinning the barriers between planes of existence and some practitioners getting pulled into the darkness."

"Yes, it can happen. It's risky. But I think that you're strong enough to handle it and that unlike those who've been pulled into the darkness, you have much to hold you here to his plane."

Nate banged a fist on the table. "No way! She *died* last night, Simon! She's only been doing this magic stuff for less than two months. You will not risk her fucking soul!"

"Her blood ties her to you and Rhett. Her heart, her soul, is linked to you two—two very powerful vampires who hold her here. If the darkness wanted her, it would have to take you two as well, being that you're the ones who turned her. She is also tied by her biology to some of the strongest inherent witches and wizards on earth. The risk is very low, Nate. Much much lower than the certainty that the attacks will continue until she dies for good."

"Are you okay with this, Nate? Rhett?" Holly asked him and he nodded.

"I don't like it, damn it! I nearly lost you last night, I don't want you to do this." Nate began to pace and Holly ached at the pain on his face.

Rhett put his head in his hands. "Nate, we have to do something. We can't protect her this way."

"You're a Charvez and a Decatur. And that combination is going to protect you. Once we find your grandfather we can stop this," Simon said. "Nate, Rhett, I know you are worried but I love her too. She's my daughter and I didn't just find her to lose her again. I swear to you."

Holly sighed. She stood up and went into the hallway, pulled a mirror that had belonged to her grandmother off the wall and brought it into the dining room and laid it on the table.

"I'll need some candles. Lee, they're on the mantle, can you bring them?"

Lee nodded and went to get them.

Alex sat down at the table on one side of her and Simon on the other. Eli, Josh and Penn were across from her.

"We need a circle," Holly said and Penn nodded and grabbed the container of salted and spelled sand.

"Lee, get everyone else in a circle and don't let anyone out until I say so. I mean it," Holly said.

"You're not doing this," Nate said, touching her arm, unease written into his normally beautiful features.

She smiled up at him, tracing the line of his cheek with her fingertips. "Nate, I am and you know why. I have to do this. We don't have the luxury of choices right now. I have a lot of strength with me in that circle, I will be fine. Accidents are rare. Wizards scry all the time."

"Dark wizards scry!"

"Okay, yes, that's true. But not all who do are dark and it's going to be fine. I did not foresee anything about this. I did foresee last night's attack." She kissed his lips and then Rhett's. "I love you and everything will be fine. Stay in the circle or you risk everyone when you leave it," she urged them both and stepped back and felt their circle seal with the last of Lee's spell.

"Okay, let's rock," she said to the wizards, who then closed their circle.

"I'm going to give you the spell, repeat it as you spill your blood on the surface of the mirror, mixing it with the ritual oil," Simon said and she nodded. He spoke the words to her and they lodged in her head like they'd always lived there.

Taking up the cutting blade, she began the spell as she sliced into her palm. She had to do it a few times because her body kept healing so fast. Drops of crimson fell into the oil that pooled on the surface of the mirror and the liquid rippled and suddenly looked miles deep and then glassy clear again as the spell ended and she touched the bell with the athame held in the hand she hadn't cut.

Concentrating, she felt the way begin to open. She felt the dark things press up against the thin membrane between worlds but ignored them and felt the strength of her father, brothers and Alex instead.

There he was! She saw Daniel Pilotte and he was in Las Vegas. He had a gambling problem and he knew he should leave town as he'd been instructed but he had to go to the blackjack tables just once more to try to win back what he'd lost.

She simply *knew* where he lived and what casinos he played in and she stored that information and began to pull back, ignoring the mental brush of things best not thought of until she was back at the table in her house in New Orleans. She said the words that broke the spell and rang the bell again.

She stood up and closed her eyes, holding hands with the others, and once they ascertained that nothing had come back with her she turned to Lee and broke their circle and Lee did the same with a nod.

The magic rushed out into the room like a warm tide and everyone soaked it up for a few moments until they all went into the living room to talk about what Holly had seen.

She told them where he was and Con immediately shimmered to get him and bring him back. They crafted a containment circle that would exclude a Faerie and waited. It was mere moments until a weary and frightened Daniel Pilotte was standing there, held captive by his own granddaughter's magic.

"Em, can you sense any magic on him? Trap spells or a geas?" Holly asked.

Em looked and shook her head. "No. He's scared but there's actually a small bit of empathy deep inside him. I daresay even a bit of love and regret."

"I can't feel anything either and I know the feel of my father's magic," Simon said.

Holly turned to Rhett and kissed his lips softly, "Honey, find what we need to know."

He touched her hair, this woman who was his everything, and turned back to Daniel. He didn't bother with any preliminaries and pushed the power of his voice as high as it would go. "Tell me what really happened nearly twenty-five years ago when Elena Charvez left New Orleans."

Daniel sat cross-legged on the floor with a sigh. "Elena had turned fifteen that summer and got secretive. Her mother told me that it wasn't a problem, that our Ellie was a smart girl with a good head on her shoulders." He paused to snort in derision.

"One day in town, a man approached me and told me that a Simon Decatur Senior wanted to meet me for drinks and dinner at Galatoire's. Who was I to turn down an expensive meal at a fine restaurant?" He shrugged.

"Decatur told me that his son was seeing Elena and that he wanted it stopped. As the son was two years older, I was behind that plan one hundred percent! When I got back I watched her like a hawk. She wasn't allowed to go anywhere alone, or that's what I thought at the time.

"But she came to me one morning in tears and told me and her mother that she was in a family way. Oh I was so angry! What would people think of her? Of us? I told her that her mother and I would have to think about it and that we would talk more later. I sent Elise out to her crazy sister's for the day and called Decatur and told him.

"The man flew into a rage and showed up at the house with that crazy lackey of his, Piven. He went into Elena's room and said a bunch of stuff, some kind of wizard bullshit, and she asked him what he'd done.

"He told her he'd cursed her."

At that, Simon, Alex and the boys all gasped in horror but Daniel just shrugged and went on with the story.

"He told her that she'd better hightail it out of town right then. That if she ever told anyone about the baby being a

Decatur, ever got in contact again with her family, that every last Charvez would die, including the she-bitch in her womb."

Daniel looked up at Holly. "You look like her. Your mom. Coloring is different but you have her features. Can I have a drink? I just signed my own death warrant, I need a stiff one."

Holly went to the liquor cabinet and poured him two fingers of scotch. She handed it to Con who gave it to Daniel through the circle. Daniel polished it off in several gulps and put it on the ground next to him.

"So anyway, Elena looked crushed. My heart went out to her because despite being a slut, she was loyal and a Charvez and you know how they are," he said to the men in the room. "She'd never risk any harm coming to her family or to the baby she was carrying. She packed up some of her things. He wouldn't even let her leave a note. Instead he made her write one to the boy, saying she didn't love him and had run off with some other guy. Decatur gave her some cash and I gave her all the money we had in the house, it wasn't much, and then Decatur did something else to her, said it would disguise her trail, and Piven drove her somewhere and I never saw her again."

Holly was crying and Isolde was next to her, holding her hand. "That's why she never let me use my gift. She was afraid he'd find me! And that's why she didn't save her own life, she chose to die over risking me or anyone else. My god! She never dated, she lived alone without anyone but me for twenty-four years and all because Simon Decatur Senior—what, didn't like witches? I mean, what was his reasoning behind it? It's not like it was fifty years ago. Teenage pregnancy wasn't such a huge stigma that he'd curse my mother to a life alone without her family—so cruel—just to stop his son from looking bad. Would he?"

"I don't know, Holly. My father cursed another person, that's an executable offense for wizards on the path of light. Worse, he placed a death curse on humans and witches, which

220

makes the death sentence automatic. He wouldn't risk that for any old reason." Simon paced.

"Well, we've got him. He's trying to kill Holly because she could find out about the curse. But why didn't he kill Daniel?" Nate mused.

"He needed me to back up his story to the boy and to the family. I been around witches enough to know how to extract a promise. He said that as long as I never told the truth he wouldn't kill me or have me killed. I don't know why I'm telling you all this now, it's my death, but I can't seem to stop it."

Holly didn't bother telling him about Rhett's voice. Daniel told them about how after Elise tossed him out Senior had given him half a million dollars and a new identity and he'd moved to Vegas, where he'd been living for the last twenty-two years. He also told them about Piven calling three years prior when Simon found out about Holly and the most recent call.

"We've got to confront him tonight!" Holly exclaimed and began to pace. "That bastard! My mother, alone and scared her whole damned life because of this! I will hear his reason why before he dies!"

"Honey, while this side of you is delicious and sexy, I think we should do some planning first," Rhett said and everyone else agreed.

"I know you're angry and hurt for your mom, but Rhett is right. My father is a really strong wizard and Piven is strong and insane. We can't just barge in there. He keeps his cadre of loyal wizards living with him at his house. We have to have a plan or we won't make it five steps into the hall," Simon explained, appreciating how Rhett and Nate protected his daughter.

"What then?" Holly cried out.

"We need to get him away from the house. It's his magical center of power and also where his power base is people-wise. If we can get him into a containment circle much like this one, only charged so that use of magic in it wouldn't work, then we could question him."

They planned on getting him to the Decatur mansion that next evening, where some members of the Keepers of the Accord, the wizard police, would be waiting to hear Senior's confession. Holly had just wanted to kill him but that would have left her father vulnerable to a death sentence as well.

"Rest up, darling. Tomorrow night is important and dangerous and you'll need to be ready when you go up against my father." Simon kissed her on the cheeks and he and her brothers all went upstairs to sleep, refusing to leave the house until the next day when they'd all go to the Decatur mansion to implement the plan.

Some of the Charvezes went home for a while and others ensconced themselves in guestrooms or on couches and cots that Con conjured up for them. They left Daniel in the containment circle with a blanket, pillow and some food, and knowing he was safe in there and in there only, he was in no hurry to go anywhere.

Rhett and Nate said their good nights and followed Holly upstairs to the master bedroom.

* * * * *

Once the door was closed Holly slowly removed her clothes and walked naked over to the bed. She would grieve for the life her mother could have had later, but for now she needed to reconnect with Nate and Rhett, remind herself why it was so important to be alive and fight.

She sat at the foot of the bed and opened her thighs. She slid fingertips up her legs and lightly touched her pussy, over her mound and belly. She cupped her breasts in her hands and flicked her thumbs over her nipples and a wicked smile curved her lips when she watched both of them yank their clothes off.

But instead of rushing over to her, Rhett grabbed Nate and pulled him tight against his body and began to kiss him.

Holly watched, getting wetter and unbelievably turned on, as the kiss became one of those raging inferno kisses of teeth and tongue and lips. Rhett's hands were on Nate's ass, pulling him cock to cock. Nate growled as they pushed and pulled past Holly and ended up on the bed, first with Nate on top, then Rhett. Café au lait skin against olive complexion, the rough ropes of Nate's dreads falling over and against the ebony silk of Rhett's hair.

Holly watched for long minutes as they thrust against each other and continued to kiss. It was a thing of intense beauty, the two men muscled and powerful, bodies sliding and grinding against each other. After she couldn't take it anymore, she pulled her braid loose, walked on her knees to where they were and pushed a hand between them and sighed when she felt the pre-cum that had made them both slick. She wanted to watch until they made each other come and she promised herself she'd do just that when this whole thing was over but if someone didn't push inside of her in under three minutes she'd expire.

Nate snaked out a hand and pulled her down flat on her back. "Hello, sweetness," he purred.

She didn't know if she had finally seen how much they desired her or if it was part of the transformation but she felt like a goddess and she couldn't stop herself from writhing a bit as his voice stroked over her like a physical caress. "Your voice seems more powerful now," she said, breathless.

"Now that you're a vampire the bond is even stronger. You're more sensitive to your mate. Mates," Rhett said and she could tell that he worked his voice for her benefit because her back arched and her toes curled in delight.

They both laughed. "I think that one night we'll have to make her come over and over with the voice," Nate said.

"Hmm, maybe you'll be the ones I use the voice on," she said, her words projecting sex. Both of them groaned.

"Oh yeah, that's the ticket. Holly, you were dead sexy before but your voice is really good," Rhett moaned.

"So fuck me already," she said with a laugh.

Suddenly she was astride Nate and he was lowering her down onto his cock. "Oh yessss," she hissed as he filled her up.

Rhett was behind her, cock against her back. "You remember what I promised? Tonight's the night, honey. I'm so sick over almost losing you and then you scrying and this whole plan for tomorrow. I want to make this a true threesome," he whispered in her ear and she heard the top of the lube open up.

"Yes, oh yes," she moaned as she felt two slicked fingers stroke over the rosette of her anus. "I want your cock in there, Rhett, please."

"Holy shit. If you don't fuck that tight little ass, Rhett, I'm going to," Nate moaned as Holly's pussy rippled around his cock.

"Hold your horses, Nate, I'm not going in cold. Let me stretch her a bit," Rhett mumbled as he pressed those lubed fingers into her and scissored them to loosen her. "That's it, honey, relax."

Nate's clever fingers played at her nipples and clit, keeping her just on the edge of climax, and at last Rhett pulled his fingers out and he took his cock in hand and guided himself against her.

Murmuring gentle sounds, he urged her to relax and bear down as he pushed the head of his cock into her.

"Ow!" she cried out.

"Shhh, honey, you need to relax and bear down, I promise that once you do that, it'll be better," Rhett said in a shaking voice.

"Better make it quick, I'm gonna blow," Nate added.

Holly did as Rhett told her and indeed it worked and he was able to continue to press his cock into her. Once the burning sensation passed she could feel the pleasure in the fullness of it.

She was so hot and so tight that Rhett thought for a moment that he was going to come before he even got halfway inside of her.

The way she was writhing, impaled between them, and making low moaning and whimpering sounds in her throat was only pushing both men closer to climax.

"Now! Oh god, both of you, fuck me now!" she cried out, caught in a web of their erotic torture.

It took a few strokes but soon as one man pulled out, the other pushed in, see-sawing into her body in rhythm.

Holly couldn't think. All she could do was feel, allow herself to drown in the overwhelming sensations of all of those nerve endings being sparked. She was surrounded by flesh and instead of feeling claustrophobic, it felt comforting. When Nate's hand went back to her clit it only took just the smallest of touches to set off the chain reaction of her orgasm.

On and on it roared through her in wave after wave of extreme pleasure. Her eyes were open but she saw nothing. She could feel the vibrations of Nate's roar as he came and of Rhett's long moan of her name but she didn't hear. She only felt. Her body was part of a machine made up of the three of them. Slipping, sliding, thrusting, together that way they created a sexual engine.

She felt herself being lowered to the mattress and moments later a warm, wet cloth cleaned her up and she allowed herself to be ministered to, unable to let go of the ripples of pleasure still moving through her.

"Now that's what I'm talking about," she mumbled dreamily and curled up against Rhett and sighed when Nate settled in behind her.

Chapter Ten

ဢ

Fed and dressed and steeled as much as they could be against what was to come, they stood and went over the plans once again. Simon took the boys back home and Con would shimmer Holly in first and then Nate and Rhett. Aidan had already been put in place with Alex in the house, awaiting Senior's arrival, and Simon and Alex would create the containment circle before Senior got there.

Several members of the Keepers of the Accord were placed strategically around the house so that they could hear the confession.

Nate was not happy that Holly was going first but she wouldn't hear it any other way. "Look, it's going to be a matter of seconds until you are both there with me. It's my fight, I'm going first. For my mother and the life he stole from her."

Nate had tried for several more minutes to change her mind but Rhett already knew it was a lost cause and finally just interrupted and said so. As long as they were both at her side, they'd make it work. They had to. Throwing his hands up with a sigh, Nate gritted his teeth.

"Damn it, Holly! I am an FBI agent. Can't you trust me to do this for you? You don't have the training for this. You could get hurt. Or worse."

"Nate, I do trust you. But this man ruined my mother's life! I have to be there when he gets taken down. I swear to you on my life that I will let you do the leading and the work. I don't want to get hurt and I respect your training. Please, please don't make this about stuff it isn't. I'll choose you if that's what you're asking. I'll stay here. But I want to be there.

For closure." Her eyes were sad and the anger drained from him.

Rhett looked at Nate with one brow raised and Nate sighed. "You really should bottle that up. No one else in the world could have made that argument to me and won. But you. Stay behind me and Rhett and do what you're told. Okay?"

She smiled and went on tiptoes to kiss his chin. "Okay."

Holly waited while Con got Rhett and Nate in place and took his place with them.

The house was quiet but Holly felt the tension in the air as Senior arrived with Piven and an argument ensued with Simon. Holly stood at the top of the stairs, just out of sight, and listened.

"I'm going to give you one last chance to tell me what happened with Elena, Father," Simon said.

"You know what happened, I told you twenty-five years ago, I told you again three years ago and I'm telling you again today. She was a whore, she got knocked up by some loser and took off with him. She probably had ten kids off him and lives in some hovel in the middle of nowhere."

Holly's eyes narrowed but Nate squeezed her shoulder to keep her still.

"How about this? You knew that she and I were seeing each other secretly. You went to Daniel Pilotte and conspired to keep Elena and me apart. But that didn't work, did it?"

There was a long silence and Simon continued. "Yes, you should look worried. Shall I go on? Yes? All right then. When you found out from Pilotte that Elena was carrying my child you rushed over there and you cursed her and forced her to get out of town. You bastard. You placed a death curse on her and she ran for her life and the lives of my child and her family. You paid off Pilotte and you've lived knowing that you utterly devastated Elena Charvez's life as well as my daughter's and my own. What I don't understand is why?"

"Come on, sir, let's get out of here, you shouldn't have to take this!" Piven said urgently to Senior.

"Oh yes, turn tail and run, Father. That's what you do best, isn't it? Were you so scared of a fifteen-year-old witch who had a gift with healing that you ruined her? I've always known you were ruthless but I had no idea you were cruel."

Holly stood and waited but heard nothing. They hadn't gotten him into the containment circle yet or her father would have used the code.

"You have no idea what was at stake," Senior said at last.

"So tell me!" Simon yelled. "Come on over here and face me like a man and tell me why the hell you did it because I can't understand it! Tell me why you had my daughter killed the night before last while you're at it."

"She didn't turn up at the morgue, Simon. Don't lie to me. I'm guessing that those breed vampires made her into one of them." Senior made a derisive snorting sound and Rhett narrowed his eyes at the slight. "Breed" was a derogatory term for vampires who were made instead of born.

"You still took her life as a human. She'll never see another sunrise because of you and I'll know why!"

"You know you can't record my voice, don't you, Simon?"

"There are no recorders or cameras on trying to capture your confession, Father," Simon said.

"I can tell you're not lying. And it'll just be your word against mine if you try to push this. She can't testify, she's not alive anymore."

Man, these wizards were some kind of people! Holly couldn't believe that she wouldn't be able to testify against him because she was a vampire! Jerks!

"Just tell me already!"

Holly could tell the plan wasn't working. He wasn't moving from wherever he was at and if he didn't, they couldn't put him in a circle. She chewed a fingernail as she considered what she'd do.

"She was just some girl from a family below our status. She trapped you, Simon. You're so stupid sometimes. Your emotions never were very disciplined. She trapped you into getting her pregnant so she could get married into our money and our family. I wasn't going to risk your future for some slut."

"She wasn't a slut! She was good and kind and compassionate and I loved her. She wasn't capable of that kind of behavior," Simon said angrily.

Holly turned to Nate. "I know I promised to wait but please! Nothing is happening down there. Let me go."

Nate's eyes widened and his face hardened. Rhett banded his arm around her waist and she leaned into him. "Please."

Rhett looked at Nate over the top of her head and Nate exhaled agitatedly. "Fine. But stay behind us or I'll kick your hot little ass, got me?"

Smiling, Holly nodded and Nate looked at Rhett, who grinned and rolled his eyes.

When the three of them entered the drawing room everyone else looked up in surprise. Her father looked frustrated, pissed off and worried.

She turned and saw her grandfather sitting behind the desk in the corner. *Ah, the vision she had.* But he didn't know she was a seer and already had dismissed her being a witch. Being underestimated had always been a powerful tool and she used it now and gathered up the spell to rebound his magic. She'd wait to use it in defense but one way or another she was going to stop him and find out the truth.

"Hello, Grandfather," she said, drawing into her power and using the voice threaded with fear and awe, and she saw his pupils widen and gave him a smile that showed her incisors.

"I am not your grandfather, girl." Sitting there behind that big desk, he looked less threatening than she'd imagined.

She laughed and sat across from him in one of the chairs and Nate stood to one side and Rhett on the other.

"Oh two of them, that's right. Well, the apple doesn't fall far from the tree," he said with a leer that made her skin crawl.

"That's enough! You won't speak to my daughter that way!" Simon yelled but Holly shook her head.

"It's bravado. Now that you've called me a slut, why don't you go on with the rest of the story? You cursed my mother and had her escorted out of town, alone, practically penniless and without anyone in the world to turn to. Then you paid Daniel Pilotte off and he left town. Why? What threat could my mother have been to you?"

"Girl, she was nothing to him. Nothing to anyone."

Holly turned and faced the voice and the woman it belonged to as she came into the room.

Nate moved so that he stood between them and Rhett protected her from Senior.

"Mother? What are you doing here?" Josh asked.

The petite, dark-haired woman looked at him and took in the rest of the room and sighed. "I'm here to clean up messes, as usual. Men, so goddamned ineffectual!" She dropped into the chair next to Holly. "I can see you have those same swamp genes, girl."

Holly raised an eyebrow. "And you are?"

"Your better, don't you forget it. I am Violet Decatur. My father is Alexander Morgan."

Holly waited to hear something impressive but it didn't come.

Violet sighed. "Dumb as a post, just like your mother and father. Thank goodness my sons take after my father."

Holly looked to her father. "*This* is who you married? What, were you smoking crack?"

Simon gave a pained laugh. "It was arranged by my father. I was twenty, what did I know?"

"Yes, Simon, what did you know? Nothing. Your father had your entire life mapped out and you blew it by knocking up some slut from the swamp! My father knew what had to be done and he made sure he applied the right leverage to get it done. Of course, he was livid when he found out that Senior here allowed the bitch to get away alive and carrying your bastard but Senior assured us that the girl would go to her family and we'd be rid of the problem. Only she never did."

Holly sat there, nails digging into the wooden arms of that chair so hard that they pressed through the wood.

"One thing men don't understand is loyalty. Your mother may have been stupid and unworthy of the Decatur name, but she was loyal, I'll give that to her."

"You bitch!" Simon cried out. "Your father was behind this? Why? For god's sake, why?"

"Simon, does it have to be spelled out for you? I can't believe you have a degree from Yale!"

But Holly interrupted Violet. "Dad, your father and her father did a bit of empire building. I don't know who is he but apparently he had something old Grandpa needed and they made a deal with you and Violet as the bargain. When you dallied with my mother, the deal was in danger." She turned back to Senior. "But I have to hand it to you, a death curse on an innocent, a big bit of overkill, wasn't it? I mean, I'm sure you could have dealt with it without breaking the laws that bind you to your power."

Senior hit the desk with his fist. "Damn it! I didn't want anything to do with any of this! I thought your mother was beneath my son but I certainly didn't want to ruin her so cruelly. But I had my own curse to fight off. She ruined my entire plan for the future and I had to do it!" He looked at Violet, who started to stand but Holly stood up and shoved her back down and was sitting before the other woman knew what hit her.

"Thank you." Senior nodded to Holly and continued. "Alexander Morgan is a very rich man and I had some debts. He and I worked some magic together and I got in over my head. The marriage cleared the debt but then he got your mother pregnant." He shook his head in disgust. "Condoms, son, a thousand times, condoms! When Morgan found out he was livid. He wanted me to kill the girl but I didn't want to risk the cost of killing an innocent so I crafted a curse that would allow her to live if she stayed smart, and she did.

"But then she died and when she did, the curse was broken. I traced it back to you in Seattle and Morgan got concerned that she'd told you on her deathbed or that you'd gotten a letter after she died. He wanted you dead. I sent the burglars in Seattle, who bungled it. They were supposed to search the apartment and question you, not assault you. And then you joined with vampires and came here and I had no choice because Alexander takes every opportunity to remind me — *painfully* — of the obligation I have through my own curse. Yes that's right, I'm cursed too, although I've just signed my own damned death warrant by telling you all this but I have had it hanging over my head for a quarter of a century and I'm sick of it."

Two tall men walked into a room holding a book and a big wooden box. Senior stood up and tried to deflect their spell and it rebounded toward Holly, who had to use her own magic to deflect it toward the ceiling. Her vision wasn't about her grandfather trying to kill her, not then anyway, it was about this.

She allowed Rhett to pull her out of the way as the Keepers took her grandfather into custody. Violet was moving toward the door when Holly moved to intercept her.

"Oh no, you're not going anywhere. You were a part of this. My mother suffered most of her life and you were a knowing party!"

"The Keepers have no authority over me. What are you going to do, call the human cops and tell them about this? What are they going to do?" Violet taunted.

"Alexander Morgan has just been taken into our custody and will be charged with using dark magics against a wizard and conspiracy to curse an innocent. You will be part of that investigation, Ms. Decatur. Come with us," one of the Keepers said and suddenly they were all gone from the room.

Simon rushed to Holly and hugged her tight. "I'm so sorry, what a terrible father I've been. I haven't protected you a moment since I created you. How you must hate me for what you and your mother suffered."

"Dad, it wasn't your fault. You were a victim too." She looked up into his face. "You're here now and that's what counts. Now is what counts. I have quite a long life ahead of me and I want to have as many people in it whom I love as I possibly can and that includes you and my brothers if you'll still want me after I caused your mother's arrest," she said around her father's body to her brothers, who all came to her and joined the embrace.

Nate looked down at her and then over at Rhett. Holly turned and slid her arm around both their waists. "Thank you both for letting me be here for this. I know you were scared for me. I needed it. It's done now."

"I love you." Nate shrugged. "What else could I have done but see to it that you were happy?"

"Honey, we have all the time in the world now. Our whole future stretches out in front of us. I think some celebrating is called for."

His lips slid into that sexy smile and she knew just what he meant and her body throbbed for them, for their touch.

"Let's get going then. I have a lot to celebrate."

Why an electronic book?

We live in the Information Age—an exciting time in the history of human civilization, in which technology rules supreme and continues to progress in leaps and bounds every minute of every day. For a multitude of reasons, more and more avid literary fans are opting to purchase e-books instead of paper books. The question from those not yet initiated into the world of electronic reading is simply: *Why?*

1. *Price.* An electronic title at Ellora's Cave Publishing and Cerridwen Press runs anywhere from 40% to 75% less than the cover price of the exact same title in paperback format. Why? Basic mathematics and cost. It is less expensive to publish an e-book (no paper and printing, no warehousing and shipping) than it is to publish a paperback, so the savings are passed along to the consumer.

2. *Space.* Running out of room in your house for your books? That is one worry you will never have with electronic books. For a low one-time cost, you can purchase a handheld device specifically designed for e-reading. Many e-readers have large, convenient screens for viewing. Better yet, hundreds of titles can be stored within your new library—on a single microchip. There are a variety of e-readers from different manufacturers. You can also read e-books on your PC or laptop computer. (Please note that Ellora's Cave does not endorse any specific brands.

You can check our websites at www.ellorascave.com or www.cerridwenpress.com for information we make available to new consumers.)

3. *Mobility.* Because your new e-library consists of only a microchip within a small, easily transportable e-reader, your entire cache of books can be taken with you wherever you go.

4. *Personal Viewing Preferences.* Are the words you are currently reading too small? Too large? Too... ANNOYING? Paperback books cannot be modified according to personal preferences, but e-books can.

5. *Instant Gratification.* Is it the middle of the night and all the bookstores near you are closed? Are you tired of waiting days, sometimes weeks, for bookstores to ship the novels you bought? Ellora's Cave Publishing sells instantaneous downloads twenty-four hours a day, seven days a week, every day of the year. Our webstore is never closed. Our e-book delivery system is 100% automated, meaning your order is filled as soon as you pay for it.

Those are a few of the top reasons why electronic books are replacing paperbacks for many avid readers.

As always, Ellora's Cave and Cerridwen Press welcome your questions and comments. We invite you to email us at Comments@ellorascave.com or write to us directly at Ellora's Cave Publishing Inc., 1056 Home Avenue, Akron, OH 44310-3502.

COMING TO A BOOKSTORE NEAR YOU!

ELLORA'S CAVE

Bestselling Authors Tour

UPDATES AVAILABLE AT

WWW.ELLORASCAVE.COM

erridwen, the Celtic Goddess of wisdom, was the muse who brought inspiration to storytellers and those in the creative arts. Cerridwen Press encompasses the best and most innovative stories in all genres of today's fiction. Visit our site and discover the newest titles by talented authors who still get inspired - much like the ancient storytellers did, once upon a time.

Discover for yourself why readers can't get enough of the multiple award-winning publisher

Ellora's Cave.

Whether you prefer e-books or paperbacks,

be sure to visit EC on the web at
www.ellorascave.com

for an erotic reading experience that will leave you breathless.